A Woman's Worth

Also by Nikita Lynnette Nichols

None But The Righteous

A Man's Worth

Amaryllis

A Woman's Worth

NIKITA LYNNETTE NICHOLS

URBAN
CHRISTIAN

www.urbanchristianonline.net

Urban Books, LLC
1199 Straight Path
West Babylon, NY 11704

A Woman's Worth copyright © 2010 Nikita Lynnette Nichols

ISBN- 13: 978-1-60162-874-9
ISBN- 10: 1-60162-874-9

First Printing January 2010
Printed in the United States of America

10 9 8 7 6 5 4 3 2 1

This is a work of fiction. Any references or similarities to actual events, real people, living, or dead, or to real locales are intended to give the novel a sense of reality. Any similarity in other names, characters, places, and incidents is entirely coincidental.

Distributed by Kensington Corp.
Submit Wholesale Orders to:
Kensington Publishing Corp.
C/O Penguin Group (USA) Inc.
Attention: Order Processing
405 Murray Hill Parkway
East Rutherford, NJ 07073-2316
Phone: 1-800-526-0275
Fax: 1-800-227-9604

Acknowledgments

Father God, you are my first love. I acknowledge you as the true author of this book.

My parents, William and Victoria Nichols, I love you both for loving me first.

My brother, Raymond, and my sister, Theresa. You are my armor bearers.

Tabitha, Toiya, Ta'Shea, William II, and Kenneth. Auntie loves you.

My uncle, Kenneth Caridine, thanks for supporting all of my book signings and buying books at each and every one. Love ya!

My especially gifted and talented editor, Joylynn Jossel. You push me, poke me, nudge me, and won't let me sleep. But I'm so grateful to have you in my corner. You're the best.

My publicist, Denise Glesser. You rock, you rock, you rock. That's all I can say.

Honey, I'm so glad you're a chubby chaser. You really have me convinced that thick is the new thin. You're my Adonis and you make me feel fabulous!

Dedication

I wish to dedicate this novel to all of my fans and the book clubs that have supported me throughout my writing career.

And to all of my sistas: Latricia Collins & Yolunda Cooper (both of whom are characters in this novel), Jamia Ray, Daphne Smith, Kara Perry, Cherritta Smith, Shlotta Gilbert, Felicia Hill, Latanya Hicks, Drusilla Lee, Anastasia Baker, Paulette Turner, Michellene Anderson, Ja' Nae Garay, Audelia Alvarez, Ginger Gilbert, Taryn Maclin, Carmela Bailey, Tanya D. Bell, Keisha Pierce, Valerie Dansby, Kimberly Ivy, Kimberly Nelson, Michelle Vaughn, Latoya Davis, Saminta Harris, Latonya Davis, Phyore Montgomery, Denita Hill, Karen Williams, Karyn Muldrow, Cortney Rogers, Kimberly Johnson, Marlo Jean Mason, Linda O'Neal, Eve Pullum, and my "Amaryllis" book cover model, the beautiful Latoyia Jones.

Chapter 1

"**W**ho is *that*?" Arykah Miles put special emphasis on the word 'that' as she leaned into her best friend, Monique Morrison, sitting next to her. Monique followed Arykah's gaze to the front of the church. The musicians were assembling themselves behind the instruments next to the pulpit, in preparation for the sanctuary choir to march down the center aisle and into the choir stand. Because there was only one new member to the church band, Monique knew exactly who Arykah was speaking of.

"That's the new keyboard player," Monique answered.

Arykah's mouth began to salivate. "Girl, he is *foine* with a capital F."

Monique looked at her best friend of ten years with a shameful expression. "Your lustful horns are showing, Arykah. And your pupils are dilated. Sit back, calm down, and close your mouth because you're drooling. He's just a man."

Arykah couldn't avert her eyes from the very tall specimen at Morning Glory Church of God in Christ. She was mesmerized at his short, wavy cut, Black Caesar style. Looking at his hair reminded Arykah of the man advertised on the Duke hair products box. His well-groomed mustache melded with his goatee. Skin the color of caramel, with a soft touch of butterscotch, brought a certain song to Arykah's mind.

"Just like candy. It's no mistaken, I'm clearly taken."

Surely, the R&B group, Cameo, was referring to this man, who sat no more than twenty feet away from Arykah. She watched as his long fingers pressed down on the keys. She imagined what it would feel like to have those fingers pressing on her body.

Monique knew Arykah well and could tell by her starry eyes what she was thinking. "Stop it, devil. You're in church. Have some dignity about yourself."

Arykah fanned her face with the church bulletin as she tried to defend herself. "Stop what? I'm only admiring him."

"You are lusting after him," Monique scolded. "I know you like the back of my hand."

Arykah smiled seductively. "Is that right? Well, since you know me, tell me what I'm thinkin' now." There was never any shame in Arykah's game. Whenever her eyes set on a handsome man, she couldn't stop herself from blurting out the first thing that came to her mind.

Monique frowned at the sinful sneer on Arykah's face and shook her head from side to side, in disappointment, as she watched her best friend mentally undress the man. "You know what? I'm not going there with you today. He could be married or engaged for all you know."

"I've already peeped that. There is no ring on his finger."

"So? That doesn't mean anything. He could be dating someone."

"A man that *foine* should be handcuffed to his woman." Arykah thought for a minute. "Find out if he's dating anyone for me."

"And how do you suppose I do that?" Monique asked.

"Boris is your man and the head musician. You can easily find out if the new kid on the block is spoken for."

Monique released a knowing snicker. Truth be told, she already knew the mystery man's name and marital status. "Uh, uh. No way, Arykah. The last two guys I hooked you up with were perfect gentlemen and you dogged them out. I happen to know that this guy is saved and sanctified. He's respectful, and he's serious about God."

"And how do *you* know so much about him?" Arykah asked.

"Because he's Boris's cousin. And your trifling behind will detour him in a hot second."

Arykah's head quickly snapped backward. She looked at Monique with a shocked expression on her face. "How can you say something like that about me?"

Monique exhaled. This wasn't the first time she had to take Arykah on a stroll down memory lane. "Arykah, didn't you cheat on Tyrone Jackson? And did you not cheat on Demetrius Wellsby as well?"

Arykah waved her hand to dismiss both of Monique's questions because according to her, they had nothing to do with who was in her vision today. "That's ancient history. You're always bringing up the past."

"It was only two months ago that Demetrius saw you downtown enjoying a horse and carriage ride while snuggling up to someone other than himself."

"Whatever, Monique. Just tell me this new guy's name."

"Nope. 'Cause if you dog this one, I'll have to deal with Boris. You're on your own this time, girlfriend."

The congregation stood as the sanctuary choir made their entrance into the church. Arykah's eyes never left the mystery man. He and Boris Cortland sat side-by-side, one on the keyboard, and the other on the organ. Boris spoke to him and the mystery man smiled in agreement. Looking at his bright, sparkling teeth was like staring directly at the sun. Arykah had to squint her eyes and blink a few times to keep from going blind.

Before the choir rendered in song, Boris removed himself from the organ and stepped to the podium. "Good morning, saints. First and foremost, I give all glory to God. It is truly a privilege to be back in the house of prayer one more time. I stand before you to introduce our newest member to the musician staff."

Arykah's mouth salivated again. Monique saw her scoot forward on the pew, hanging on to Boris's every word.

"He's twenty-six years old and fresh out of music school. And if I do say so myself, the boy is bad on the keys. And I'm not just saying that because he's my cousin."

The congregation chuckled.

"He's gonna accompany the sanctuary choir with 'The Lord's Prayer.' I introduce to you all, Chicago's own, Mr. Adonis Cortland Jr.," Boris announced proudly.

Arykah was in another world as she spoke dreamily, but loud enough for Monique to hear. "*Adonis*. Boris, you sho ain't lying there."

"You ought to be ashamed of yourself," Monique said.

"Well, I ain't. Do you even know what an Adonis is?"

"You act like he's a piece of candy."

There goes that word again, Arykah thought. *Just like candy.* "You took the words right out of my mouth, Monique. He's church candy and I can lick him like a lollipop."

At that moment, Monique felt embarrassed. She looked all around them, hoping and praying that the mothers of the church, who were seated on the pew directly in front of them, hadn't heard Arykah's comment.

After the benediction, Monique sat in the back of the church to wait for Boris. An usher greeted her as she was leaving the sanctuary. "Hey, Monique."

"How are you doing, Sister Daniels?"

"Tired. I got my praise on today."

"Yeah, I saw you back here in the corner cuttin' a rug."

"Bishop wore me out, then it took us forever to count the tithes and offerings."

"Speaking of that, is Arykah still in the finance room?" Monique asked.

"Yes, but she'll be out in a minute. You're waiting on Boris again?" Sister Daniels asked.

"You know it. Every Sunday, he's the last to leave the church."

"He's a musician. You know how they are about their equipment. Everything has to be secured." As Sister Daniels walked away, Monique saw Arykah practically running toward her.

"Girl, he wrote a check to the church for four hundred fifty dollars," she announced excitedly.

"Who?" Monique asked.

Arykah gave Monique a dumb look as if she should've known who she was speaking of. "Adonis Cortland. *Duh.* He put a check mark in the tithes box on the front of the envelope."

Monique shrugged her shoulders, wondering what the

big deal was. "So? The man pays his tithes. That's a good thing. I told you he was serious about God."

Arykah rolled her eyes while thinking that sometimes her best friend could be so slow. "I'm not talking about *that*, Monique. Please flow with me. I'm talking about the amount of money he gave. Four hundred fifty is ten percent of forty-five hundred. That means he's making a lot of loot."

For the second time in one day, Monique looked at her best friend shamefully. "Arykah, you have stooped to an all time low. First of all, as a member of the finance committee, you have no business telling me or anyone else what the people are tithing because it's personal information. How much did *you* tithe today?"

"We ain't talking about me," Arykah answered.

"How much did you put in the offering basket?"

"We still ain't talkin' about me. What does Adonis Cortland do for a living?"

"I ain't telling you." Monique folded her arms across her chest.

"Why?"

"Because, you're foaming at the mouth," Monique said disgustingly.

"Please, Monique," Arykah whined. Monique knew that Arykah could play the detective role real well. In only a few days she would have had the answer to her own question.

"He's an electrician, like Boris. They work together," she relented.

Kaching. Kaching. Arykah looked toward the front of the church and saw a huge dollar sign, in the shape of a man sitting behind the keyboard.

If Monique hadn't known any better, she'd swear that at that moment the heavens had opened up and shown a ray of light down on Arykah. She stood up and snapped her fingers in Arykah's face to bring her back from dreamland. "You ain't nothing but the devil."

"Why do I have to be the devil? Just because I see an attractive man and want to get to know him doesn't make me a bad person."

"No, it doesn't. But undressing him with your eyes, *while in church*, and focusing on his money makes you a bonafide hoochie."

Arykah placed her right hand on her hip. "Excuse you. I am not a hoochie. You got me confused with Kita. She and Cherry left the club and came straight to Sunday School this morning."

"The only way you'd know something like that is if you were with them," Monique said.

"I don't get down like that with those two. I could look at their faces and tell. Cherry's eye shadow was faded; needed to be retouched badly. And Kita's lipstick bled past the line of her lower lip. Trust me, Monique, fresh make-up doesn't look like that."

Monique laughed. "Kita and Cherry have been club hopping for years. But they're always the first to enter the choir stand on Sunday morning. I know you're cool with them, Arykah, but you need to watch your step with those two. Everywhere they go, trouble isn't too far behind. Boris told me that Cherry was peeping Adonis in choir rehearsal this past Wednesday night."

Arykah's eyebrows rose and so did the octave in her voice. "*My* Adonis?"

"He's not *your* Adonis. But you should know that you're not the only one who's mesmerized by him."

They both sat down. Arykah watched Adonis. His eyes, along with the other musicians', were focused on Boris as he filled them in on what songs they would be working on in choir rehearsal Wednesday night. Boris made one last statement, and the musicians nodded in agreement, then they were dismissed.

After the drums, horns, tambourines, and keyboards had all been secured in a locked room behind the pulpit, Boris and Adonis came to the back of the church where Monique and Arykah sat.

"Monique, you ready?" Boris asked.

She took note of Boris's rude greeting. He completely ignored Arykah seated next to her. Monique stood up. "Hello to you too, Boris, and yes, I'm ready." She then turned her attention to his cousin. "How are you doing, Adonis?"

Adonis stepped to Monique and kissed her cheek. "I'm good, Monique. How did I sound on the keys?"

She smiled and gave a short wave of her hand, dismissing his ridiculous question. "Adonis, please, you know you're the bomb."

"Don't tell this Negro nothin' like that. It'll go straight to his head," Boris joked.

Feeling left out of the loop, Arykah stood and nudged Monique's side with her elbow.

Monique saw a silly grin on Arykah's face, nodding her head toward Adonis. "Oh, uh, Adonis, this is my very best girlfriend, Arykah Miles."

Adonis extended his hand to Arykah and smiled. "It's a pleasure to meet you, Arykah."

She got a close-up of the whitest teeth she'd ever seen in her life. According to Arykah, Adonis missed his true calling. It's *his* mouth that millions of viewers should see in the Dentyne and Colgate commercials. Arykah became self conscious of the gap between her teeth.

Monique and Boris looked at Arykah, who seemed a billion miles away. Monique grabbed her best friend's right hand and placed it into Adonis's left hand. Arykah's eyes roamed from his pearly teeth, to his perfect nose, up to his starry eyes. "My name is Arykah."

"I just told him that," Monique said.

Adonis became uncomfortable with the way Arykah's eyes gazed at him. As he attempted to withdraw his hand from her tight grip, she held on. "The pleasure is all mine, I promise," she said. "Your name fits you and you wear it extremely well."

At her compliment, all thirty-two of Adonis's pearly whites became even more visible.

Monique took Arykah's hand out of Adonis's. "Okay, that's enough of that. Let's go eat."

"Where are we going?" Boris asked.

Monique looked at him as though he were crazy. "Where were you when I baked a honey ham, macaroni and cheese, and cooked mustard and turnip greens this morning?"

Arykah rubbed her stomach. "Ooh, Monique, you got down like that, girl?"

"She sure did. That's all I kept thinking about in church today," Adonis confessed.

Boris turned his nose up at Monique's menu. "Well, I don't want that. I got a taste for pizza."

A deacon turned off the lights in the sanctuary.

"What are you doing, Deacon Brown?" Arykah asked.

"Y'all ain't got to go home, but you got to get out of here." The deacon then ushered them out of the sanctuary.

The four of them walked out of the church, and Monique whispered to Boris. "I know you're not going to order a pizza when I cooked Sunday dinner."

"I told you I don't want that today."

Monique exhaled a sigh of frustration. She couldn't believe Boris's gall. "Well, why didn't you tell me that before I put the ham in the oven? You saw me making the macaroni and cheese this morning."

Boris didn't respond as he walked down the church's steps toward his Lincoln Navigator. Adonis and Arykah came and stood next to Monique. They witnessed her and Boris's exchanged words and knew by the expression on Monique's face that she was upset.

"What was that about?" Arykah asked.

Monique was on the verge of tears. "I am so sick of his crap. Are you coming over to eat?"

"Girl, yeah. When have you known me to pass up your famous mac and cheese?"

"I can't believe Boris would rather get pizza than eat what I cooked."

Adonis kissed Monique's cheek again. "Don't get upset over that. If Boris doesn't want to eat, that's his loss. The way I look at it, he's leaving more for me. You know I love everything you cook. That sausage omelet you made this morning was off the chain."

Though Adonis's comment was meant to make Monique feel better, it didn't pacify her one bit. She was fed up with Boris's disrespect and ungratefulness. But she couldn't blame anyone but herself. She'd made a conscious decision to move in and play house with a man who wasn't her husband. So she had to deal with the consequences.

Arykah opted to trail Boris's Navigator to his and Monique's house on the south side of Chicago. Adonis mentioned that Monique had made him breakfast that morning. Arykah made a mental note in her mind to ask Monique if Adonis was living with her and Boris, or if he had been invited over that morning for breakfast.

When Monique and Adonis got into the SUV, Boris was

on his Blackberry completing his pizza order for delivery. When he disconnected the call, Monique looked at him. "I can't believe you're disrespecting me like this, Boris."

"What is your problem, Monique? I don't want ham and greens, I want pizza."

Adonis sat in the backseat listening to them go at it again. He had moved into their basement three days ago, just after graduating music school. While he was hunting for a place of his own, Boris invited Adonis to stay with him and Monique. This was the eighth argument he'd heard already between his cousin and his fiancé.

"It's the principle of the matter, Boris. All of us could've gone out for pizza, but I cooked a full course meal this morning before we came to church. You need to go home and eat what's been prepared for you."

Boris raised his voice. "I'm a grown man. You don't tell me what the heck to eat."

"Calm down, cuz. It ain't that serious, man," Adonis said from the backseat.

Boris adjusted the rearview mirror to look at Adonis. "You see what I gotta put up with? Do you see what I have to go through?"

Adonis didn't answer him. Boris was his cousin, but he felt that Monique was too good to him. Adonis would give anything to have a devoted woman like Monique run his bath water and cook his meals. When Adonis didn't respond to his questions, Boris started the truck and pulled away from the curb.

Adonis sat behind Monique. He couldn't see her face, but he heard her sniffles. He wanted so badly to give her the handkerchief from his jacket pocket, but thought better of it. He didn't want to overstep his bounds.

An hour later, Boris was in the living room enjoying his pizza while watching a basketball game. Monique and

Arykah were sitting at the kitchen table when Adonis came upstairs from the basement dressed in a nylon jogging suit.

"Is it cool enough down there for you, Adonis?" Monique asked.

"Yeah, it's all good," he answered. "The washer stopped. You want me to put your clothes in the dryer?"

"No, I'll get them after dinner. The food is hot; come on and eat." Arykah watched as Monique got a plate from the cabinet and began to fill it with macaroni and cheese.

Her kindness stunned Adonis. "You ain't gotta fix my plate, Monique. I can do it."

"I don't mind. What do you want to drink?"

"Any grape Kool-Aid left?" he asked.

"If there isn't, I'll make a pitcher for you."

"Don't go through any trouble. I'll drink whatever you have."

Monique stopped preparing his plate and looked at him. "Adonis, you're a guest in my home. Go into the living room and watch the game with Boris. I'll bring your plate and Kool-Aid to you."

Adonis smiled and kissed her cheek a third time in less than two hours. "Thanks, Monique, you're somethin' else," he complimented.

When he left the kitchen, Arykah looked at Monique. "Since you're being so helpful, *Alice*, can I get another slice of ham?"

"Who are you calling Alice? You're trying to be funny?"

"I just figured that since you're so ready, willing, and able to meet Adonis's needs, I wanna get treated like royalty too. And why didn't you tell me you had such a handsome house guest?"

Monique placed another slice of ham on Arykah's

plate. "He just moved in on Thursday, Arykah. Have I talked to you since Thursday?"

"You could've called and said somethin'."

Monique stirred sugar into a pitcher of grape Kool-Aid. "Something like what?"

"How about, 'Arykah, girl, you better get over here. There's a mad cutie in the house. '"

Monique laughed as she poured the Kool-Aid into a glass filled with ice. "Arykah, you need prayer. And you need to ask God to help you keep your legs closed. As a matter of fact, you should put that ham down, 'cause a request like that can only come by fasting and praying." No sooner than the words were out of her mouth, Monique realized that she was the pot calling the kettle black.

Arykah held the floor and could've reminded Monique which of the two of them was shacking up with a man, but she let it go. She had a more important issue to tend to. She leaned back in her chair and looked around the corner and got a peep of Adonis sitting in the living room watching the game with Boris. She licked her lips. "I'll fast and pray for something all right."

"Thanks, Monique. It smells great." Adonis said when Monique set his dinner tray in front of him.

"You're welcome. Oh, I forgot your napkin. I'll be right back." Monique turned toward the kitchen, but Adonis stopped her.

"That's okay. You've done enough; I'll get it."

She stopped him from getting up. "Adonis, it's not a problem. Go ahead and eat. I'll be right back with your napkin."

Without taking his eyes away from the game, Boris said, "Bring me a napkin too."

Monique returned to the living room with two napkins. Of course, Adonis did the gentlemanly thing and thanked her, but when she laid Boris's napkin on his tray, he instantly held up an empty glass for her to take. Monique stood looking at him. "What am I supposed to do with that?"

Boris removed his eyes from the television and looked up at her. "Fill it."

Adonis watched Monique snatch the glass from Boris and leave the living room. He'd wait until after she brought the drink back before he said anything to his cousin.

Monique returned and placed the glass of Pepsi, his favorite, on Boris's tray and waited for a response.

Boris looked up and saw her standing with her arms folded across her chest. "What's up?"

"Can I get a 'thank you'?" Monique sucked her teeth.

"For bringing me something to drink? Heck, I bought it and you drink more Pepsi than I do. The least you can do is pour it for me. Do I hear you thanking me when I drop the mortgage payment in the mailbox?"

"I thank you by keeping this house clean and by keeping your belly full."

Boris turned his attention toward the game. "Monique, you better step away from me with that crap. You see I'm watching the game; I ain't tryin' to hear that ying yang on a Sunday. Why do you always wait until a game comes on to nag the heck out of me?"

Monique was stunned that Boris would treat her this way in front of company. Out of the corner of her eye, she could see Adonis looking at her. To keep him from seeing her cry, she left the living room and went back to the kitchen.

Adonis spoke to his cousin. "Boris?"

He answered Adonis while looking at the television. "What's up, man?"

"Why you gotta talk to her like that?"

He looked at Adonis. "Like what? All I did was ask for something to drink."

"You didn't ask, you demanded. You ain't even thank her, man. What's up with that?"

"Monique needs to know her place. I pay the mortgage."

"I understand that, cuz. But since I've been here, she's done nothin' but bend over backward for you *and* me. I'm just saying that you shouldn't be dissin' her like that. She's a good woman."

Boris turned his attention back to the television. "Adonis, do not let Monique fool you. She ain't perfect."

Darn near. Adonis thought.

Monique sat at the kitchen table with a tear-stained face, trying to finish her dinner.

"Monique, why do you serve that fool?" Arykah asked.

"What's wrong with a woman serving her man?"

"Nothing, if he appreciates it. But Boris doesn't respect you. And the more you do for him, the more he expects you to do. And what do you get in return? Absolutely nothing; not even a simple thank you. It's June and your wedding day is less than three months away. Do you think he's going to change by then? You allow Boris to treat you like you're a two-year-old. Umph, Boris got the right woman, because it sure couldn't be me."

Monique blew her nose into a napkin. "I'm so tired of him, Arykah. I swear I am."

Arykah stood and took her empty plate to the sink. "Nah, you ain't tired, 'cause you're still with him."

"Am I wrong for trying to make my relationship work?"

Arykah came back and sat at the table. "First of all, a

couple shouldn't have to *make* a relationship work, Monique. If God ordained it, then it should just flow. And what you and Boris have is not a relationship. It's a dictatorship. He dictates and you do what he says. In relationships, people relate to each another. And as far as trying to make something work, you have to realize who and what you are working with. You might come to the conclusion that it ain't worth working on at all."

Monique blew her nose into a napkin. "What are you saying?"

"Look, Monique, I don't have a man, so it's really not my place to tell you what to do with yours. But I will say this: I'd rather spend every night alone in my own bed than spread my legs and give up my goods to a man who I know in my heart has proven over and over again that he doesn't love or respect me."

Monique knew Arykah was speaking the truth.

At ten minutes to eight that evening, Adonis heard Monique in the kitchen scrambling around. He walked in and saw her wrapping what was left of Sunday's dinner in Saran Wrap. He noticed she was in a hurry. "You all right?" he asked her.

Monique looked at him and smiled. "I'm just trying to wash these dishes and clean the kitchen before my eight o'clock movie comes on the *Lifetime* channel."

"Go ahead and get ready for your movie. I'll clean the kitchen."

Monique stopped gathering the plates and glasses and looked at Adonis. "Say what?"

He took the dishes from her hands and put them in the dishwater. "I said, I'll clean the kitchen. You've done enough; it's time for you to relax. It's almost eight o'clock now get out of here."

Monique stared into Adonis's eyes. Could he be serious? It was hard to believe that he and Boris shared the same blood. Boris had never offered to relieve her of kitchen duty.

"Thanks, Adonis. I've been waiting three weeks to see this movie."

On her way out of the kitchen, Adonis called her name and she turned around.

"Thanks for cooking breakfast and dinner. I appreciate everything you do for me."

Monique didn't say anything. She just smiled and turned toward her bedroom. She saw Boris in the living room asleep in his La Z' Boy recliner. He was laid back and snoring. On his dinner tray was a half-eaten sausage pizza. Monique turned on her heels and peeked around the refrigerator at Adonis. She saw him wash and rinse a glass, then set it upside down in the dish rack. She looked at Boris again, slouching in his chair, then she looked at Adonis and saw him dry a plate before placing it into the cabinet.

I appreciate everything you do for me. Adonis's words ricocheted through Monique's mind as she closed the door to her bedroom.

Chapter 2

When Adonis stepped out of the shower Monday morning, he heard Monique yelling. She and Boris were in their bedroom adjacent to the only bathroom in the house. Their bedroom door was shut, but Adonis heard every word clearly.

"Why is the gas light on in my car, Boris?" Monique asked.

"Monique, what are you hollering about now?"

"You ran all the gas out of my car Saturday. Why didn't you fill the tank up? It was full when you got in the car."

"'Cause I forgot, all right? Dang, you're always fussing about somethin'. I'll give you twenty bucks to put in your tank."

"That's not the point. This **ain't the** first time you've done this. Don't you realize that I could've gotten stranded somewhere or run out of gas on the expressway?"

Adonis heard Boris raise his voice. "Monique, are you

stranded now? Well, then shut the heck up. It's too early in the morning for this crap."

"You don't tell me to shut up; *you* shut the heck up. I'm sick and tired of you running the gas out of my car. I'm already rushing to get to a meeting that starts in a half hour; now I gotta stop for gas."

Ten seconds later, Adonis heard the front door slam. He opened the bathroom door and met Boris coming out of his bedroom. "Wow, it's a regular Fourth of July around here, cuz," Adonis joked.

Boris exhaled loudly and scratched his bald head. "More like midnight on New Year's Eve. Sorry you had to hear that, man."

"It's all good." Adonis hesitated, then spoke again. "You know she had a valid point, right?"

Boris shrugged his shoulders. "What point? I forgot to put gas in her car. It happens, and it was no big deal. You'll find out soon enough that Monique's trademark is making a mountain out of a molehill."

"Boris, Monique is an attractive female driving by herself. That alone makes her a target. So let's say for the sake of argument that she ran out of gas on the expressway and a lunatic came to her rescue before a State Trooper did."

Boris thought about the point Adonis was making. "Are you trying to make me feel bad? I messed up, all right? I admit I made a mistake. What more do you want from me, man?"

Adonis tightened the belt on his bathrobe. "Look, cuz, I ain't tryin' to be all up in your biz, all right? I just want you to understand that you need to take better care of your woman. When you make a careless mistake like that, you put Monique in harm's way. You're supposed to cover your woman at all times. Monique is worth more than what you're giving her, Boris. It's your responsibility to make sure her car is safe to drive at all times, man."

"Adonis, I'm an electrician, not a mechanic."

"I know that. I'm talking about just simply checking to make sure that her tires aren't balding, keeping the windshield washer fluid flowing, and making sure that her gas hand doesn't go below the half-full line. I mean, what's the problem with washing her car whenever you wash yours, or making sure her tires are rotated when yours get rotated? Women don't think to do stuff like that. You know you'd lose your mind if something bad happened to Monique as a result of a fault of yours."

Boris couldn't deny that Adonis had a valid point. As much as he and Monique argued, fussed, and fought, he was crazy about her.

In the conference room at the headquarters of WGOD, an FM gospel radio station, Monique stood before the executive board members. "According to the amount of calls we get on a daily basis, most of our listeners request contemporary gospel rather than the old school gospel music, such as quartets."

Edwin Wiley, the Chief Executive Officer of WGOD, leaned back in his chair and intertwined his fingers across his oversized belly. "Tell me, Miss Morrison, what do you propose we do so that the older listeners, such as senior citizens, would tune in to our station?"

As Senior Executive Producer, Monique pulled on the coattail of her ivory colored, paisley printed, brocade St. John suit jacket as she strutted across the front of the room with confidence. Monique was a confident plus size woman, and she paid a pretty penny for her size 20W

dresses, skirts, pants, and suits. Every day was like show
and tell at WGOD.

The women at the radio station looked forward to
Monique stepping off the elevator and walking toward
her office on the fifth floor just to see what she was wearing. She enjoyed putting on a show, primarily to prove to
women and men alike, that big girls can be beautiful too.
Monique once went four entire months without having
to wear a repeater.

"I've been thinking about that all weekend, Mr. Wiley,"
Monique answered, "and I've come to the conclusion
that our senior citizens couldn't care less about today's
hip hop gospel music. In my church, the seniors in the
choir would rather sing hymnals than fast songs because
they can't clap to an upbeat tune. Here at WGOD, each of
our deejays is on the air for four hours at a time. I suggest
that one of each one of their hours is dedicated to our senior citizens with old school gospel music."

Mr. Wiley smiled slightly at Monique's idea. He glanced
around the table at the board members for responses.
Everyone agreed with Monique. He stood and shook her
hand. "I'm impressed, Miss Morrison. Have this proposal
in writing and on my desk first thing in the morning."

The boardroom was empty in less than five minutes.
Monique sat down at the table and exhaled loudly. "I'm
glad that's over."

The telephone rang, and she answered on the first
ring. "Boardroom. Miss Morrison speaking."

"Mr. Wiley just walked past my desk. Is your meeting
over?"

Monique exhaled again as she spoke to Theresa, her
secretary and right hand woman. "Yep, and not a moment too soon. What's up?"

"Have you forgotten that Edward Primer and The Voices of Joy Community Choir is scheduled to sing live on the air at noon today?"

Monique sat straight up in her chair and looked at her wristwatch. "Oh, my God. It's eleven thirty. Yes, I had completely forgotten that. Are they here?"

"They're in the green room practicing as we speak."

"Okay, have Mr. Primer escorted to my office. I'm on my way."

Five minutes later, Theresa saw Monique rushing toward her. "Edward Primer is in your office per your request."

"I can't believe I let something like this slip my mind. I forgot to prepare a list of questions for him."

Theresa held up an index card to Monique. "The Voices of Joy is releasing their new CD next week. I took the liberty of jotting down a few questions pertaining to that."

Monique looked over the questions and smiled at her secretary. "Theresa, I could kiss you."

"Well, you ain't gotta do all *that,* but you can hook a sista up with one of the tenors in the group. All five of them are *foine.*"

Monique chuckled, but didn't really take her married secretary's request seriously. "I'll see what I can do."

"Ed Primer is a keeper too, Monique. Try not to look at his pectorals."

"Now why did you tell me that, Theresa? Just because you said that, it's gonna be hard for me not to glance at his chest."

"I'll be glad to interview him for you. You want me to?" Theresa asked hopefully.

"Not a chance. Have the choir escorted to the studio;

they're on the air in fifteen minutes." Monique exhaled deeply, then displayed a huge grin on her face and opened the door to her office. "Mr. Primer, how are you?"

At two o'clock in the afternoon, Theresa came into Monique's office and set a bouquet of roses on her desk. Monique turned her attention away from her computer and looked at them curiously. "Who are those for?"

Theresa gave her an irritated look. "You know, Monique, to be a Senior Executive Producer, you sure ask dumb questions sometimes. Who do you think these roses are for, the cleaning lady?"

She gave Monique the small envelope that accompanied the roses. Monique silently read what was written on the card inside.

'I hope the rest of your day goes better than the morning you had. I appreciate everything you do for me.'

Theresa leaned over across the desk to try and see what was written on the card. "I didn't know Boris had it in him. He must be in the dog house."

Monique quickly placed the card back in its envelope. "They're not from Boris."

Theresa's eyes bucked out at Monique and the corners of her lips turned up in a sly sneer. "Aah, sooky, sooky, now. Somebody's creeping."

"Ain't nobody creeping."

"Who sent them then?"

"None of your business," Monique answered.

"I knew I should've steamed the envelope open. Why won't you tell me who sent them?"

"The card isn't signed. I don't know who sent them." Monique didn't lie about the card not being signed, but she definitely knew who had sent the roses to her.

Theresa looked deeply into Monique's eyes. "You're a liar."

"Excuse me?"

"You're lying, Monique."

Monique leaned back and crossed her legs. "Uh, Theresa, don't you have some work to do?"

"Nope, I'm done for the day."

"No, you're not. I need a proposal typed for Mr. Wiley."

Theresa put her hand on her hip. "I'll get back to work when you tell me who sent the roses."

"Is that right? How about you get back to work right now before you find yourself standing in the unemployment line this afternoon?"

Upon leaving Monique's office, Theresa said, "Where there's a will, there's a way. And I'm willing to find out who sent those roses."

When Theresa shut the door behind her, Monique took the card out of the envelope and read it again. She read the card a third time before inserting it and its envelope in the paper shredder. Back at her desk, she smiled as she dialed Adonis's work number. It was a familiar number to Monique. Boris had gotten Adonis hired at the electric company making good money. Monique keyed in his extension, and her call was answered on the second ring.

"Hi, it's Monique. You busy?"

"Never too busy to talk to you."

Her smile got wider. "I just wanted to call and thank you for my roses. They're beautiful."

"Beautiful roses for a beautiful lady. They're my way of

saying thanks for accepting me into your house and making me feel at home."

"You are family, Adonis. Of course, Boris and I would welcome you."

"That means a lot to me. Aunt Myrtle raised me and Boris to always appreciate the people who go out of their way for us. My father's sister is more like a mother to me than an aunt."

Well, at least one of you listened to her, Monique thought. "After graduating from music school, I could've moved back in Aunt Myrtle's house until I got on my feet, but to me, that would be like taking a step backward in life. But I promise to be out of your basement within a couple of months. I'm sure I'll find a nice condo real soon."

"Where are you looking to buy?"

"Somewhere in the south suburbs; possibly Burr Ridge."

"Arykah is a realtor. You should give her a call. I'm sure she'll be glad to help you find something. Really, really, glad." The city of Burr Ridge was big money, and Monique knew that Arykah would jump on that.

Adonis remembered the vibes Arykah gave him in church yesterday. "Uh, thanks but no thanks. Nothing against your friend, but I've already contacted a realtor to help me."

As a best friend, Monique fulfilled her duty by referring Arykah Miles when she knew of someone interested in purchasing property. But truth be told, Monique knew that Adonis was very wise in seeking an agent elsewhere because Arykah would be on him like white on rice. "Well, take all the time you need. I enjoy having you, and I'm sure Boris does too. I'm sorry for the spats you have to witness on a daily basis. I know our basement hasn't turned out to be the peace and quiet you thought you'd get."

"Monique, you don't have to apologize for anything. I grew up with Boris, remember? Aunt Myrtle raised us as brothers. He is the same today as when we were teenagers. When you left this morning, I told Boris about himself. I tried to get him to see that he was wrong for not refilling your gas tank."

"And I can just bet he tried to make you think I was overreacting by complaining about it, didn't he?"

"Of course. It's just like Boris to do that. But I had serious man to man words with him, and I think he understands that he needs to be more attentive to you and your needs."

Monique became speechless. Boris was three years Adonis's senior, yet he had to take love lessons from his younger cousin. As far as Monique was concerned, Adonis could stay with them forever. With his foot constantly up Boris's butt, she was guaranteed to be treated like the queen she was.

Adonis's two-way pager beeped. "Well, it looks like I have a job to do. I'm being summoned to Loyola Hospital. Apparently, one of the elevators lost power and someone's stuck inside."

"Oh my, that's terrible," Monique said. "I'll let you go so you can get over there. I'll see you at home, and thanks again for my roses." Monique disconnected the line and dialed Boris's cellular number.

"Talk to me," he said.

"Hey."

"You sound like you're still in the bed. You ain't up yet? I didn't know I could put it on you like that."

Monique frowned. Did she dial the correct number? "Boris, it's me. What are you talking about?"

Immediately the telephone line went dead. She removed the receiver away from her ear and stared at it in disbelief. Instead of pressing the numbers of Boris's cellular number again, Monique opted to redial the last call to see if she had accidentally dialed the wrong number. Her call was sent directly into Boris's voicemail. Monique placed the receiver on its base and thought about what Boris had said. There wasn't any touchy feely activity in their bedroom that morning, so Monique wondered who he was talking about or who he thought he was talking to.

It was twenty minutes later when Theresa sent Boris's call through to Monique.

"What's up?" he asked.

"Why did you hang up on me when I called the first time?"

"When did you call me?"

"So, now you're gonna play stupid, huh? I called twenty minutes ago, Boris. You said something about me being asleep and putting it on me."

"Monique, my cell phone ain't rang all day. I don't know what you're talking about. You sure you dialed *my* number?"

It really ticked Monique off when he tried to play her for a fool. "I've been dialing your number for two years, Boris. I think I got it right by now."

Boris heard the hostility in her voice. "Look, Monique, I'm at a job site, and I don't have time for this. I don't know who you talked to, but it wasn't me, okay? I was just calling to see how you're doing, but as usual, I see you have an attitude for no reason, so I'll talk to you later." Boris disconnected the call.

Monique sat at her desk steaming. There was no question she had dialed the correct number, and it was no question that Boris had answered. The question to ask was, 'Who was he messing around with?'

She took one of Adonis's long stemmed roses from the vase and inhaled the scent. *Never too busy to talk to you . . . It's my way of saying thanks . . . You've done enough, it's time for you to relax, I'll clean the kitchen . . . Thanks, Monique, you're somethin' else . . . I appreciate everything you do for me.*

"Monique."

She blinked her eyes a few times and saw Theresa standing on the opposite side of her desk. "I'm sorry, Theresa, what is it?"

"Didn't you hear the intercom? I've been buzzing you for the past five minutes. Mr. Wiley is holding on line three."

Monique reinserted the rose in the bouquet, dismissed all thoughts of her houseguest, and pressed the third button on the telephone. "Sorry to keep you waiting, Mr. Wiley. What can I do for you?"

Monique drove into the driveway at 6:30 that evening. She saw Adonis pushing the lawnmower back and forth across the front lawn. She'd bet Boris was in the house with his eyes glued to the *ESPN* channel while his cousin played the role as man of the house. This was probably Boris's way of saving money. Normally, he'd pay the thirteen-year-old boy next door to mow the lawn.

Before she exited the car, Monique sat behind the wheel and watched Adonis. Under the hot June sun, his muscles glistened and sweat soaked through his white tank T-shirt. Adonis walked behind the lawnmower to one side of the lawn, took a pair of scissors from his back pocket, then knelt to cut weeds.

Monique got out of the car and strutted up the walk-way. "Hey, you."

Adonis looked up at her. Monique saw streams of sweat cascading down the sides of his face. Adonis's complexion was like none other, and Monique understood why Arykah was so smitten with him. The sun beamed on his skin and made it shine.

"Welcome home. How was work today?" Adonis asked.

Monique shrugged her shoulders. "Okay, I guess. Work was work, nothin' to brag about."

Adonis stood and wiped his face with a towel.

Sweet as candy. Monique had to mentally check herself. She was thinking like her best friend. What was wrong with her? This man was her fiancé's cousin, which meant he was off limits. Arykah's devilish ways were rubbing off on her.

"That's a nice suit you're wearing, and your hair is pretty," Adonis complimented.

Monique was confident in her own skin. Men of all ages and races were attracted to her pretty brown features and voluptuous curves upon first sight. But compliments had stopped flowing from Boris's lips to her ears long ago. Adonis confirmed what she already knew; she was a beautiful black woman. "Thanks, Adonis, but as big as I am, I need to be on a diet."

"Monique, unless your health is at risk, you shouldn't change anything about yourself. You're gorgeous."

She blushed and looked down at her ivory-colored stilettos.

Adonis sat on the first step of the porch. "Tell me about your day at work. This morning, I heard you say that you had a meeting."

Could Adonis be for real? She'd been with Boris for

two years, and he had never asked about her day at work. The times she tried to share with him the details of her day, he'd blown her off. Monique set her briefcase on the bottom step and leaned against the banister. "Well, WGOD has lost a lot of listeners over the age of fifty. In the meeting this morning, I suggested that our deejays dedicate an hour of their airtime playing gospel music from the fifties, sixties, and seventies."

"That sounds cool. Did your boss like your idea?"

"Yep, he loved it. He ordered all of the old school music to be brought up from the archives. The new WGOD goes into effect at midnight tomorrow."

Adonis clapped his hands and applauded Monique. "Congratulations. If you keep solving problems, a promotion may present itself."

It saddened Monique that Boris wasn't as enthusiastic about her work. It was a shame that his cousin could so easily step in and play the supportive role. "I hope so, Adonis. Where's Boris?"

"He left about a half hour ago. He said something about getting Aunt Myrtle's prescription for her diabetes refilled."

"Her prescription was just refilled on Saturday."

Adonis threw his hands in the air and stood. "Hey, I thought that's what he said, but don't quote me on it. I could be mistaken."

Monique picked up her briefcase and went into the house. She poured Adonis a glass of grape Kool-Aid on ice and brought it outside to him. "You look like you could use this."

Adonis graciously took the glass from her. "Monique, you're a godsend."

Mesmerized, she stood and watched his Adam's apple

move up and down with each swallow he took. Beads of
sweat ran down his neck and dissolved into his tank.

He gave the almost empty glass to her. "That was right
on time, I appreciate it."

Monique took the glass into the kitchen. Before she
placed it in the sink, she looked at the sip of Kool-Aid
Adonis had left. She ran her finger along the entire rim of
the glass, then swallowed what was left in it.

In her bedroom, Monique undressed and stepped into
palazzo pajama pants with a matching tank top. She
hung her suit in the closet, sat on the bed, picked up the
telephone and called her mother-in-law to be. "Hey,
Gravy, how ya doin?"

According to Monique, Myrtle made the best homemade gravy in the world. Since the first time she sat at
Myrtle's dinner table, Monique had been calling her 'Gravy'
because that was her specialty. When other members of
Boris's family called Myrtle by the nickname Monique
had given her, Myrtle put them in their place. She said
that name was for Monique's use only. Boris was Myrtle's
only child, and she had always told Monique she thought
of her as the daughter that she never had.

The two women were very close. There had been times
when Monique shared things with Myrtle that she hadn't
shared with anyone else. Having lost her mother to a
brain tumor at the impressionable age of sixteen, Monique
was happy to have Myrtle Cortland. Myrtle always favored Monique during the spats she had with her son.
Many times she told Monique to leave Boris because he
didn't realize how special she was.

*"Baby Girl, one man's loss is another man's gain. I
don't care if he is my son, you deserve better,"* she'd said.

"I'm still in the land of the living, so I guess that's a
good thang. How's my Baby Girl?"

'Baby Girl' was the nickname Myrtle Cortland assigned to Monique the first time she had met her. She said Monique's skin was as soft as a baby's bottom.

"I'm fine, Gravy. I'm looking for Boris. Is he there?"

"Is he supposed to be? 'Cause I ain't seen him if he is."

That was the reason Monique loved Myrtle. She never covered for Boris, no matter what. "Adonis said Boris was getting your diabetes medication refilled."

"I got my medicine refilled two days ago. Boris ain't been here."

Once again, Monique's suspicions had been confirmed.

It was just about midnight when Boris came into the bedroom. Monique lay on her side facing away from him, staring at the wall. Boris didn't bother turning on the light. He undressed as quietly as he could, put his clothes in the hamper and went to the bathroom. When Monique heard the water in the shower going, she got out of bed, stormed in the bathroom, and snatched the shower curtain back.

"Where have you been, Boris?"

He stood in the shower with soapsuds covering every inch of his body. "What?"

"Where . . . have . . . you . . . been? And before you say 'my mother's house,' I already called her."

Boris knew his absence would raise Monique's red flags. Earlier in the evening, he had called his mother and asked her to lie about his whereabouts, should Monique call her house looking for him. Myrtle had informed Boris that Monique had already called and she didn't lie for him. But Boris had come up with a back-up. "Monique, can I finish my shower first?"

She ignored his question. "Where have you been?"

"I was at church, practicing."

"Practicing what?"

"I was getting ready for choir rehearsal on Wednesday."

Monique shifted and placed all of her two hundred plus pounds on her right leg. "If the musicians were rehearsing tonight, why was Adonis here?"

"I was practicing by myself."

She knew Boris was lying. "So, you're telling me that you've been at church all this time. Is that what you're saying?"

"Yeah."

Monique walked out of the bathroom and slammed the door. She got back into bed and stared at the dark ceiling, contemplating. When she heard the water in the shower stop, she turned toward the wall and closed her eyes.

Downstairs, Adonis lay awake in bed listening. He wondered why his cousin refused to honor and respect his good thing.

As soon as Monique strapped herself in the seatbelt Tuesday morning, on her way to work, she took her cellular phone from her purse and called Arykah's house.

"It's seven thirty. You better be on your deathbed," Arykah answered sleepily.

Monique chuckled. "Good morning to you too. It's time for you to get up."

"No, it's not. I got about seven minutes of good sleep left. I hit the snooze button five times."

Monique frowned. "You must be talking in your sleep, because I don't have a clue what you just said, Arykah."

"Who is this?"

"Arykah, will you wake up and talk to me?"

"Who is this?"

"It's me, Monique, and I got an issue."

"You ain't got no tissue?"

Monique wanted to cuss. Her gut instinct told her to hang up on Arykah but she wanted to talk. "Arykah, wake up."

"Call me back in five minutes."

"See, I wouldn't do this to you, Arykah. If you called me early in the morning, I'd talk to you."

"First of all, I have enough sense not to call anyone's house this early in the morning."

"I need to talk. I'm serious."

Arykah lazily sat up on the bed. "This better be good, Monique. What is it?"

"The finance committee meets on Monday nights, right?"

"Uh-huh."

"Were you at church last night?"

Arykah yawned in Monique's ear. "Uh-huh."

"What time did you leave?"

Arykah stopped her. "Uh, hold up. What's up with the third degree?"

"I wanna know if you saw Boris at church last night."

"Yeah, that fool was there."

"What was he doing?" Monique asked.

"He was grinning all up in Kita's face, but she didn't seem to mind. She met his smile tooth for tooth."

"Kita? What was *she* doing there?"

"She's a praise dancer. The dancers rehearse on Monday nights.

Monique's anger was on level seven, slowly rising. "What were they talking about?"

"The heck if I know. I wasn't that close to them. I don't even think Boris saw me because he wouldn't have been x-raying Kita's tonsils if he had."

Monique entered the Dan Ryan Expressway at 95th

Street and headed north. "Would you believe Boris didn't get home until almost midnight? Why didn't you call and tell me what you saw?"

That question caused Arykah to become fully awake. "Monique, you act like you don't know Boris is a ho. How many times have I come to you with somethin' that I've seen him do? Whatever I tell you makes no difference in the status of your relationship or living arrangements, so why should I bother?"

"It is not like that, Arykah."

"Then how is it?"

"It ain't like *that*."

"Okay, you ain't gonna like what I'm gettin' ready to tell you, but you need to know this. Last night I was in the bathroom behind the stall when Cherry and the new praise dancer, Tracy, came in. Of course, they had no clue I was in there. I heard Tracy ask Cherry where Kita had disappeared to. Apparently, Kita ditched dance rehearsal. Cherry told Tracy that Kita told her that she and Boris were going out to eat. Then Cherry lowered her voice and told Tracy that Kita told her not to wait up for her."

Monique squealed. *"Not to wait up for her?"*

"Uh-huh. You know Kita and Cherry are roommates."

Monique's anger had reached level ten. "That fool thought I was asleep when he came in last night. He took his clothes off and got in the shower, and when I confronted him, he gave me some lame excuse about being at church practicing for choir rehearsal."

"I don't know if he practiced or not. I was on my way to the finance meeting when I saw him and Kita cheesing at each other. Um, I don't mean to change the subject, but how is Adonis doing?"

At the mention of Adonis's name, Monique smiled. "He's fine. Arykah, he did the sweetest thing yesterday."

"Like what?"

"Boris and I had an argument before I left for work, and apparently Adonis heard us. He sent a dozen roses to my job to cheer me up. Wasn't that sweet?"

This was not what Arykah wanted to hear. "Too sweet, if you ask me."

Monique exited the expressway at Pershing Road and drove two miles west. "Why do you say that?"

"Think about it, Monique. You and your man had an argument, but instead of Adonis taking his *cousin* to the bowling alley or to the park to shoot some hoops to cheer *Boris* up, he sends *you* flowers. You don't think that's a little odd?"

"Arykah, he did it to be nice."

"If you say so, Monique, but you need to watch that."

"There's nothing to watch. Adonis was just being Adonis." Monique pulled into her assigned parking spot at WGOD. The placard displayed on the building read: RESERVED FOR MONIQUE MORRISON, SENIOR EXECUTIVE PRODUCER. She bid farewell to Arykah and entered the radio station.

Monique got to her desk and thought about her situation and wondered what she should do about Boris. She picked up the telephone and dialed her cousin, Amaryllis. She'd know exactly what to do.

Chapter 3

Amaryllis Price, Monique's cousin, listened patiently while Monique gave her the details of her and Boris's relationship. "I'm saved now, but I'm wondering if the saint in me should tell you what you need to hear, or if the crazy in me should tell you what you wanna hear," Amaryllis said.

"Well, tell me both. But first tell me what I need to hear," Monique said.

"Are you sure you want me to? 'Cause, you know I ain't one to bite my tongue or sugarcoat nothin', Monique. I may be saved, but I'm still ghetto with a capital 'G'."

Monique laughed. "Yeah, I know, Amaryllis. That's why I called you. I know you'll come correct and set me straight. So go ahead and lay it on me. I can handle it."

"Okay. Remember that *you* called *me*, all right? I don't want this conversation to come between us."

"It won't. I promise." Monique wasn't so sure. Amaryllis was the queen of tough love.

Amaryllis saved the data she entered into her computer at work. Next she moved back from her desk, crossed her right leg over her left knee, then moved in for the kill. "Why are you acting like a fool, Monique? I taught you better than this. You make me ashamed to say we're cousins." She came out of the bag on Monique.

Though she knew Amaryllis was rough, Monique wasn't prepared for this.

Amaryllis noticed Monique didn't respond. "You want me to shut up?"

"Say what you gotta say, Amaryllis."

"It sounds to me like you're waiting for Jesus to become flesh, swoop down, and look you in your eyes and verbally tell you that Boris is not the man for you. You got good sense. Why are you acting so dumb?" She heard Monique sniffle. "You created this mess yourself. Boris couldn't care less if you died tomorrow, and he's proven that over and over again.

"You are a twenty-eight-year-old, beautiful, black woman. First and foremost, you're a role model. Learn to represent your sistas. Our women ancestors went through rape and too much mental, verbal, and physical abuse on our behalf, for us to be living beneath the standards they've set for us. If Harriet Tubman was alive to witness the crap you are taking off of Boris, she'd put her foot knee deep in your behind, Monique. She didn't risk her life bringing our great, great, great grandmother through the Underground Railroad for you to act as though your life ain't worth nothing.

"Never, under any circumstances, allow a man to control you, because it motivates you to make bad judgments. Start loving yourself, and put Monique first. To heck with Boris, because in so many ways, he's saying 'To heck with Monique. '

"He presented you with an engagement ring that another woman gave back to him. And like a fool, you accepted it. It ain't even a fourth of a carat. You gotta put on contacts, a pair of bifocals, then hold binoculars up to your eyes while looking through a telescope just to see the darn ring. You're allowing Boris to treat you like trash. A man will only do to you what you allow him to do."

Tears dripped from Monique's chin onto her desk. She knew Amaryllis was speaking nothing but the truth.

"You still love me?" Amaryllis asked her.

"Yeah, I love you." Monique was barely able to whisper.

"Good, 'cause I ain't finished. I'm getting ready to give you a ghetto Bible lesson." She cleared her throat and began. "God took Eve out of Adam because he was nothing by himself. He was alone, bored, and dumb. When Eve was made, all of that changed. Why? Because she had the tools to make his days fulfilling and his life complete. Women are powerful creatures. *We* cook the meals, *we* clean the house, and *we* carry the babies for nine months. This world belongs to women, and most of us don't even know it.

"See, both Adam and Eve were told not to eat from the tree of good and evil, but the enemy tricked Eve. And when she gave Adam the fruit, he knew better. But Eve was so beautiful and seductive to the point that Adam didn't care what God said, he did whatever he had to do to get some nooky."

Monique hollered out and laughed. "What? Amaryllis, you are crazy."

"I may be crazy, but I'm truthful and smart. I've figured this thing out since I've been saved. Eve set an example for us, and when I get to heaven, I'm gonna kiss her feet. She showed us that we have the power to make men do whatever *we* want. Men can't function without us, and I bet if you pack up your stuff and leave Boris, he'd get his act together."

"But my name is on the mortgage too. I own half of that house."

"I don't give a . . . ! Girl, you almost made me go to hell. I could've said something that would've cost me my salvation. I don't care whose name is on the house. Forget about a house. What about *you*, Monique? What are you willing to do to make Boris realize that you won't be disrespected anymore? And you were dumb as heck to co-sign your name to a mortgage with a man who was not your husband. You need to leave him. If you don't want to sign an apartment lease, rent a hotel room.

"Show Boris that you can make it without him. Don't even go to your church on Sunday. Visit other churches. You can hang out with me and my roommate, Bridgette, at Progressive Ministries in Hillside. But you gotta be careful at 'Gress' though. You can get hooked in no time. The praise over there is just ridiculous."

Amaryllis uncrossed her left leg from her right leg and switched. "Once you prove to Boris that you ain't a punk, and you ain't taking his crap no more, he'll change his ugly ways. He's not stupid; he knows he can clown on you because you accept everything he throws at you. And whoever this Kita chick is, she won't be in the picture long. See, some women, especially women in the church, feel that if they can take a man from his wife or woman, they've accomplished somethin'. But all they're really doing is putting themselves on blast and showing how insecure they are.

"Obviously, Kita doesn't know the real Boris, or she wouldn't be wasting her time pursuing a man who has no morals. But this is her little red wagon; let her pull it any way she wants to. And what is it about musicians and preachers, anyway? For some reason every woman feels the need to be hanging on the arm of one. Don't give this girl the satisfaction of seeing you sweat and thinking she's got one up on you. Do yourself a favor and wrap Boris's tail up nice and pretty with a big red bow and serve him to her on a silver platter with all the trimmings. You don't have to put yourself in competition with any woman for anything, because you are God's daughter, a King's kid, and you're second to none. And I promise you this, Monique; when Kita sees that you don't care what she and Boris do, she'll lose interest and move on to her next prey. This is only a game to her."

Monique listened to Amaryllis in awe. Just hearing how much knowledge she'd gained in the short time she'd been saved was mind blowing. Monique remembered it wasn't that long ago when Amaryllis herself was a professional man stealer.

"Do you understand the words that came out of my mouth, Monique?"

"Yeah, I understand everything you said. And I know what I gotta do."

"Sometimes we have to trust wisdom and not our hearts."

"I love you, Amaryllis. Thanks for setting me on Straight Street."

"Anytime, sweetie. You can put my check in the mail."

"What check?" Monique asked.

"My honorarium. I did just preach, you know. The topic of my sermon was, *Every Woman's Middle Name Ought To Be Eve*."

Monique informed Theresa that she'd be out of the office for the remainder of the day and to forward all of her calls to her voicemail. On her way back home, Monique's cellular phone rang. She recognized the familiar number. "Why aren't you at work?" she asked Arykah upon answering.

"After I talked to you this morning, I laid back down and overslept, so I decided to take a vacation day. I just called your office, and Theresa said you left for the day. What's up?"

Monique's adrenaline was flowing. "I'm on my way home to pack my clothes. I'm checking into a hotel."

"Whaaat? Where's the brick that fell on your head?" Arykah was impressed with Monique's courage, though this was the third time in she and Boris's two-year-old relationship that Monique had separated herself from him. Each time before, she'd gone back after only a few short days.

"Ha-ha, very funny. A brick didn't fall on my head."

"Well, something must've knocked some sense into you, because you and I both know that you didn't have any."

Monique was surprised yet happy to see Arykah sitting on her front porch with two large authentic Louis Vuitton suitcases next to her. "I figured since I didn't have anything better to do on this bright and sunny day, like go to the mall or pamper myself with a Swedish massage, I'd help you pack. And I brought two suitcases so you won't have to stuff your clothes in hefty bags. You know you're ghetto like that."

Monique hugged her best friend. She knew she could always depend on Arykah to be by her side through thick and thin. "Thanks, Arykah. I love you."

"Yeah, yeah, yeah. Come on, let's get this packing party started."

Never in her wildest dreams did Monique ever think she'd be in the position of preparing to leave Boris again. This was not how she envisioned her life to be. As they were packing the second suitcase, Monique broke down and cried. She sat on the bed and covered her face with her hands.

Arykah sat next to her and pulled Monique in her arms. "It's gonna be okay, sis. I know it hurts."

"Why can't Boris do right?"

"Because Boris is a man, and that's all I gotta say. Just be glad you don't have any babies by him." Arykah pulled away and looked Monique sternly in her eyes. "When was your last period?"

At seven thirty that evening, Adonis came upstairs from the basement. As usual, Boris's eyes were glued to a basketball game on the television in the living room.

"Hey, cuz, where's Monique? She's usually home from work by now."

Boris waited to see if a player scored before he answered Adonis. "Aw, man, he could've made that shot. It was wide open. I don't know where she is."

"You haven't talked to her?" Adonis was concerned.

"Nope. She's probably somewhere with Arykah, getting her hair and nails done."

"You ain't worried, man?"

"Worried about what? She's all right." Boris dismissed all thoughts of Monique and concentrated on the basketball game.

Adonis shook his head in disgust at Boris's unconcern for Monique's absence in that late hour of the day. Of course, he could've called Monique's cellular phone himself just to make sure she was okay, but he knew it would be out of order to do so. Adonis had to constantly remind himself that Monique was his cousin's girlfriend, not his.

He took Sunday's leftovers out of the refrigerator, made himself a plate, then warmed it in the microwave and took it downstairs.

Adonis's cellular phone woke him at 10:30 P.M. He didn't bother looking at the caller identification. He answered in a daze.

"Hi, Adonis."

He opened his eyes at the sound of her soft voice. "Monique? Where are you?"

"Are you near Boris?"

"Nah, I'm downstairs. Where are you? Are you okay?"

"I'm at a hotel downtown. I moved out."

Adonis sat up on the bed. "What?"

"I couldn't take him anymore, Adonis. It's time for me to love Monique."

"I knew something was up when you didn't come home. Boris thinks you're out getting your hair done."

"Well, he hasn't called my cell phone to verify that, so apparently he ain't too worried."

"What hotel are you at?"

"I'm not telling you because I don't want Boris to know."

"Monique, you don't need to be out there by yourself without anybody knowing where you are."

"Arykah knows where I am, and I'll call Gravy when I get to work in the morning."

"Monique, please tell me where you are. Are you hungry? Do you need anything? Is your door locked securely? Let me come to you." Adonis was losing his self-control.

Monique's heart leapt in her chest. Why couldn't these caring words come from the other Mr. Cortland? "Adonis, I need to do this, and I need to do it alone. But you can always call my cell phone or my office number."

"What do I tell Boris?"

"Boris doesn't care about me. I'm willing to bet fifty bucks that if you or Gravy don't mention my name to him, a week will pass before he even realizes that I'm gone."

Monique hung up from Adonis and called Amaryllis. "I just wanted you to know that I checked into the Hilton hotel downtown."

"Good for you, Monique. Does Boris know you're missing yet?"

"Probably not, but you know what? I couldn't care less. Listen, earlier you told me what I needed to hear, you never told me what I wanted to hear. What was it?"

"Well, if I weren't saved, I would've suggested that we call Nana in Baton Rouge and tell her to send us something to put in Boris's food that will put a root on him. Nana will have him on the lakefront, barefoot in his drawers, walking up to people, scratching his head saying, 'What's my name? Where do I live? Can you take me home?'"

"Amaryllis, you are crazy." Monique laughed so loud, the people in the suite next door banged on the wall to shut her up.

"Boris doesn't know whom he's messing with. We Creole women gotta stick together. Nana would've shipped us some stuff overnight. By this time tomorrow, Boris would've been in a padded room, sitting in the middle of the floor with his legs folded in a pretzel, wearing one of those white jackets that made him hug himself, blowing spit bubbles. The doctor's report would've read: *Boris Cortland showed signs of suffering from Shaken Baby Syndrome.*"

Monique screamed out in laughter. The people in the

suite next door banged on the wall again. "Amaryllis, I gotta go, girl. I'll see you at your church on Sunday."

Monique's father and Amaryllis's mother were brother and sister but the two cousins were like night and day. Boris and Adonis were also the offspring of brother and sister, and Monique often wondered why she wasn't lucky enough to have met Adonis first.

Adonis woke Boris by tapping his leg. He opened his eyes slightly. "What's up, man? Who won the game?"

"Never mind the game, cuz. Your woman is gone. She ain't coming home."

"What are you talking about?" Boris asked the question half caring.

"Monique just called and said she moved out."

Boris looked up at Adonis. "Moved out?"

"Yeah, man; she's gone. What are you gonna do about it?"

"Monique is a grown woman. She can do whatever she wants to do. I told you she's a drama queen. When she sees that I ain't chasing after her, she'll be back. This ain't the first time she called herself leaving."

Adonis couldn't understand Boris's nonchalant attitude. "You ain't going out to look for her, man? She's out there by herself."

Boris positioned himself comfortably in his La Z Boy and closed his eyes. "She'll be back. She always comes back."

Adonis headed back downstairs. He laid on his back and stared at the dark ceiling. His heart went out to Monique, and he felt the need to protect her. But from who? His own cousin? Boris and Monique were adults, and every couple had their issues. But Monique was pulling on Adonis's soul. He sat up on the side of his bed and bowed his head.

"Almighty Father, I may be out of place talking to You about this, but I feel the need to cover Monique. I don't know where she is or what she's doing at this moment, but I humbly ask that You surround her with Your glory. Please anoint her car as she drives to and from work, and I bind accidents and mechanical failures in Your holy name. Dispatch Your angels all around her. Father, in Your name, this I pray." Adonis paused before he spoke to God again. "And Father, I need You to do one more thing for me. Please don't let me fall for this girl."

He searched for the right words to pray for Boris, but couldn't find any. Adonis didn't feel led to talk to God on his cousin's behalf. When he realized sleep wasn't coming anytime soon, he turned on the radio to V103 FM, then lay down. The words to a song paralyzed him. He could do nothing but lie there and listen.

"Tell me what kind of man would treat his woman so cold? He treats you like you're nothing when you're worth more than gold."

In the song, a male singer told a woman, who had been mistreated by her man, that she deserved much more than what she was receiving. He exposed his heart to her and let it be known that he wanted to do all of the things for her that her man wouldn't do.

Adonis closed his eyes and imagined himself as being the song artist, and the lady he was singing to was Monique.

Adonis called Monique's cellular phone at 5:45 A.M. "You wanna meet at the lakefront and watch the sun come up?"

"I would love to," she answered.

"Let's meet at Lake Shore Drive and Sheridan Road in a half hour."

Monique was sitting on a bench looking at the tides when Adonis walked up. He stood behind her admiring her silhouette. Sitting pretty in a beautiful yellow sundress with her hair dancing to the beat of the breeze and the water waving in front of her, made the perfect picture for a postcard.

He approached Monique carrying two Styrofoam cups and a small white bag. "Sorry I'm late. I stopped for breakfast. I hope you're hungry."

Monique smiled. "I'm famished. What did you get?"

He sat down next to her. "For starters, I got hazelnut flavored coffee with extra cream and extra sugar with a pinch of cinnamon."

Monique was floored. "I love hazelnut coffee when it's light and sweet with cinnamon in it. How did you know?"

"I did my homework," he answered.

Her grin got wider. "I'm impressed so far. What's in the bag?"

"What do you *want* to be in the bag?"

Monique looked out at the lake and thought about the question he asked. "How about a life with no stress, no worries, no disappointments, and no bills?"

"Is that all? Girl, you ain't asking for nothing." Adonis sat the bag in the palm of his left hand and held it out in front of him at arm's length. He waved his right hand over it three times. "Abracadabra, in this bag shall be what the lady requested."

Monique laughed. "Adonis, you are so silly. That was cute though; real cute."

He opened the bag and looked inside, then frowned at the contents. "Uh, I'm gonna have to work on my magic skills. What would be the next thing you'd want?"

"You think your magic skills can make a raisin bagel that's lightly toasted with butter appear in the bag?"

Again, Adonis held the bag at arm's length and said the magic words. Without looking into the bag, he smiled and gave it to Monique. "Your wish is my command."

In the bag, Monique saw two raisin bagels lightly toasted with butter. At this point, her mind was completely blown. Without thinking, she leaned over and kissed his lips.

Before she had a chance to pull away, Adonis pressed the back of her head forward to keep her lips where they were. Monique allowed herself to get lost in the forbidden passion she felt for him.

He pulled away and looked deeply into her eyes. "I'm in love with you, Monique. I wanna take care of you and do all the things for you that Boris doesn't do."

She was at a loss for words. For so long she had been longing for Boris's undivided attentiveness, for him to say to her the things his cousin said, and for Boris to make her feel the way his cousin had. "Adonis, I, uh—"

"Adonis, I what?" The deep, angry voice came from behind them. They looked over their shoulders, startled to see Boris. He walked around the bench and stood directly in front of Monique and Adonis with one hand behind his back. "Go ahead, Monique. Finish what you were saying. Tell him how much you love and want to be with him."

Monique didn't say a word. Boris turned his attention toward Adonis. "What the heck is going on, cuz? How long have you been screwing around with my woman?"

To Adonis, Boris appeared to be lethargic and high on drugs. "Boris, slow your roll, because it ain't like that."

"Oh, it ain't like that, huh? How is it, Monique? Is this the reason you won't let me touch you anymore? You've been giving your stuff to my cousin?"

Adonis stood and took two angry steps toward Boris. His disrespect toward Monique had to end today, Adonis would make sure of it. "Watch how you talk to her, man. I said, it ain't like that."

Boris brought a .25-caliber semiautomatic Beretta from behind his back and pointed it at Adonis's nose. "Fool, who the heck are you walkin' up on?"

Adonis stopped dead in his tracks and raised his hands.

Monique screamed.

Boris's nostrils swelled when he inhaled. "Come on, punk. Take another step forward so I can blast you."

Adonis kept his hands in the air. He swallowed, paused, then spoke to Boris calmly. "Cuz, you're high and overreacting. Don't do nothing crazy."

Boris stood flatfooted. "Crazy? I'll show you crazy." He pointed the gun at Monique's chest and pulled the trigger.

The gunshot was the loudest noise Adonis had ever heard. It jolted his body awake.

His eyes opened wide, and he quickly sat up on the bed. It was moments before the familiar surroundings in the basement came into clear view. Sweat dripped from his chin onto his chest. Adonis was panting for air as though he were having a seizure. He reached over to the nightstand and turned on the lamp and saw that his T-shirt and pillowcase were drenched with sweat. His alarm clock read 5:45 A.M.

"Oh, my God," he said. In his dream, that was the exact time he had called Monique. He wanted to make sure she was okay, but was afraid that if he called, his dream would become a reality. He got out of bed and walked upstairs to the kitchen. He filled a glass with tap water from the sink. He brought the glass to his lips, looked out of the window and saw the sun rising. He had to admit to himself that slowly but surely he was falling for Monique, but he didn't want to. Why hadn't God answered his prayer?

Chapter 4

Monique's intercom buzzed.

"Yes, Theresa?"

"Arykah Miles is on line one."

Monique picked up the telephone and pressed the first button. "Good morning, sis."

"Don't we sound like we're bright-eyed and bushy-tailed this morning. I take it that you survived your first night of celibacy."

"Girl, please. Boris ain't been gettin' any on a regular anyway. I love the king-size bed though. I'm gonna have to put one on my Christmas list this year for Santa."

"Has the fool called you yet?" Arykah asked.

"Nope, he hasn't called my cell, and I've instructed Theresa not to send his calls through. No matter how many times he calls, she's to tell him I'm in a meeting. The security guard downstairs is familiar with Boris and won't allow him into the building."

"My, my, my. I guess it's true what they say about a woman scorned. It's a shame when a man can't appreciate a good woman when he has one. I hope you realize something, Monique."

The word appreciate sent Monique's mind miles away. *I appreciate everything you do for me.* "What did you say, Arykah?"

"I said, I hope you realize somethin'."

"What?" Monique asked.

"You didn't go home last night, and Boris hasn't called to check to see if you were all right. This proves that you're not a priority to him."

Just then Monique's cellular phone rang. She looked at the caller identification.

"Arykah, my cell is ringing."

"Is it Boris?"

"No, but I gotta answer the call."

"Okay, call me later, and remember what I said."

Monique was anxious to answer the call before it went to her voicemail. "Okay, I will." She placed the receiver on its base and brought her cellular phone to her ear. "Monique speaking."

"Hi, it's Adonis. How are you?"

She smiled. "I'm good. How are *you*?"

"I'm good too. I'm sitting at my desk browsing through my emails before I head out to a job site. But first I wanted to check and make sure you're okay and to see if you needed anything."

I guess this is what Arykah meant by 'priority.' Monique didn't know why she was smiling. This man was her fiancé's cousin, and she knew the right thing to do was to fight whatever feelings she may be developing for Adonis. "You are so sweet, and I thank you, but I'm fine. I don't need anything."

"Promise me you'll call if you do. No matter what time, **day** or night. I'll make myself available to you."

Monique's mouth dropped wide open. If someone had been standing in front of her, they would have been able to see what her last meal consisted of. She could hardly get the words out. *You're gonna make me love you,* is what she wanted to say. "Okay, I promise."

"How did you sleep last night?" he asked.

"Pretty good; I was all over that huge bed. My room has a balcony that faces Lake Michigan. I saw the sun rise this morning, and it was beautiful. It's a shame how we take things for granted. Watching the sun come out of the water was a sight to see. I've never witnessed it before."

Adonis's heart started to race. "You were up that early?"

"Uh-huh. My alarm is set for five forty-five every morning."

"How ironic is that? I woke up at four forty-five this morning." Adonis prayed she wouldn't ask why.

"Oh, really? We could've met for an early breakfast. I get up early to pray and meditate before my day starts. Why were *you* up so early?"

Adonis's brain scrambled for words, any words. "I pulled a muscle in my leg. It must've happened when I was turning over or somethin'."

"I know how painful that can be. How's your leg now?"

"It's all right. Um, I told Boris you called and said you moved out."

"And what did he say?" Monique asked.

"I don't know what's going on with him, but he definitely needs to get himself together."

"Adonis, is that your way of saying he didn't care?"

Actions most definitely spoke louder than words, and Boris's actions were heard clearly, that he didn't care for his woman, but Adonis refused to confirm it. In his eyes, no woman should ever feel that she wasn't cared for. "It's my way of saying Boris has issues." Adonis heard his name being paged. "Looks like I got an assignment. I'll call you back when I break for lunch."

After a three and a half hour meeting, Monique stopped at Theresa's desk on the way into her office.

"How was your meeting?" Theresa asked.

Monique exhaled a sigh of relief. "Too long. I'm glad it's over. Any messages?"

Theresa read a handful of 'While You Were Out' memos. "Mr. Wiley called wanting to see the number of calls that came in on the midnight show. Boris called; I told him you were in a meeting. He said he'd call back. Arykah left a message for you to meet her at Macy's at 1:00 P.M. She says there's a mad shoe sale going on."

Monique glanced at her wristwatch. "It's almost two o'clock, I guess I missed out. Anyone else?"

"Yep. Someone named Adonis called, but he didn't want to leave a message."

Monique smiled and took the messages from Theresa.

"So, uh, who's Adonis? And why is your fiancé banned from the building?"

Monique looked at Theresa sitting on the edge of her chair. "Not that you're entitled to know my business, but I'll tell you because I know you won't get any sleep tonight if I don't. Boris is tripping so I'm taking a breather from him. My current address is the Chicago Hilton, and that's my personal business, Theresa. The entire office staff need not know."

"Monique, I've been your personal secretary for three years. When have you known me to spread your business?"

"I want it to stay that way."

"It will. Who's Adonis?"

Monique didn't feel the need to keep Adonis's identity in the closet. "He is Boris's cousin and a friend of mine."

Theresa looked at Monique curiously. "Mm-hmm. A friend, huh?"

"Before you let your wild imagination fly out of the window, Adonis is *only* a friend."

"Monique, who do you think you're talking to? I can put two and two together. Boris is acting a fool and his cousin is acting right. If I ask a question, will you tell me the truth?"

"Depends on the question."

"Is Adonis cute?"

"That's a safe question. Yes, he's very cute."

"Did he send the roses?" Theresa asked.

"That's two questions, and yes, he sent the roses. But only to cheer me up."

"Uh-huh. One more question."

"No, Theresa, you know too much already." Monique walked into her office and closed the door behind her. She sat at her desk and checked her cellular phone messages.

"What's going on with you, Monique? You call yourself moving out again? What? You expect me to chase you or somethin'? Why are you trippin'? You must be on your period, huh? Why you gotta act a fool while my cousin is living with us? What? You're tryin' to make me look bad in front of my peeps? You ain't gotta . . . " (Beep)

Monique saved the message. Boris placed the blame for their separation on her. How typical of him to refer to her monthly flow as the reason for her leaving.

"YOU GOT MAIL." Her computer sang the words after she logged on.

She turned toward her computer and typed in the password that opened her mailbox. The message was sent from Adonis. They had exchanged email addresses over the phone last night.

ACortland_music@yahoo.com >>*Monique, I will be dining at Houston's downtown at around 5 o'clock this evening. Can you join me?*

Monique leaned back in her chair and thought about it, then sat up to answer him.

MissMo@WGOD.org >>*I have another meeting at four this afternoon and I'm sure I'll be held up until seven tonight. Can I take a rain check?*

She sent the message through.

ACortland_music@yahoo.com>>*Are you absolutely sure you can't make it?*

She typed in her response.

MissMo@WGOD.org>>*I'm sorry; I can't get out of it. What are you doing later this evening?*

ACortland_music@yahoo.com>>*Choir rehearsal from 7 to 9.*

MissMo@WGOD.org>>It is Wednesday, isn't it? How about lunch tomorrow?

ACortland_music@yahoo.com>>*Sounds like a plan. I'll get back to you. Have a good meeting.*

Monique pressed the intercom. "Theresa, can you come in here please?"

"I'll be right in." Theresa came and sat across from Monique with a notepad and pen.

"I want you to call a florist downtown and order a dozen roses to be sent to Adonis Cortland at Houston's at five thirty. I want the card to read: Sorry, I can't make dinner *this* time. Don't put my name on the card. I don't wanna leave a paper trail."

Theresa smiled. "So, that's why he called three times. Why can't you make dinner?"

"Because I've got a finance meeting."

"Mr. Wiley canceled the meeting."

Monique quickly sat up in her chair. "What?"

"I'm sorry, I forgot to tell you. It's been rescheduled for eleven a.m. tomorrow. And before you get your panties in a bunch, I said I'm sorry."

Monique didn't hear Theresa because her mind was elsewhere. The finance meeting had been canceled. That changed everything. She began locking her desk drawers in preparation to leave. "You can go home, Theresa. I don't need you anymore today."

Theresa was stunned. "Say what?"

"I'm leaving for the day. You can too."

"Monique, it's a little after two. Are you for real?"

"Forget the flower order and get Starr on the phone. See if she can fit me in for a wash and blow dry in fifteen minutes."

Theresa didn't ask any more questions. Three minutes later, she buzzed Monique.

"Starr says she's booked."

"Tell her I need an emergency appointment right now, and I'll pay double."

A few seconds passed. "She said come on."

"Thanks, Theresa. I need you here at seven in the morning to prepare for the finance meeting."

"Gotcha, boss lady. I'll be here. Enjoy your dinner."

Suddenly Monique was on an emotional high. She knew it was wrong for her to accept Adonis's invitation to dinner because of the feelings she was developing for him. But she couldn't remember the last time Boris had taken her out. She didn't even know for sure if Adonis would still dine at Houston's that evening since she had declined to join him, but she was hopeful.

* * *

"Excuse me, is this seat taken?"

Adonis looked up from the menu he was holding. It was a good thing he was seated. He would've hit the floor if he hadn't been. Monique's beauty and scent took his breath away. He could do nothing but look at her.

"Has the cat got your tongue?" she asked.

Adonis stood. "Monique, you are breathtakingly beautiful. I love what you've done to your hair. And this dress; have you worn it before?"

"No, I just bought it today."

"It looks lovely on you." He stepped across the table and pulled Monique's chair out for her. "I'm glad you are able to join me. How did you get away?"

"My meeting was canceled."

"I love the scent you're wearing. What is it?"

"It's Ralph Lauren."

Adonis couldn't take his eyes off of her. "I really love your hair like that. Did you get it cut?"

Monique ran her fingers through her new tapered look. Her shoulder length tresses had been introduced to a pair of shears. "Yes, I thought it was time for a change."

The waiter approached their table. "Hello, my name is Pierre, and I'll be your server this evening. Would either of you care for a glass of wine?"

Adonis quickly spoke. "No, we'll have two pink lemonades."

Monique's eyebrows rose. When Pierre walked away, she looked at Adonis. "What makes you think that I don't want a glass of white wine to go with my dinner?"

Adonis raised his hands. "My bad. I'll go to the bar and get you one."

"I don't want wine, I want the lemonade."

He looked at Monique like she was crazy.

"Don't look at me like that. I wanna know why you chose lemonade over wine."

"Because Boris told me that you only drink alcohol when you're at home, away from the public eye. And I also know that you love pink lemonade and grape Kool-Aid. Those are the only two beverages in the house. I told you I did my homework," he said.

"When did you tell me that?"

Adonis had to catch himself. Monique sitting pretty on the beach in the yellow sundress was messing him up big time. He'd told her that in his dream. "Uh, I, um . . ."

Pierre returned with their drinks and set them on the table. "Here we go. Two pink lemonades. Are you ready to order?"

"Yes," Adonis quickly answered, thankful for the interruption.

From his apron's pocket, Pierre withdrew a notepad and pen. "What can I get you folks?"

Monique looked at Adonis. "Why don't you order for me since you did your homework. And you better not mess up, because I'm hungry."

"Don't worry, I got this," Adonis said most assuredly. He looked at Pierre. "I'll have the full slab of barbecue ribs with French fries, and the lady will have the grilled chicken Caesar salad. She'll also have a baked potato with sour cream and chives, cheddar cheese, bacon bits, and butter."

Monique sat across from Adonis in complete awe. She was grinning from ear to ear. Pierre waited for her approval. When she nodded her head, he walked away.

Pride had Adonis's chest protruding like The Incredible Hulk's. He looked at Monique with a sure smile on his face. "So, how did I do?"

"You've been following me around, haven't you? You ordered exactly what I would have."

Adonis laughed. "Nah, I ain't been following you around. It's a man's job to know what his date likes and dislikes."

Monique threw a ball into Adonis's court to see what he'd do with it. "Is this a date, Adonis?"

He knew what she was doing. She was trying to intimidate him, but he could do one better. "Do you *want* this to be a date, Monique?"

She laughed out loud. "Okay, you got me. You're good. I think we're two friends having dinner and enjoying each other's company."

Adonis picked up his glass of lemonade and held it across the table. "Touché."

Their glasses made contact, and they each took a sip without taking their eyes off of one another. Their meals were served, and they dined in style after Adonis blessed the meal.

"Boris called me today," Monique said.

Adonis swallowed his food before he spoke. "I was wondering if he had, but I wasn't going to bring it up."

"It's okay, I don't mind talkin' about it." Monique dialed her voicemail on her cellular phone and gave it to Adonis. "Listen to this."

After he heard Boris's message, Adonis gave Monique the telephone. "Seven questions of blame; eight if he hadn't gotten cut off. And not one of them was 'Baby, what I gotta do to get you back home?' or 'I'm sorry, can we get together and talk?'"

"How was he at work today?"

"Boris and I rarely see each other at work. Our desks are in separate buildings and we hardly ever get assigned to the same job sites."

Pierre approached them again. "How is everything?"

"Everything was wonderful. May we have two takeout containers, please?" Adonis asked.

As Adonis was looking over the check, Monique's cellular phone rang. "Yes, Arykah, my love," she sang into the phone.

"Don't give me that *my love* crap. Did Theresa give you my message?"

"Yes, she did. I was in a meeting when you called."

"Where are you now?" Arykah asked.

"I'm at Houston's having dinner."

"With who?"

"By myself." Monique looked at Adonis and placed her index finger on her lips.

"Yeah right, Monique. You want me to believe that you went all the way downtown to Houston's to eat by yourself?"

"Arykah, I live downtown, temporarily. Have you forgotten?"

"Okay, I'll give you that. You owe me one hundred thirty-seven dollars and twenty-six cents."

Monique frowned. "What for?"

"Because I bought you two pairs of sandals from Macy's."

"You are so sweet, Arykah."

"I ain't *that* sweet, because I want my money."

"Okay, I'll bring it to you when I leave here. I'm on my way."

"Bring me a baked potato. You know how I like it."

Monique ended the call and placed her phone in her purse. "Adonis, the only reason I lied to Arykah is because she has a major crush on you. If she had a clue that you and I were here together, she'd bust a blood vessel."

In the back of their minds, Adonis and Monique knew

they were sneaking around. What would seem like an innocent dinner between friends to an outsider, wasn't so innocent in reality. They were developing deep feelings for one another. Forbidden feelings that could create friction among family if the secret was ever found out.

"I understand. I'm way ahead of you. No one needs to know we had dinner together," Adonis said.

When Pierre came for the check, Monique placed Arykah's order to go. Pierre said it would take ten minutes.

"So, you're on your way to choir rehearsal, huh?" Monique asked Adonis.

"Yep. And you're on your way to Arykah's house?"

"Yep. She bought me sandals today. She does that so I don't ask to wear hers. Our tastes are exactly alike, especially when it comes to shoes. We always buy each other the same pair of shoes when we buy for ourselves."

"Are you telling me that you and Arykah have the exact same shoes in your closets?"

"Yes."

"Monique, I never heard of two friends doing that before. Can I ask you a question? Since you and Arykah are as tight as two friends can be, I'm curious as to why she didn't offer you to stay with her."

"This isn't the first time I've left Boris. I left twice before, but the first time I stayed with Arykah. She has a two-bedroom town home in Lansing. But that experience proved that two grown women can't live together and remain friends. We fought over everything from who would cook on which days to not having enough respect to call each other when one of us was extremely late coming in. So to keep our friendship, we decided to never live together. And it works because Arykah and I have been friends for a long—"

"You are so beautiful," Adonis interrupted.

Monique was caught off guard and mesmerized. Her deep dimples showed. "Thank you."

"I mean it. You are especially radiant this evening."

She couldn't remember the last time Boris told her she was beautiful. Come to think of it, had he ever told her?

Pierre set Arykah's order on the table. "Here you go."

Adonis told him to add Arykah's order to the bill.

"Well, in that case, your new total comes to seventy one dollars and sixteen cents."

Adonis gave him four twenty dollar bills. "Thanks Pierre, no change is necessary."

Outside of Houston's, Monique tried to give Adonis the money for Arykah's order.

"Monique, put that money back in your purse. What's eight dollars?"

"What are you talkin' about? As high as gasoline is these days, eight dollars can go a long way."

"Well, put it in your gas tank, because your money is no good to me."

The valet brought Monique's car first. She stood on her toes and kissed Adonis's cheek. "Thanks for dinner."

"You're welcome. I know you're on your way to Arykah's, but when you get to your hotel room tonight, can you please call me so that I'll know you made it to your room safely?"

She looked into his eyes. The way Adonis cared for her made Monique feel warm and very secure. "Adonis, you are too much, and yes, I will call you; I promise."

He walked Monique to her car and closed her driver's door after she got in. He stood in the street and watched her car turn left at the corner.

*   *   *

Monique was on cloud nine when she got to Arykah's house. She squealed in delight when she saw the sandals. "These are beautiful, Arykah. That's why I love you, because you take such good care of me."

Arykah sat down at the kitchen table and dug into her baked potato. "Monique, I ain't trying to hear that. Where's my money?"

Monique looked at her. "Do you hear me hollering about you paying me for that potato you're eating?"

"Give me my money, Monique. I ain't playing with you."

"I don't have enough cash on me."

"Write me a check," Arykah said.

"Arykah, you can't wait until tomorrow? You're gonna get your money."

"Uh-uh. I can't wait. Write me a check."

Monique sat down at the kitchen table and wrote Arykah a check. "This is a shame. You act like you ain't gonna get your money."

Arykah swallowed. "*You* act like I ain't gonna get my money."

Monique gave Arykah the check and recorded the amount written in her register.

Arykah looked at Monique's hair and dress. "You look cute. Do you always cut your hair and buy a new dress when you go out to eat by yourself?"

Again, Monique ran her fingers through her new short, wavy 'do. "Oh, you like my hair? I didn't think you noticed."

"Oh, I noticed all right. I couldn't help *but* notice the way you sashayed in here looking good and smelling good. I don't even remember seeing your feet touch the floor while you were walking. So who is he?"

Monique's heart skipped two beats. Was she wearing the high that Adonis was responsible for on her sleeve? "What are you talking about, Arykah?"

"Monique, don't play with me. You are glowing because you have a distraction."

"What kind of distraction?"

"The kind of distraction that makes a break-up go a little easier. You don't cry as much, and you're not depressed like you would normally be if there wasn't anyone to help take your mind off of your situation. So I'll ask the question again. Who the he . . . heck is he?"

"You need to take your mouth to the altar, because you almost cussed," Monique said.

"Oh, honey, you ain't heard nothing yet. Yeah, I almost cussed. But I got an emergency key to your hotel room. You let me walk in on something, then you'll hear some cussing."

Monique laughed at her best friend.

Arykah was chewing fast. "Ha-ha, my behind."

Choir rehearsal had already started when Adonis took his seat behind the keyboard.

"You're late, cuz. Where you been?" Boris asked.

"I stopped for a bite to eat and I lost track of time."

"Look, man, rehearsal starts at seven p.m. sharp. The choir members and musicians know that I don't tolerate tardiness, never have. I don't have time to keep going over the same material for latecomers. So you can drop me ten on the organ for being late."

Adonis didn't have a clue what Boris was talking about. "Ten what?"

Taj, the drummer, spoke up. "Ten dollars, man. That's the fine we pay for being late."

At that exact moment, Adonis witnessed an alto walk

up to Boris and place a $5 bill on the organ before taking her seat in the choir stand.

"What's up with that? Why I gotta pay *ten* dollars?" Adonis asked Boris.

"As a musician, you are in leadership. You set the example for the choir members to follow. Pay up so we can get back to rehearsal."

Adonis placed a ten dollar bill on top of the organ. Boris folded the money and put it in his pocket. The church's new music equipment fund was now $15 richer. Adonis blew it off. Ten dollars was nothing to pay considering the reason why he was late. Dinner with Monique was worth millions.

Boris spoke to the choir members and musicians. "I hope everybody left their problems outside of this church. Do not, and I repeat, do not bring the stress and worries of your day into my rehearsal. If I call your name to sing a note, don't play with it. Hit it hard so we can move on. I'm not puttin' up with anybody's laziness tonight. If you cooperate with me, I'll cooperate with you, and we can all be out of here no later than nine fifteen. If anyone has to leave early, sit on the end of the pew so that you don't disturb me or the person seated next to you.

"Everyone here is an adult, so I trust you took care of bathroom duty before you came into the choir stand. And from now on, if you're late, do not walk into the choir stand while I'm teaching. Show respect and wait 'til I acknowledge you. Please turn off all cell phones and pagers. We're gonna run through a quick warm up, then we'll touch on the song I taught last week. Everyone sittin' straight up with your backs away from the bench, please. All minds are clear?"

"All minds are clear," the choir and musicians responded as Boris opened with prayer.

Ten minutes later, Kita strolled into the sanctuary laughing and talking on her cellular phone. Adonis watched as she took her time walking right past Boris, without placing any money on the organ, and took her seat in the soprano section. She finished her conversation, then put her phone in her purse. Adonis was stunned that he alone seemed to notice that she didn't give up any money. Everyone behaved as though this was her normal routine. Kita openly disrespected Boris, didn't pay her fine and no one said anything.

Boris played a key on the organ. "Kita, sing what I just played."

"I don't know it," she responded with a bit of irritation in her voice.

"I made you the section leader because I know you can hit high notes." Boris played the note again. "Sing it, Kita."

She looked at Boris as though she were ready to attack. "I said I don't know it."

Boris played a lower key and moved to the alto section. "Sing, Jennifer."

Jennifer did as she was told, and she did it perfectly.

After choir rehearsal, Deacon Brown locked the church doors, and everyone stood outside talking. Adonis saw Boris and Kita down the street exchanging words.

"Hi, Adonis."

Adonis turned around and saw Kita's best friend. "Oh, hey, Cherry. How are you?"

Cherry took a step closer to him as if he wouldn't be able to hear her from where she was standing. "I'm fine."

Adonis took a step backward. "That's good."

"That's not what you're supposed to say."

He didn't understand. "I beg your pardon?"

"You're supposed to say, 'I didn't ask how you're look-ing, I asked how you're doing. '"

Are you for real? "Oh, uh, sorry about that." He thought Cherry to be plain looking.

"Don't you think I'm fine, Adonis?" Cherry asked.

"Uh, you're all right, I guess." That was the best he could do. He didn't want to hurt her feelings.

Cherry placed her hand on her hip and rotated her neck. "You guess?"

Before she had a chance to cause a scene, Adonis ex-cused himself and walked over to Boris. "I'm heading home, cuz, what about you?"

"Me, Kita and Cherry were gonna go and get some grub. Come on and roll with us."

Adonis wasn't interested in becoming involved in whatever game Boris was playing. "Nah, man, that's all right. I ate before I got here."

"Come on, Adonis, man. You can't hang with your cuz?"

Adonis saw how Kita was leaning on Boris's arm. He didn't see what Boris saw in her. A trophy she was not. Like her friend, Cherry, Kita was plain looking. Monique was the cream of the crop. "Uh, let me holla at you for a minute." They walked a few feet away from Kita. "What are you doing?" he asked Boris.

"Nothing."

"It doesn't look like nothing to me, man. Why are you hanging out with Kita?"

"We're just going to get something to eat, that's all."

"Come on, Boris, it's me you're talkin' to. I saw her come in to rehearsal late, talking on her phone, and not pay her fee."

"Kita can do that," Boris said.

Adonis cocked his head to the side and raised his eyebrows. "Why? Because she's payin' in other ways?"

"Look, I need you to do me a favor and keep Cherry company while me and Kita do our thang."

Adonis quickly shook his head from side to side. "Nah, man; I can't do that. And you need to cut Kita loose and work on gettin' your woman back."

"Monique made her choice; she left *me*. Now, are you gonna help me out tonight or not?"

"This is some wild crap. I can't get into nothing like this, cuz. You, Ronnie and Trixie do y'all's thang. I'm going home." The characters from the movie, *The Players Club,* were exactly who Kita and Cherry reminded Adonis of.

On his way home, Adonis checked his voicemail. After keying in his security code, he listened to the first of four messages.

"You ain't been by here to check on your Aunt Myrtle in two days. Don't let my no good son's ways rub off on you." (Beep)

"Hi, it's me. As promised, I'm callin' to let you know that I'm safe and secure in my hotel room. Arykah bought the prettiest sandals. If I had my toes done, I'd sport a pair tomorrow. Thanks again for a lovely dinner. You have—" (Beep)

Adonis was bummed that Monique's message had gotten cut off. He anxiously waited for the third message, silently praying that it was from her.

"As I was saying, you have a way of brightening my darkest days. I got a confession to make. I was kinda excited when my secretary told me that my meeting was canceled. I was like a schoolgirl with a crush. I went and got my hair done and bought a new dress just to impress you. I hope it worked."

"Oh yeah, it worked." Adonis smiled to himself, re-membering just how lovely Monique was earlier that evening.

"You know, Adonis, I don't know why I'm tellin' you all of this. I'm sittin'—" (Beep)

Adonis got frustrated. "Shoot. I hope you called again, Monique."

"These phone companies should give you more time to leave a message. You're probably gonna kill me for using so many of your minutes. Let me know how much time I used, and I'll reimburse you."

"Don't worry about that, just keep talking," Adonis said to himself.

"I'm sittin' on my balcony, on the eighteenth floor, looking out over the lake. The breeze is intoxicating. I love when it blows through my hair."

Adonis immediately made a U-turn and headed down-town.

"Well, my battery is low, so I'm gonna place it on the charger for a while. I guess I'll hang out on the balcony until I get sleepy. I'll talk to you later, Adonis. Bye."

Adonis saved all three of her messages and kept driv-ing. If Monique's room overlooked the lake, the hotel might be on Lake Shore Drive. He dialed Monique's cel-lular phone, hoping and praying she'd answer. Chances were it might not ring if it were on the charger. Immedi-ately, her voicemail picked up, and he chose not to leave a message.

Adonis got to the south end of Lake Shore Drive, set his cruise control at thirty miles an hour, and sailed north looking at all of the balconies of every hotel along the way. Twenty-five minutes lapsed before he reached the exit at Sheridan Road. He made a U-turn and reentered Lake Shore Drive, heading south. He set his cruise control again and searched and searched for Monique, but she was nowhere to be found.

Frustrated that he didn't see her, he made a call on his cellular phone. "Hi, Aunt Myrtle?"

"It's about time you called me," Myrtle fussed. "Where are you?"

"On my way home from choir rehearsal. How are you doing?"

"How am I doing? I wonder why you ain't been by here to see me."

"You know, Aunt Myrtle, adjusting to my church schedule and my job keeps me pretty busy, but I promise to come by on Saturday and take you shopping."

"Okay, baby, I'm holding you to that, hear? I just wanna lay my eyes on you."

"I promise. Have you talked to Monique this week?"

"I sho ain't. Not since she called here Monday and caught Boris in a lie. She's all right, ain't she?" Myrtle asked.

"Yeah, she's fine. I was just wondering if you talked to her, that's all. Well, I'm just about home, Aunt Myrtle. I'll give you a call on Saturday morning, okay?"

"Okay, baby. Bye-bye."

"Bye."

Apparently Monique hadn't told Myrtle she'd moved out. But there was one person he figured knew for sure where Monique was staying. Adonis wondered what kind of plan he could come up with to get that information out of Arykah?

Chapter 5

At offering time, Adonis was able to get Arykah's attention as she walked to the altar and placed her envelope in the basket. She read his lips as he mouthed the words, "I need to talk to you." One would've thought somebody told Arykah she'd won the lottery. She strutted back to her seat as though she were about to cash in.

After Boris gave the musicians his weekly speech to prepare them for the upcoming Wednesday night rehearsal, Adonis approached Arykah. "Hey, Arykah, thanks for waiting. How are you doing?"

Well, it's about time you pay me some attention. "I'm fine, Adonis. How are *you*?"

"I'm good. Can we step outside for a minute? I want to ask you something."

"Sure." Arykah stood, grabbed her purse from the pew, and gently placed her hand in Adonis's hand.

His first instinct was to withdraw his hand, but decided against it. He knew that once they were outside and he told her why he needed to talk to her, Arykah would remove her own hand from his. They strolled past Kita and Cherry on their way out of the church. The two women saw Arykah's hand in Adonis's hand. The expression on their faces was a Kodak moment for Arykah.

Cherry called out to him. "Hey, Adonis. How are you doing, sweetie?"

He didn't get a chance to answer for himself. Arykah released his hand and wrapped her arm around his waist. "He's doing fine, can't you tell?"

Adonis shook his head from side to side as he and Arykah stepped outside. "I need to ask you something."

She pictured Adonis going down on bended knee, reaching for her left hand. Of course, it was too soon for a marriage proposal, but a dinner date would be ideal.

"What is it?" she asked excitedly.

"Can you tell me where Monique is staying?"

Adonis totally threw Arykah for a loop. That was absolutely the last question she thought he'd ask her. "Monique?"

He knew Arykah was hot on his trail, but there was nothing he could do about it. She was the only one with the information he needed. "I need to talk to her. It's important."

"Adonis, you can just call her cell phone."

"I know, but she won't tell me where she's staying."

Arykah frowned at him curiously. "Why do you need to know where Monique is staying?"

He wondered how he could answer Arykah's question without revealing his true feelings for Monique. He placed his hands in his pants pockets. "I just wanna make sure she's all right, that's all."

Arykah saw that he was becoming uncomfortable with her interrogation. She looked deep into Adonis's eyes and saw a need much more than just making sure Monique was all right. "She's fine, Adonis. And I'll be sure to tell Monique you asked about her."

Adonis couldn't risk blowing his cover. Arykah was Monique's best friend. There was no way he would get her to talk. "Okay, uh, yeah, tell Monique I asked about her. Thanks, Arykah." Adonis turned and walked toward his car.

"For a man who's in love, you give up mighty easy."

He stopped in his tracks, then quickly turned around and looked at Arykah. "Excuse me?"

She walked over to him and looked in his eyes. "The roses, the kisses on her cheek, and wanting to know where Monique is are signs of a man in love."

Adonis could've told Arykah she was delusional and talking crazy, but she had just read him like a book. He smiled in embarrassment. "Is it *that* obvious?"

"Well, at first I wasn't sure. I saw the kisses you planted on her, but didn't make anything out of them. But then she told me about the roses you sent to cheer her up, and I kinda thought you were sweet on her, but I still wasn't sure. But today, the look, the concern in your eyes when you asked her whereabouts, confirmed it for me."

"Arykah, I don't want you to think that I'm the cause for Monique leaving Boris. She doesn't even know what I feel for her."

It was at that moment that Arykah knew she had to dismiss all hopes of her and Adonis getting together. He was in love with her best friend, which meant he was off limits to her. "Adonis, you don't have to explain anything to me. We can't help whom we fall in love with. Monique is a wonderful woman, and you are a wonderful man. And I don't think your cousin deserves her."

Adonis put his hands in his front pockets again. "Arykah, please tell me where she is."

Arykah had every intention on telling him where Monique was staying, but she wanted to make him sweat first. "Why should I? What's it worth to you and what's in it for me?"

"You should tell me because I'm having trouble sleeping at night without knowing. It's worth everything I possess, and what's in it for you is I promise to treat her like the queen she is."

After worshiping at Progressive Ministries with her cousin, Amaryllis, and her roommate, Bridgette, Monique walked into her hotel suite and saw twenty-five vases of white lilies. At first she thought she was in the wrong room. She took another look at the number on the door. "What in the world?"

Monique sat her purse on the bed because there was no room on the dresser. She opened the small white envelope from one of the vases and read it.

'I appreciate everything you do for me.' She smiled. "Adonis."

She read another card. *'I appreciate everything you do for me.'*

She laughed out loud and moved to the third envelope. *'I appreciate everything you do for me.'*

Monique saw that all twenty-five cards read the same. "Oh, my God. Adonis. How in the world did you find me?" She dialed his cellular number. The ringing she heard was close by. Monique opened her balcony door and saw Adonis looking out over Lake Michigan.

He knew she stood behind him. Without turning around, he spoke. "This view is spectacular."

Monique stepped onto the balcony next to him. "Adonis, what are you doing here? Better yet, how did you find me and who let you into my room?"

Adonis kept his eyes on the waves rushing against the shoreline. "I couldn't stay away."

His words touched Monique mentally, physically and emotionally. "Adonis, you are so awesome."

He kept his focus on the lake and didn't comment.

"Why won't you look at me?" she asked.

"I can't."

"Why not?"

"Because I'm afraid you'll see me for who I am."

Monique placed two fingers on the right side of his chin and gently turned his face toward her own. "Who *are* you?"

In Monique's eyes, Adonis saw his future. He saw her as his wife, he saw their children, he saw the house with a white picket fence, and he saw Monique and himself sitting in rocking chairs on the front porch with a quilted blanket spread across their legs, watching their grand-children play in the front yard.

"I'm the man who loves you, Monique. Every inch of my body aches because I know I can't have you. Yester-day, I was in Ford City Shopping Mall sniffing Ralph Lau-ren perfume just to remind myself what you smell like. Do you have any idea how many times I have dialed your cell phone and hung up before it rings? I do that because I really ain't got nothing to say; I just wanna hear your voice. I call my voicemail every night and listen to your messages that I saved. I do that so your voice can rock me to sleep."

"Why?" Monique asked.

"Because all I can do is wish that I wasn't in love with you. You are engaged to my cousin. So you know what I did at church this morning, Monique? I tripled my tithes and took it to the altar and knelt before God. I paid Him to take you out of my soul because I don't wanna love you anymore. But even after I did that, I still couldn't stay away."

Without another word between them, Adonis walked away from Monique and left the hotel room. She leaned against the railing and looked down at the traffic on Lake Shore Drive. She didn't know she was crying until a tear dripped onto her chest. She was holding her cellular phone in her hand when it rang.

"Don't be mad, Monique. He talked me into telling him where you were." Monique didn't respond, but Arykah could hear her sniffles. "Monique?"

"Arykah, you won't believe what he did and what he said to me."

"What happened? Never mind, tell me when I get there. I'm on my way."

Chapter 6

Monique opened the door for Arykah and sat down on the bed. Arykah was surprised to see what Adonis had done. The lilies took up every inch of the room and smelled pretty. She sat on the bed next to Monique. "You wanna talk about it?"

Monique didn't respond.

"First of all, I don't see why you're having mixed emotions, Monique. I mean, heck, on one hand, you got a man who practically worships the ground you walk on. On the other you have a man who is a ho and doesn't give a darn about you. Are you *that* dense that you can't see who the right man God has for you is?"

"I'm engaged to Boris, Arykah. Have you forgotten that?"

"You're engaged to a moron. Have *you* forgotten *that*? Explain to me this hold Boris has on you, because I'm confused."

"He doesn't have a hold on me. I love him."

Arykah threw frustrated hands in the air. "Why?"

"What do you mean, why?"

"What do you love about Boris?"

"It doesn't matter what I say about him, because you never liked him from Jump Street."

"Because he was a jerk from Jump Street."

"See, that's what I'm talking about, Arykah."

"Actually, Monique, you ain't talking about nothing. If Boris is so good, and since you love him so much, why are you living in this hotel?"

Monique didn't respond, and Arykah scooted closer to her. "Look around this room, Monique. Look at all of these flowers Adonis bought you. The closest thing to a flower you got from Boris was the wreath he brought home from his uncle's funeral last year. Now, I can understand your hesitation if you don't feel anything for Adonis because that's a whole different ballgame."

Monique exhaled and looked at her friend. "Arykah, isn't it wrong for a woman to leave her man and start dating his cousin? Isn't that what we call skanks and skeezahs?"

"Monique, people on the outside looking in will always form their own opinions. But ain't nobody got a heaven or hell to put you in. A woman sexing two men, who share the same blood *is* wrong, but you're not sleeping with Adonis. Boris is a donkey. You know it, I know it, Adonis knows it, and even Boris's mother knows it.

"I'm gonna tell you like I told Adonis. We can't help whom we fall in love with. Happiness and true love only come around once in a lifetime. Adonis adores you, and if you were true to yourself, you'd realize that you care for him too. Heck, how can you not when he's at your every beck and call? So if they label you a skeezah for giving up on a useless man who sleeps around and abuses you mentally and falling into the arms of his cousin who treasures you, I say to heck with what the folks on the outside looking in say. Wear your title well because you'll be a skank who's happy and in love and a skeezah with a man who loves and respects you. Most of the time when folks talk about you, it's because they want what you have.

"Now, you can be a fool and let Adonis get away if you want to. You'll be like Brian McKnight in his music video rolling on the floor, clutching your pillow, singing your shoulda's, woulda's, and coulda's."

Monique laughed, then became serious. "I know you like Adonis."

"Look, Monique, Adonis is fine as heck. He's a prize with legs shaped like parenthesis, but the man ain't thinking about me. You need to snatch him up quick, fast, and in a hurry, and that's all I gotta say about the situation. I'm hungry, let's go eat."

"Where do you wanna go?" Monique asked, wiping her tears away.

"We're in downtown Chicago, there are plenty of restaurants to choose from."

Monique turned up her nose. "I don't think so." She made a call on her cellular phone. "Hey, Gravy."

"Baby Girl, where are you? What's this I hear about you moving out and how come you ain't been by here to cut and polish my toenails? These thangs so long, they're slicin' my sheets when I turn over in the bed. This morning they ripped right through my brand new pantyhose."

"I just gave you a pedicure two weeks ago, Gravy."

"Heck, I can't tell," Myrtle responded sarcastically.

"What did you cook today?"

"I got ham hocks, black-eyed peas, hot water bread and gravy."

"Is Boris over there?"

"Uh-uh."

"What about Adonis?" Monique asked.

"I ain't seen him since church."

"Okay, then go ahead and soak your feet in Epsom salt. Arykah and I are on our way."

"Where are you staying at? And why weren't you in church today?" Myrtle asked.

"I'll talk to you about that when we get there."

After dinner the ladies sat in Myrtle's living room. Arykah made herself comfortable and leaned back on the loveseat and propped her feet up on the cocktail table, then belched loudly. Monique sat on the floor in front of Myrtle and dried her right foot, then massaged it with Johnson's Baby Oil.

Myrtle looked down at her. "I'm waiting."

"Waiting for what, Gravy?" Monique asked without looking up.

"For you to tell me why you moved out."

"Can I tell it?" Arykah asked.

Myrtle looked at Arykah. "Yeah, tell me."

"Mind your business," Monique scolded Arykah.

"Somebody's gonna tell me something," Myrtle insisted.

Monique began filing Myrtle's toenails. "Gravy, it's about Boris, and I don't wanna discuss it with you."

"Why, because I'm his mother? I know my son ain't no good. I told you a long time ago to leave him alone. I'm just glad you finally listened. I wanna know what he did that pushed you out the door."

"I can't say it's one particular thing that he did, Gravy. I just got tired of being tired; you know?"

"Baby Girl, we all have our limits. What gave you the guts to pack your bags?"

Arykah raised her hand in the air as though she were sitting in a sixth grade classroom, eager to solve a mathematical problem. "Ooh, ooh, can I tell it? Please, Miss Morrison, can I tell it?"

"No. And I told you to mind your business," Monique said.

Arykah let her head fall back on the loveseat and closed her eyes.

"I'm still waiting," Myrtle said to Monique.

Monique dried Myrtle's left foot and exhaled. "Gravy, do you know who Kita is? She sings and she's a praise dancer."

"You're talking about Sister Vickie's daughter?"

"I found out that she and Boris are keeping close company."

Myrtle sat up in her chair, stunned at what Monique had just told her. "What? I thought she was going with Sister Jackson's boy."

"You're talking about Trevor. He canceled Kita last summer when he found out she was snuggling up with Deacon Woolford. Where have you been, Gravy? You gotta keep up with the current events."

Myrtle leaned back as Monique massaged her toes. "Chile, I try not to get in nobody's business. Wait a minute, Deacon Woolford is in his late sixties."

"And? Kita doesn't care. He's also very married. Who do you think pays for that brand new Lexus truck she's driving? And you know what kind of car Sister Woolford drives, don't you, Gravy?"

"Uh-uh. What kind is it?"

"Humph, it ain't nowhere near a Lexus."

Myrtle shook her head from side to side. "That's a mess, a hot mess. That Kita girl is something else."

"She's a hooker," Arykah said with closed eyes as she shifted lazily on the loveseat.

Myrtle was ashamed of Boris. "And now my son is another experience she added to her résumé. Boris is truly his father's son."

Monique began applying red polish to Myrtle's toenails. "It ain't just this thing he's got going on with Kita, Gravy. I'm tired of the disrespect. I cook and clean for Boris, but he doesn't appreciate it. The one thing I ask him to do is to replace the gas he uses in my car, and he can't even do that. I'm sick of the late night calls he gets on his cell phone and I'm sick of him comin' in whenever he feels like it without a reasonable explanation. So I decided to pack my bags and leave, and that's exactly what I did."

The front door opened and Adonis walked in. He saw Monique and Arykah and paused at the door.

Myrtle yelled at him. "What the heck are you just standing there for? You think I got money to air condition the whole darn city in June? Close my door, and where is your cousin?"

Adonis closed the door behind him and kissed Myrtle's cheek. "Hey, Auntie. I don't know where Boris is. I haven't seen him since church let out."

Arykah was lying on the loveseat with one eye open looking at them. Monique continued polishing Myrtle's toenails without acknowledging Adonis.

"You ain't seen him since church let out? Where *you* been all this time? Church let out almost three hours ago," Myrtle inquired.

"I had to take care of some business." Adonis was anxious in Monique's presence, so he opted to change the subject. "What did you cook?"

"Ham hocks and black-eyed peas. You might have to warm your plate in the microwave."

Adonis turned toward the kitchen, and Myrtle stopped him. "Excuse me, don't you see company? You can't speak?"

Arykah decided to be messy. "You ain't gotta speak to me, Adonis, 'cause we saw each other in church today, but it's been awhile since you've seen Monique, right?"

Monique looked at her best friend, and if looks could kill, Arykah would have been six feet under.

"Yeah, it's been awhile. How are you doing, Monique? It's good to see you," Adonis said.

Monique looked up at him. "I'm fine, Adonis, how are *you*?"

"I'm good, thanks."

Neither of them wanted to be the first to take their eyes away from one another.

Myrtle looked from Monique to Adonis, then from Adonis to Monique as they held their gaze. Arykah was on the loveseat having a field day.

"Adonis, get me a glass of water," Myrtle said. When he walked away, Myrtle lowered her voice. "What was that about?"

Monique started to apply the clear topcoat to Myrtle's toenails. "What was what about?"

"Baby Girl, don't play with me."

"I don't know what you're talking about, Gravy."

Myrtle was quiet for the longest moment before she spoke. "Uh-huh." She looked at Arykah who quickly closed her eyes and pretended to snore loudly. "Uh-huh," Myrtle said again.

Adonis brought the glass of water to Myrtle, then urgently left the living room. She looked down at Monique who seemed to be in a rush to finish her toes. She then glanced at Arykah lying down with her eyes closed and a silly grin on her face.

"Uh-huh," Myrtle said a third time.

A half hour after Monique and Arykah left, Myrtle walked into the kitchen and found Adonis at the sink washing the last of the dishes.

"Since you're in a washing mood, how about coming by next weekend to help me wash the outside of my windows."

Adonis drained the sink and dried his hands. "How can I resist a chance to do hard labor? I took the garbage out and tightened the screws on this ceiling fan. It's not shaking anymore."

Myrtle looked up at the fan. "Boy, you're gonna make some woman real happy to have you as her husband. So what are you waiting on?"

"The right woman," Adonis answered.

"You think you'll know her when you see her?"

He didn't answer.

Myrtle remembered the way he and Monique were looking at each other. "*Have* you seen her?"

He leaned back against the sink, crossed his arms over his chest, and exhaled. "I thought I did, Auntie, but I was wrong."

Myrtle sat down at the kitchen table. "Adonis, sit down for a minute."

Adonis rolled his eyes. He knew those words meant it was storytelling time. "Oh Lord, here we go."

"What do you mean *here we go*? And what are you rolling your eyes at?"

He sat across from Myrtle. "Nothing, Auntie, what's up?"

Myrtle looked into the face of a man she raised since he was ten years old. "You're so handsome, Adonis. I'm so proud of the life you chose to live. For you and Boris to be raised as brothers, you're like night and day. I'm sure I don't have to say which one of you represents the day."

Adonis smiled at Myrtle's words.

"You have the same smile your daddy had. Same teeth, same dimples, and everything. My brother was a good man, and I see all of his traits in you. Do you know how he and your mother got together?"

"He met her at one of your family reunion picnics, right?"

"Your mother, Augustine, came with a girl named Sharlene Taylor, who was your daddy's girlfriend at the time. Your mother and Sharlene were first cousins."

Myrtle saw Adonis's eyes grow wide. "Why are you telling me this, Auntie?"

"Because I'm going somewhere with this story. Your father and I were in high school at the time, but he was a year behind me. Back then Sharlene was the head of the cheerleading squad at our school. Needless to say, she was a fox, and she knew it. According to your father, Sharlene could do no wrong. Whatever she said was the law. Clearly, she wore the pants in that relationship. Your grandmother and I couldn't stand the broad, but we let your father do his own thing. Since he liked her, we promised to tolerate her. Because Sharlene was the head cheerleader, she thought that gave her license to walk around as though her poop didn't stink. She had a very nasty attitude and treated your father like crap. But she had his nose wide open; he couldn't get enough of her. Sharlene knew that and used it to her advantage.

"I will admit, Sharlene was a very pretty girl, but her attitude made her ugly. I'd watch your father sit up all night and wait by the telephone for her to call. She'd make a date with him and cancel at the last minute. I don't think she appreciated him and what he did for her. With the little money he had, he would buy flowers and candy. One time she embarrassed him in front of the cheerleaders in practice. He went to the gym with six roses for her. She looked at him and said, 'All the nooky I'm giving you, and I can't even get a whole dozen?' When he came home and told me what she said, he had to sit on my legs to keep me from going to whoop her tail."

Adonis laughed. "You were a roughneck, huh, Auntie?"

"I had to be. Our mother was working two full-time jobs to help ends meet. Your father and I only had each other. We never knew our daddy. He left when your father was six months old. In high school your father had a paper route. He got up at four in the morning to deliver newspapers just so that Sharlene could take his money and do what she wanted with it. But hey, according to Mr. Adonis Cortland, as long as his woman was happy, so was he.

"One summer, Sharlene invited your mother to one of our family reunions. Augustine was staying with Sharlene's family. Augustine was just as pretty as Sharlene, but Augustine was also pretty on the inside and treated your father very differently than her cousin. At the reunion, while Sharlene was off somewhere flirting and showing the latest cheer she'd put together for the upcoming football season, your mother was the one keeping your father occupied with volleyball and the water balloon toss. Augustine was his partner in the three-legged race. When the ribs were done, Augustine brought your father a plate."

Adonis thought back to two Sundays ago, when Monique had insisted that she bring his dinner to him.

"For the rest of the summer, Sharlene made a mistake. She didn't think it was necessary to spend quality time with your father because her cousin didn't seem to mind doing it. The time Sharlene spent in practice, Augustine and your father were out walking along Rainbow Beach, sharing ice cream cones and holding hands. At the end of the summer, Sharlene asked your father for some money. He said he spent all of his money on a plane ticket to California. She asked him what was in California, and he said *he* would be when he took Augustine home."

Adonis sat at the kitchen table in awe. Was Aunt Myrtle giving him permission to walk in his father's footsteps and go after his cousin's girlfriend just as his own father had done when he ended his relationship with one cousin and eventually married the other?

"Wow, that's deep, Auntie. But why did you tell me this story?"

Myrtle stood up from the table. "No special reason, but if you can get anything out of it, be my guest." She kissed Adonis's forehead on her way out of the kitchen and left him to his thoughts. "I'm gonna take a bath. Make sure to set the alarm and lock the door when you leave."

Adonis sat at the kitchen table for a long moment. He wondered if history was repeating itself. He grabbed his keys and walked into the living room. On his way out of the door, he caught a glimpse of his parents' wedding picture on the mantel. He picked it up and saw how happy they looked. Adonis had to admit that he was a mirror image of Adonis Cortland Sr. Emotions crept on him as he looked into his parents' eyes.

He could remember being called to the principal's office in the middle of recess to find Myrtle sitting with her eyes almost swollen shut from crying. The principal left them alone in her office so Myrtle could break the news to Adonis Jr. that his parents had been killed in a car accident that morning shortly after they had dropped him off at school.

Adonis set the picture back on the mantel, wiped his moist eyes, set the house alarm, then securely locked Myrtle's front door. He arrived home at approximately nine o'clock P.M. When he closed the front door behind him, he heard laughter. With every light in the entire house out, Adonis didn't think Boris was even home. He walked through the living and dining rooms and found the voices coming from Monique and Boris's bedroom.

For a quick moment, jealously enraged through Adonis's body at the thought of Monique being with Boris. His first instinct was to go directly downstairs to the basement, but curiosity was killing the cat. He had to know if Monique had had a change of heart.

Adonis quietly crept to their bedroom door and saw it wide open. He stood in shock at the sight of three completely naked people. In the middle of the queen-sized bed, Kita was straddling Boris as he fondled Cherry. Either Boris didn't expect Adonis to come home, or he didn't care about privacy. He'd heard Boris tell Monique on more than one occasion that this was *his* house and he would do whatever he wanted in it.

The gasping sound coming from Adonis's throat caused the trio to look his way. Adonis's feet were glued to the hardwood floor. He couldn't move to save his life.

"Come on and join the party, cuz," Boris said when he saw Adonis standing in the bedroom doorway.

Adonis was in shock. "What the devil?"

"You heard Boris. It's a party," Kita said.

Cherry pointed at Adonis and motioned for him to join them on the bed. "You better come on over here and get your prize."

Adonis looked at her and felt Myrtle's ham hocks rising to his throat. He swallowed repeatedly to keep his dinner in place. Cherry blew what she thought was a seductive kiss toward Adonis, and it unglued his feet and sent him running to the bathroom. Adonis had to flush the toilet three times to prevent it from becoming clogged, he was so sick to his stomach. He envisioned the kiss Cherry blew at him, and it caused his stomach to rumble. Adonis had to flush the toilet a fourth time.

Chapter 7

At 12:30 on a Monday afternoon, Monique's intercom buzzed.

"There's a Mr. Adonis Cortland here to see you, but he doesn't have an appointment," Theresa announced.

Just the mention of his name caused Monique's heart to go pitter-patter. It had been two weeks since the last time she'd spoken with Adonis. She slowly counted to five to calm herself before she answered. "No appointment is necessary, Theresa. Show him in, please."

The door to Monique's office opened, and Theresa walked in followed by Adonis. Monique rose from her chair, walked around her desk and embraced him. "This is a surprise. What are you doing in my neck of the woods?"

It felt so good having her in his arms with her face pressed against his chest. Adonis inhaled Monique's scent, which almost caused him to lose his balance. "I finished a job early, so I decided to have my car detailed at a body shop just a block away from here. And now that I'm here, you can give me the keys to your car."

Monique looked at Adonis confusingly. "The keys to my car?"

"On my way in to see you, I noticed that your car is looking kinda dirty. I can't allow you to drive around in a dirty car when my car is shining. What kind of friend would I be?"

Adonis was too good to be true. Boris had never washed her car. Monique was at a loss for words, and it dawned on her that Theresa was standing in the doorway to her office, watching her and Adonis. "That'll be all, Theresa."

Theresa couldn't take her eyes off of the tall and handsome creature standing in Monique's office. Monique had told her that he was fine, but in Theresa's opinion, he was *stupid foine*. An 'Adonis,' he truly was.

"Can I get you a cup of coffee, Mr. Cortland?" Theresa offered.

Adonis looked at Theresa and smiled. "No, thank you."

"How about a cup of tea?"

Adonis smiled at her again. "No, I'm fine."

You sho is. Theresa did not want to leave his presence. She wanted to do something, anything to please him. "I could run down to the corner store and get whatever you like. How about fresh lemonade? I could squeeze the lemons and sweeten it to your taste."

Adonis blushed with embarrassment. Monique walked to Theresa and ushered her out of the office. Often times, Monique had to remind Theresa that she was a married woman. "Theresa, if you just *have* to get something, get me the number of calls that came in on last night's show." Monique closed the door behind Theresa and smiled at Adonis. "Do you see what kind of impact you have on women? You can't come around here and disrupt my staff. She's probably on her way to the bathroom to splash cold water on her face."

"I could've stayed away longer than two weeks, but my heart was starting to ache. I had to see you."

That remark put a lump in Monique's throat. She swallowed three times as she guided Adonis to one of the chairs on the opposite side of her desk from where she sat. He was extremely handsome that day. He wore a white v-neck New York Knicks throwback that couldn't hide his well-toned triceps and biceps. Dark denim shorts stopping just above his knees gave Monique full view of his bulging calves. The dark blue flip-flops Adonis wore showed his fresh pedicure.

"Okay, tell me the real deal why you're here. I know it's more than wanting to give my car a bath," Monique stated.

Adonis leaned back in the chair and crossed his right ankle over his left knee. "There is another reason I'm here. While my car was gettin' detailed, I got detailed too."

"What do you mean?"

Adonis removed a baseball cap from his head and Monique's, eyes grew wide.

"Oh my God. You shaved your head," she squealed.

He ran his hand over his shiny scalp. "You like it?"

I more than like it. "Yes. What made you do it?"

"To be honest with you, I don't know why I did it. I guess it was on impulse."

"It makes you look even more handsome than you already were, and I didn't think that was possible. The bald head is definitely a keeper."

Adonis grinned at Monique and she understood why Theresa's knees were weakening just being in his presence. *I can't stand to look at you, you're so fine,* she thought to herself.

The longer Adonis sat in Monique's office looking at

her, the more he loved her. He would have to find a way
to make her his. "So how about those car keys?"

Monique was in shock that he'd be willing to do this
for her. "Adonis, are you serious? You don't have to do
this."

"Yes, I do. A woman of your caliber should always have
a clean car."

"I'm very grateful."

When he took the keys from Monique's hand, he held
on to her fingers and kissed her knuckles softly. "I get joy
out of pleasing you, Monique."

"You're different from Boris, that's for sure. He's never
been concerned about the dirt on my car."

The mention of Boris brought back the image of him
and his playmates to Adonis's mind. "Hopefully, he'll get
his act together before it's too late." He stood waiting for
Monique to say that it was already too late for Boris, but
she didn't say a word. "What time do you get off work?"
he asked her.

"Whenever my work is done, and only God knows
when that'll be."

"I'll try and have your car back in two hours."

"Two hours? Are you washing it or building me a new
one?"

He smiled at Monique and walked out of her office.
Outside the door, Theresa was sitting at her desk eating a
corned beef sandwich. "Would you like half of my sandwich, Mr. Cortland?"

"No thanks, Theresa." Adonis kept walking, but he
heard her call after him.

"How about a bite of my pickle?"

After two, two and a half hour long meetings, Monique
got back to her office, kicked her heels off, and crossed

her ankles on top of her desk. She sighed and looked at the clock on the wall. It was almost 5:30 P.M. Her work was done, and she was ready to call it quits, but realized Adonis had yet to return with her car. She reached for her telephone to call his cellular phone and saw that she'd just missed a call from Adonis a minute ago. Just as she was dialing his number, her intercom buzzed.

"Theresa, tell whomever is calling I'm gone for the day."

"Even if it's a tall, butter pecan, pralines n' cream, butterscotch, caramel looking brotha calling?"

For the second time in one day, Monique's heart raced at the mention of Adonis. She pressed line one and brought the telephone to her ear. "I was about to call the police and file a missing person's report on you. Are you okay?"

"Sorry it took me so long to get your car back to you. Are you ready to go?"

"More than ready. I'm on my way out."

Monique stepped outside the radio station and didn't recognize the car Adonis was sitting in. Her late model Toyota Camry shined so bright that the dull burgundy color, caused by layers of dirt Monique had grown comfortable with, was now highlighted to candy apple red. The only other time the paint looked this good was the day Monique had driven it from the showroom floor. Also sparkling in the sun were the brand new silver chrome rims.

Monique covered her mouth that had fallen open as she walked toward her car. "Adonis, what did you do?"

He stepped out of the car and held the driver's door open for her. "Your chariot awaits you."

Monique sat in the driver's seat and immediately noticed the brand new stereo system. "Oh my God. How much did all of this cost you?"

"Monique, it's very rude to ask someone how much they spent on a gift for you. I wanna show you somethin'." Adonis reached for her hand and guided her toward the rear of the car. He opened the trunk to reveal a fifteen compact disc changer.

"Oh my God," was all she could say.

"I bought you fifteen gospel CD's and one by Luther Vandross that's playing now. On your way to your hotel, I want you to listen to track number four. It's called "A House Is Not A Home." I dedicate it to you."

Monique returned to the driver's seat and Adonis sat on the passenger side and demonstrated how to properly operate the CD player. It was then that Monique noticed the candy apple red floor mat beneath her feet. "Adonis, is there no end to your surprises?"

"I just have a couple more. When I left with your car this afternoon, the gas tank was nearly empty. It is now full and the oil has been changed. I bought new windshield wipers."

Monique looked into his eyes. "I can't believe you did all of this. I know the rims alone cost you an arm and a leg."

I'll give up both arms and both legs for you. Adonis reached inside the glove compartment and pulled out a white envelope containing a card he stopped and bought on his way back to her office. "I wanna read you something."

Monique turned the volume knob on the stereo counter clockwise so that she could give Adonis her undivided attention.

Adonis pulled the card from the envelope and read it

to her. "Since I first laid eyes on you, I knew you were someone special. It wasn't any particular thing that I've seen you do or any words I heard you say. It was God who said to me, '**BE CAREFUL WITH HER, SHE'S ONE OF MY OWN, THEREFORE SHE'S SPECIAL.**' You are extraordinary and exceptional. You are a peculiar person set aside from anyone else I've ever known. You are highly favored in my heart, and that alone makes you very special to me."

In shock, caught off guard, and being in total awe was putting mildly what Monique felt at that moment. She wanted to say something, but what could she say? She sat in the presence of a man who had spent thousands of dollars to upgrade her car and listened to him pour out his heart to her, yet no words came from her throat.

Adonis put the card in the envelope and placed it back into the glove compartment then looked into Monique's eyes. "A penny for your thoughts."

Monique met his eyes. "I don't know what to say."

Adonis looked down at his lap, then back into Monique's eyes. "Well, do you mind if I tell you what's on *my* mind?"

"I think I know," she said.

Adonis seriously doubted her statement. Had Monique an inkling of what he felt in his heart, she'd be *his* fiancé and not Boris's. "Really? Do you know how my soul cries out from within me because I can't go twenty-four hours without hearing your voice? Have you any clue how many times I wake up in the middle of the night, in a cold sweat, because your face suddenly appears in my dream? Are you aware of the countless near death experiences I've had working with live wires? Sometimes I get so caught up in wondering what you're doing or where you are that I can't concentrate on what I've been hired to do.

Are those the things you thought you knew about me, Monique?"

She desperately wanted to reach out to him, wanted to tell him that she loved him, wanted to assure Adonis that he could stop trying so hard, that he already had her, but she couldn't do any of that. "Adonis, you know my situation. Where were you two years ago, before I met Boris?"

"Two years ago, I was away at school, but I'm home now."

"And I'm engaged to your cousin. Our wedding is weeks away."

"You're still gonna marry Boris after the way he's been treating you? If you're unhappy now, what makes you think you'll be happy after the wedding?"

"Adonis, the reason I separated myself from Boris is so that he can realize what he's missing and get his act together."

Adonis looked away from Monique. If she only knew that Boris wasn't missing out on anything. Whatever Monique thought she had taken away from him was being given to him two-fold. Adonis would never forget going to the shower that morning, peeking into Boris's bedroom and seeing him sleeping peacefully with both Kita and Cherry lying on opposite pectorals. He contemplated whether or not to confess to Monique what he had walked in on two weeks ago, but decided against it. He wanted Monique's heart, mind and soul, but she had to come to him on her own.

"You know what, Monique? You make my worst days worth living. Has Boris ever told you that?" Adonis didn't wait for a response from Monique. He exited the car and shut the door.

Monique sat in silence and watched him get into his car and drive away. When Adonis was out of her sight, she found track number four and listened to Luther Van-dross explain why a house was not a home. When the song ended, she listened to it again. After the song ended the second time, Monique glanced around the parking lot and noticed that she sat in the lot at WGOD all alone. she started the car, backed out of her spot, then switched the gear and drove out of the parking lot. She turned on the air conditioner and immediately, Adonis's favorite cologne blew full blast into her face as the vents circulated Issey Miyake.

Monique's cell phone rang as she inserted her key into the lock of her hotel room door.

"Well, it's about time you answered," Arykah complained when Monique had finally greeted her after the phone rang five times.

Monique rolled her eyes into the air. "Well, you called when I was coming into my room. The only reason I answered was because I thought you were somebody important."

"Am I not important to you?"

"Sometimes," Monique responded jokingly.

"Well, how about calling me back when I make your priority list? Maybe I'll be important enough to talk to then."

Arykah slammed down the telephone. Monique could tell by the tone of Arykah's voice that something wasn't right with her. The two of them always played the dozens with each other, so Monique couldn't understand why today was different. A response like, 'Ain't nobody more important than me,' would have been a typical response from Arykah.

Monique sat down on the bed and called Arykah's number.

"What?" Arykah answered the phone coldly.

"I don't know what's going on with you, but I sure as heck don't appreciate you hanging up on me."

"And I don't appreciate you telling me that I'm not important to you."

Monique couldn't believe Arykah was acting that way for no apparent reason. "Are you on your period?"

"Are *you*?" Arykah responded.

Monique had had enough of the sarcasm. If Arykah wanted to act a fool, she was going to do it alone. "You know what? I'm gonna hang up and give you time to cool down from whatever that's got you ticked off, okay?"

Arykah didn't respond.

"Okay, Arykah?" Monique asked loudly.

"I have a lump in my left breast."

There was no way she could've heard Arykah correctly. To Monique, it sounded like she said somebody was under arrest. "What did you say?" she asked Arykah, forcing her voice to stay calm and low.

Sniff, sniff. "I got a lump in my left breast the size of a golf ball."

Monique felt her heart sink into her stomach. *Oh my God. Oh Jesus.* "How do you know it's a lump? Have you gone to see your doctor?"

Sniff, sniff. "I felt it in the shower Saturday morning. I took this afternoon off and went to see my doctor. The x-rays showed a lump, but we don't know if it's cancerous. I'm scheduled for a biopsy at West Suburban Hospital at nine o'clock, Friday morning."

Monique's heart was running a marathon, and she was breathing heavily. "Okay, then what we're gonna do is touch and agree that God is in control of this thing. We don't know what Friday will bring, but we do know the

One who holds our hands. God is a healer and a deliverer, and we're gonna trust and believe that everything will work out.

"What are you doing right now?"

Sniff, sniff. "Sitting on my living room floor."

"I'm on my way."

On her way to Arykah's house, Monique dialed Adonis's cellular number.

"Hey, beautiful," he greeted.

Sniff, sniff. Tears dripped onto Monique's cheeks. "Hey."

He could tell that Monique was upset. "You're crying. What happened?"

"I'm on my way to Arykah's house."

"Is she all right?"

"I don't know. She got some news today."

"What kind of news?" Adonis asked.

"This is between you and me, okay?"

"Of course. Tell me what happened."

"Her doctor confirmed a lump in her left breast this afternoon."

"Oh wow. Is it malignant?"

"We don't know yet. She's scheduled for a biopsy on Friday morning."

"I'm so sorry, Monique. Is there anything I can do?"

"No, I don't think so. I'm on my way to keep her from having a pity party."

"You're not gonna be any good to her if you walk in her house crying."

"I know. I'm tryin' to get it all out before I get there."

"Do you want me to go with you?"

"No, I just need you to pray."

"I can do that. Where are you?"

"Driving on the Dan Ryan Expressway at Ninety-Fifth Street."

"Keep the telephone to your ear, I'm gonna pray right now." Adonis proceeded to pray, and twenty minutes later, Monique pulled into Arykah's driveway and turned off the ignition. Adonis had prayed for Arykah's healing. He also prayed for Monique's strength and consoled her all the way to Arykah's house. "You feel better?" he asked.

Monique blew her nose into a Kleenex tissue she had retrieved from her glove compartment. "Much better, thanks to you."

"Check your face and remove all traces of tears. Stay calm, and try not to break down in front of Arykah. She needs you to be strong. Call me when you leave, no matter how late."

"I knew who to call to get me through this."

"Hey, that's what I'm here for. If I can't pray you through rough times, then I'm no good for you."

"Just know that I appreciate everything you do for me."

Adonis chuckled. "Hey, that's *my* line."

"But I *do* appreciate what you do for me," Monique said with a grin on her face.

"I just wanna make you smile."

"I am smiling."

"That's all that matters. Go ahead and take care of Arykah, and call me later."

"I will."

A pregnant pause presented itself before Adonis spoke. "Hey, Monique?"

"Yes?"

He hesitated. There were three words he'd wanted to say to her for what seemed like forever. But what if she didn't echo them back to him? Would the words place her in an awkward position and cause her to become uncomfortable with him? He couldn't chance jeopardizing the friendship they shared. "Nothing."

Monique knew what Adonis wanted to say to her. At that very moment, those words would have been music to her ears. "Don't do that, Adonis. Say what you gotta say."

"It's nothing."

"Are you sure?" she asked. *Please say it. Tell me that you love me.*

"Yeah, I'm sure."

"Okay, well, I'll talk to you later."

"I love you, Monique," Adonis said the words after she disconnected their call. He was in trouble. His heart belonged to Monique. It was unreal how quickly he had fallen for Monique in the short time he'd known her. It was almost like a fairytale. But Adonis saw it coming. He felt himself being drawn closer and closer to Monique. He forced himself to go two whole weeks without calling her. He'd hoped the distance between the two of them would give him time to come to his senses, but it didn't work. During that time, Monique was all he thought about. Adonis had paid God a lot of money to turn his heart in another direction, but He didn't do it.

Monique used the emergency key Arykah had given her and entered the living room. There were no lights on in the entire house, but Monique saw Arykah's silhouette sitting on the floor with her back against the sofa.

"Why are you sitting in the dark?"

"This is *my* house, and if I wanna sit in the dark, I'll do it."

Monique sat on the loveseat opposite of Arykah. "Well, I didn't come all this way to sit in the dark."

"First of all, I didn't ask you to come all this way, but since you're here, you *will* sit in the dark because I don't want any lights on."

Monique exhaled loudly. Consoling Arykah wasn't going to be easy.

"I don't care about you sighing, Monique. You can huff and puff all you want."

Monique felt like calling Adonis again for another dose of pep talk and encouragement. She'd been in Arykah's presence all of a minute and already she was ready to go. She knew Arykah's situation was difficult, but she had to be strong and patient no matter how Arykah responded to her. "Are you hungry?"

"Nope."

"Have you eaten anything today?"

"Nope."

"Look, you don't know what the results of the test will be. So why sit around forcing yourself to become depressed? You are a child of God. Your attitude should be as though you're already healed *if* there's anything to be healed from."

"Monique, it's easy for you to sit there and tell me how I should behave because it's not your breast with the lump in it. If the shoe was on the other foot, you wouldn't be so calm, cool, and collected."

Arykah was absolutely right. Thousands of women died from breast cancer every year. And if Monique was honest with herself, she knew she'd be hysterical if she were facing a biopsy. She sat on the floor next to Arykah. "You know what, sis? You're right. If it were me, I'd be a basket case. I'll be honest and say that I'm also afraid, but like I said, we don't know what the test will show. It's my job to hold your hand and encourage you to be strong when you don't wanna be. Trials come every day, but we can't freak out and lose our heads over them. I believe that if we pray hard enough, whatever is in your breast will be gone by Friday."

Arykah placed her face in her hands and cried. "I hope so. I'm so scared."

Monique pulled Arykah into her arms. "I know you are, but we'll get through this, I promise." She held Arykah tightly. Listening to Arykah cry her heart out, Monique couldn't help but to cry herself. "We gotta stop this, Arykah. I promised Adonis that I was gonna be the strong one."

Arykah pulled away from Monique and looked at her. "Adonis? You told him?"

"Please don't be mad at me. After you called, I had to get strength to come and comfort you. He wants you to know that he's praying ,and he told me to tell you that he's just a phone call away."

Arykah wiped the tears from her eyes. "So you two are getting closer, huh?"

"Oh my God, Arykah. This man is awesome. Today, he came by the radio station and . . ." Monique stopped herself. Surely after the day Arykah had had, the last thing she wanted to hear was how great and wonderful Adonis was.

"Yeah, and? He came by the radio station and what?"

"I'll tell you later," Monique said.

"No, you're gonna tell me now."

"I don't want you to think that I'm trying to downplay your situation by bragging on Adonis."

"Monique, please, I know the man is all that. Tell me, I really wanna know. Plus I can use a pick-me-upper."

Monique turned on the living room lamp and sat on the sofa. "Well, I told you about the roses he sent to my office and all of the phone calls just to make sure I'm all right and to find out if I needed anything. And you saw the lilies in my hotel room. Well, today he came to the radio station and got the keys to my car. He claimed he was gonna get it washed, but when he returned it to me, it was shining like new gold. He bought brand new chrome rims, new floor mats, and installed a fifteen CD changer. Girl, he even bought new windshield wipers, plus he filled my gas tank."

Arykah was impressed. "Does this blessing come with a house, two kids and a dog?"

"Humph, even if it did, I couldn't take the blessing."

Arykah looked at Monique like she was from another world. "Excuse me?"

"Don't look at me like that, Arykah. You know I can't go there with Adonis. He's Boris's cousin."

"And that means what, Monique? I can't believe you're still holding on to Boris."

"I'm engaged to the man. What do you expect me to do?"

"I expect you to drop him like he dropped you."

"Boris didn't drop me, I moved out. Remember?"

"Oh yeah, I remember. I also remember you telling me that you were done with him for good, but if the wedding is still on, I guess this time is no different than all the other times you left him."

"What are you talking about?"

"You really had me fooled this time. Packing up all your clothes, going to a hotel, not taking Boris's calls and having him banned from the radio station showed me that you were really gonna leave that fool alone. But I see that you're only going through the motions. But what I wanna know is why you're wasting your time. Why bother putting on a front for everyone else? If you're still engaged to the man, you may as well go on back home and stop pretending like you're teaching Boris a lesson, because he ain't trying to learn a darn thing. Boris is gonna do what he wants to do. He always has and he always will."

"That's not true, Arykah. Every time I leave Boris, he apologizes and promises to do better."

Arykah exhaled loudly and looked into her best friend's eyes. "Monique, your behind is dumb all day long. Did you hear what you just said? You said 'every time I leave Boris.' Why should you have to keep packing your bags every six months for this fool to realize he's messing up? Can't you see that this is a pattern with Boris? He ain't never gonna change because he knows you're gonna eventually come back to him, which is saying you accept the crap he puts out. And it's wrong for you to string Adonis along."

"I'm not stringing Adonis along. He knows what I'm going through, and he's only a friend."

"Monique, you're playing with his emotions. You know the man is in love with you."

"I can't help that, Arykah. You act like I did something to lead Adonis on."

Arykah's eyebrows raised and she cocked her head to the side. "Did you?"

Monique became quiet. She slowly stood and walked halfway across the living room then turned around and looked at Arykah. "This is why I didn't want to tell you what Adonis did for me today, because I know you still have a crush on him."

Arykah leaned back against the sofa and crossed her ankles. She'd been doing good controlling her mouth, but right then, the devil was really trying to make her curse. "You need to bring your fat, wide, black behind back on over here and sit down, because I'm getting ready to check you real fast."

Monique didn't move from her spot. She kept her gaze on Arykah.

"For the record, whatever feelings or *crush*, as you call it, that I may have had for Adonis went out the window the moment I learned he only had eyes for you. And just so you know, I'm for the two of you getting together because I think you'll make a great couple. What I'm telling you ain't got nothing to do with me having a crush on Adonis because that's not the case. This is about you permitting him to get closer and closer to you when your every intention is to go back to Boris.

"You're allowing Adonis to invest his time, money, *and* his heart in something that you don't want to prosper, and I'm telling you it's the wrong thing to do. He's gonna end up getting hurt and feeling like you used him, which is exactly what you're doing."

Monique's head snapped backward. *"I'm using him?* First of all, you and I wear the same size in clothes, so if I'm fat, you're fat. And how am I using Adonis? I don't ask him for anything. He sends flowers to *my* job and *my* hotel room. He calls *me* all the time. What do you want me to do?"

"I want you to act like you got some morals and an ounce of dignity. Adonis is head over heels in love. He's buying you things and reaching out to you because he thinks he may actually have a chance of being with you. So you need to do the right thing and set him straight before he becomes more involved than he already is."

After the argument over Adonis, Monique talked Arykah into putting some food in her stomach. At nine o'clock P.M., they drove to Lem's Bar-B-Que on 51st and State Street. Back at Arykah's house, they sat at the kitchen table, licked mild sauce from their fingers, and talked until the wee hours of the morning. Finally, at three in the morning, Monique announced to Arykah she was headed back to her hotel suite.

"Girl, it's too late and dangerous for you to be out alone. You're gonna stay the night," Arykah demanded.

"I don't have a change of clothes."

"I have a closet full. You can shower and go to work from here."

"I would rather sleep in my own bed."

Arykah rose from the table and threw their trash into the garbage can. "And I would rather be in a size twelve. You are not leaving my house at this hour. So come on upstairs and get in the bed with me."

"Arykah, I can be downtown in twenty minutes. I'll call you when I get in my room."

Arykah removed Monique's car key from her key ring. "I'm gonna put this under my pillow. If you take it and leave my house before I wake up in the morning, you'll have hell to pay."

As they walked upstairs to Arykah's bedroom, Monique figured out a way to get her key back. "Well, you know I sleep naked, right?"

"Not in my bed."

"That's the only way I can get a good night's sleep, Arykah."

Arykah opened her top dresser drawer and gave Monique a nightgown. "Monique, don't play with me. Put this on, get in the bed and shut up. And I know you're going through a drought season right now, so make sure to stay on your side of the bed and don't try anything funny."

Chapter 8

The alarm clock woke Arykah up at six o'clock A.M. Lazily, she reached over to the nightstand to shut it off. She sat up on the bed, then looked over at Monique still sleeping. Arykah silently thanked God for her. If there was ever a true friend in this world, Monique Morrison was the one. In the ten years they'd been best friends, Arykah couldn't remember a single time when Monique hadn't come through for her. Whether it was money, a prayer partner, advice, a shoulder to cry on, or a swift kick in the butt, Monique was there to deliver whatever Arykah needed, and for that, she was grateful. Even during the situation with her breast, it was just like Monique to come running to Arykah's side to hold her hand. Whatever the outcome of Friday's test, Arykah was glad she didn't have to face it alone.

She tapped Monique's shoulder. "Wake up, sleepyhead."

Monique turned onto her side, facing away from Arykah with her eyes closed. "It can't possibly be morning already."

Arykah got out of bed and went into the bathroom to brush her teeth.

"Can you please turn the water on in the shower?" Monique asked Arykah as she walked out of the bedroom. She lay in Arykah's bed another three minutes, then forced herself to get up. She walked into the bathroom and saw Arykah standing at the sink examining her naked left breast.

"You wanna feel the lump?" Arykah asked Monique. Without waiting for an answer, Arykah grabbed Monique's hand and pressed it directly beneath her left breast then rotated her hand in a circular motion. "Can you feel it?"

"No."

She pressed Monique's hand deeper into her breast and kept rotating.

"Now I feel it. I would say it's about the size of a golf ball."

"That's what my doctor said."

Monique pulled the shower curtain back. She raised the gown over her head, let it fall to the floor, and stepped in the hot running water. "Well, don't worry about it, because it'll be gone by Friday."

In spite of her ungodly relationship and prior living arrangements with Boris, Arykah knew Monique had a divine and direct connection with the Lord. When it came to petitioning the throne of grace, Monique was a powerhouse in the Holy Ghost. At church, her prayers brought the house down many a day.

"You promise?" Arykah asked.

"Yep, I got the hook up. Me and Jesus, we're tight. We're here." Monique brought two fingers up to her eyes and moved them back and forth in front of her face.

*   *   *

After her shower, Monique opened Arykah's closet door to select something to wear to work. Arykah walked up behind her. "You can't wear anything that has a price tag on it."

"Why not?"

"Because, I haven't worn it yet."

Monique chose a two-piece navy pantsuit by Chanel. Arykah took it out of her hand and hung it back in the closet. "Nope, not this one. I paid fifteen hundred dollars for it."

Monique's next selection was a red, silk, knee length sarong dress. Arykah grabbed it and hung it back in the closet as well. "Uh-uh. No can do. That's a Donna Karan original."

Monique's temper was on level five and slowly rising. If it got to ten, all heck was going to break loose. Since Arykah was acting funny with her dress clothes, Monique opted for something casual. She didn't have any meetings scheduled that day, so casual wear was ideal. She chose a black cashmere sweater and a pair of black denim jeans.

Again, Arykah hung what Monique had selected back in the closet. "You can't wear this outfit either. It's Tommy Hilfiger, and I only wore it once."

Monique stepped back and looked at her. "Why don't you just give me a Hefty garbage bag? I'll cut a hole in the bottom of it and slip it over my head."

"I think I can do a little bit better than a Hefty bag," Arykah said.

Monique sat on the bed and waited for Arykah to decide what she'd allow her to wear. "This is why I should've taken my behind to my hotel room."

Arykah didn't respond. She brought Monique an

A-line, plain looking, khaki colored dress that buttoned down the front.

Monique eyed the dress in disgust. "You gotta be kidding me, Arykah. Gravy's got a dress just like that and she's fifty-three years old."

"This happens to be a Claire James, Monique."

"Who is Claire James?"

Arykah shrugged her shoulders. "The heck if I know."

Monique had reached level ten. If Arykah wasn't facing a biopsy on Friday, Monique would've gone to war with her. She snatched the dress from Arykah and laid it on the bed.

"Oh, my God. It's almost seven o'clock. I gotta get in the shower," Arykah said. She gave Monique an air kiss, then rushed into the bathroom. Monique waited five minutes, then went into the bathroom and flushed the toilet. Suddenly cold water attacked Arykah's body. She screamed, and the name she called Monique wasn't nice, but Monique felt justified.

Adonis came upstairs from the basement, on his way to the shower, only to find Kita standing at the stove scrambling eggs. What stunned Adonis was the pink lace bra and panty set she was modeling. She looked at Adonis standing at the top of the stairs in his pajama bottoms. In his hands were a towel, a toothbrush and a bar of soap.

"Good morning, handsome. Can I make you some breakfast?" Kita asked Adonis seductively.

"You can't do nothing for me," he responded disgustingly.

On his way to the bathroom, Kita admired his physically fit torso. "You should let me rub baby oil on your chest to lay those hairs down."

Adonis made a beeline to Boris's bedroom and saw

him getting dressed. "Look, cuz, if you're gonna have that broad up in here, the least you can do is tell her to put some clothes on. You ain't the only one living here, and personally, I don't wanna see her naked tail."Adonis didn't wait for Boris to comment or respond. He went into the bathroom and slammed the door.

Ten minutes into his shower, Adonis heard the bathroom door open and close. He peeked from behind the shower curtain and saw Kita prepare to use the restroom. Adonis couldn't believe the gall of her. "What the heck are you doing?" he frowned.

"What does it look like?" She answered a question with a question.

Adonis snatched the shower curtain closed. He heard the toilet flush, then the water turned cold and chilled him. When the door opened and closed, it dawned on him that Kita didn't even bother to wash her hands. "Nasty broad," he said to no one in particular.

Monique came from her office and approached Theresa's desk. "Theresa, I need you to pull some files for me."

She looked at the way Monique was dressed. "What are you wearing?"

"I didn't go home last night."

Theresa's mouth dropped open. "Ah, sooky, sooky, now."

"Don't go there. I spent the night with Arykah. This is her dress."

"Monique, tell that to somebody who doesn't know any better. I know Arykah's style. Every time she comes here, she is as sharp as a tack. She wouldn't be caught dead in that dress."

Monique folded her arms across her chest and looked at her secretary. "You think you have it all figured out, don't you?"

"Yep, I'll tell you what happened," Theresa said.

Monique exhaled. "This should be good."

"You hooked up with Adonis last night. Next thing you knew, you were singing that Shirley Murdock song. *It's morning and we've slept the night away.*" Theresa sang the lyrics and swayed in her chair.

Although Monique didn't want to, she had to chuckle. She shook her head from side to side, but couldn't deny the fact that Theresa amused her. "Girl, would you please do me and the rest of the world a favor and get saved?"

"I'm right, Monique, and I know it. You didn't have time to go to your hotel room and change clothes this morning and you were forced to stop at Wal-Mart and buy something to wear to work because Saks, Lord & Taylor, and Macy's weren't open yet."

"You know what I'm gonna do for you, Theresa? I'm gonna recommend that you see the company's therapist, because there is really something wrong with you."

"Monique, no one's judging you. You and Adonis can do whatever you wanna do."

"Look, Theresa, whatever you have concocted in that twisted mind of yours ain't happening, okay?"

"But I bet you wouldn't mind if it did. Monique, you ain't fooling anybody. This is me you're talking to. Adonis is righteously gorgeous. He's built like his middle name should be Hercules, and he worships you. Can you honestly look into my eyes and tell me that if the opportunity presented itself, you wouldn't jump his bones?"

Even though Monique was dark skinned, her cheeks turned crimson red. "Theresa, I refuse to answer a ridiculous question, and this inappropriate conversation is over."

Theresa studied her face. "You're blushing. I didn't mean to get you riled up."

She gave Theresa a list of names. "Ain't nobody riled up. Get me these files, and please stay out of my business."

When Monique sat behind her desk and picked up the telephone to call Arykah, her computer spoke to her. *"YOU GOT MAIL"*

She placed the receiver on its base and typed in the password to open her mailbox.

ACortland_music@yahoo.com>>*Good afternoon, beautiful. I'm worried because you didn't call last night. How's Arykah?*

Monique thought what a wonderful man Adonis was. It was just like him to be concerned about someone else's friend.

MissMo@WGOD.org>>*I'm sorry, I didn't call. Arykah's fine. I stayed the night with her. She appreciates your concern and prayers.*

ACortland_music@yahoo.com>>*You two must've been up all night talking.*

MissMo@WGOD.org>>*Yep, that's exactly what we did. I didn't have time to go to my hotel room for a change of clothes. Arykah was stingy with her clothes this morning; she gave me a dress that makes me look like Aunt Jemima's granddaughter.*

ACortland_music@yahoo.com>>*LOL . . . I find that hard to believe. I'm sure you're still a shining star in whatever you're wearing.*

Monique felt her cheeks get warm. She knew Adonis was trying to make her love him.

MissMo@WGOD.org>>*I know what the mirror shows me, Adonis.*

ACortland_music@yahoo.com>>*Monique, beauty is in the eye of the beholder. Always remember that. I* *think someone has a birthday coming up. Who might that be?*

She smiled.

MissMo@WGOD.org>>*That would be me. This Saturday is the big 2-9 for me. How did you know?*

ACortland_music@yahoo.com>>*I have my ways of finding things out. What are your plans?*

MissMo@WGOD.org>>*Everything revolves around Arykah's test on Friday. I'm taking the day off to be with her. I don't make any plans to celebrate my birthday. Arykah usually goes all out with a shoe shopping spree, balloons, and a cake, but I'm sure my birthday is the furthest thing from her mind right now.*

ACortland_music@yahoo.com>>*That's understandable, given the circumstances and stress she's under.*

Theresa came into Monique's office and set the files on her desk. She saw Monique smiling at the computer. "You must be chatting with Adonis 'Hercules' Cortland."

MissMo@WGOD.org>>*Adonis, I got a nosy person looking over my shoulder trying to be all up in my grape Kool-Aid.*

Theresa's eyes grew wide. "I can't believe you sent that through."

Adonis knew whom Monique was referring to.

ACortland_music@yahoo.com>>*LOL . . . Good afternoon, Theresa.*

She hurried around the desk to type a response, but Monique beat her to it.

MissMo@WGOD.org>>Adonis, *you can't say anything like that to her.*

ACortland_music@yahoo.com>>*Why not?*

MissMo@WGOD.org>>*Because she'll twist it around and think you're asking her to marry you.*

Theresa shrieked. "Oh, my God. I can't believe you sent that through."

ACortland_music@yahoo.com>>You two are crazy, and it's great that you have a fun working relationship. My job is so serious that I have to literally put my life on the line every day. On that note, I gotta go. Give Arykah my love. Theresa, have a great evening. And Monique, the most beautiful Aunt Jemima's granddaughter on this side of heaven, I'll give you a call later on.

Monique signed off and saw the silly grin on Theresa's face. "What's that look for?"

Theresa clapped her hands together and imitated Eddie Murphy from a scene in *The Nutty Professor* movie. "Hercules, Hercules, Hercules."

After choir rehearsal Wednesday night, Adonis and Taj were the last to leave the sanctuary.

"Hey, Adonis, you live south, don't you, man?" Taj asked.

"Yeah."

"Can you give me a lift to Seventy-Ninth Street? I can catch the bus home from there. I asked Boris, but he said he wasn't going south tonight."

Adonis wondered if that meant Boris wasn't coming home at all. "Yeah, man, I'll give you a lift. What's wrong with your ride?"

Taj exhaled. "Man, what *ain't* wrong with it? It needs a muffler, brakes, new tires and a wheel alignment. And my battery needs charging. This morning I tried to start it, and I swear my car laughed at me, man."

Adonis chuckled. "Taj, you need to trade it in. Have you been car shopping?"

"I kinda like not having a car note. But my ride *is* kinda raggedy, huh?"

"My aunt Myrtle used to always say that a raggedy ride is better than a dressed up walk any day." Out of the corner of his eye, Adonis saw Arykah come out of the Bishop's office with a tear stained face. "Taj, I'll meet you outside."

Adonis caught up with Arykah just as she was on her way into the ladies room. "Arykah."

She stopped, then turned to look at him. Adonis saw her red, puffy eyes, and immediately pulled her into his arms and held her tight. Arykah wrapped her arms around his neck and allowed her weight to fall against him. He heard her exhale loudly in his ear.

"I got you, sweetie," he whispered to her. Adonis knew Arykah needed to release the cry she held inside.

Just when Arykah thought she couldn't shed any more tears, they fell down her cheeks. Adonis felt her body shaking, and he was glad to be the shoulder she needed at that moment. She pulled away from him and wiped her eyes. "I'm sorry, Adonis."

"Don't you dare apologize. I knew you needed to get that out. Did the Bishop pray for you?"

Sniff, sniff. "Yeah, he did. Listen. Monique told me that you were praying for me and I appreciate that."

"Praying is the least I can do. James, chapter five, verse sixteen says: *Confess your trespasses to one another and pray for one another, that you may be healed. The effective, fervent prayer of a righteous man avails much.*"

Arykah looked into his eyes in amazement. "All right, Adonis, you better quote that scripture, boy."

He chuckled. "You sound surprised. It would be a shame to sit in Sunday School week after week, and not get anything out of the lesson."

"Yeah, you're right about that."

Adonis placed a finger under Arykah's chin and lifted

her face toward his own. "Keep a positive attitude about Friday. God always has the last word."

"I know He does. I'm still scared though."

"What time is the biopsy?"

"It's scheduled for ten o'clock."

"At ten o'clock Friday morning, I'll remember to stop what I'm doing and pray."

Arykah couldn't believe the magnitude of Adonis's character. "Thanks, Adonis."

"I gotta go. Taj is waiting on me." He kissed Arykah's cheek then turned to walk away when she stopped him.

"Monique's birthday is Saturday."

"Yeah, I know. Are you planning anything?" he asked.

"Monique loves shoes; I'll probably take her shoe shopping Friday evening. Every year she spends her entire birthday married to the *Lifetime Movie Network*. I ordered an Atomic Bomb cake."

He frowned. "Atomic Bomb?"

"It's a cake with fresh strawberries and bananas and it *is* da bomb. You should come by my place Friday night and help us celebrate."

Adonis smiled at Arykah. "I'll be there."

Arykah couldn't resist her question. "What are *you* planning for her?"

"I don't have anything planned. Monique ain't *my* woman."

The way he answered her told Arykah he was lying about not having anything planned. "You're up to something. You can tell me. I promise to keep it on the down low."

"There's nothing to tell." Adonis smiled and walked out of the church.

* * *

Early Friday morning, Monique was on her knees praying. She decided to spend Thursday night with Arykah for moral support. As Arykah slept peacefully, Monique knelt next to the bed. She placed her hands softly on Arykah's left breast, closed her eyes and talked to God in unknown tongue so the enemy and his camp couldn't comprehend what she was saying to the Father.

Dr. Biesterfield, the head oncologist at West Suburban Hospital, came into Arykah's room with the latest x-ray of her left breast in his hand. She was lying in bed as Monique sat in a chair holding her hand.

"Miss Miles, I'm sending you home with a clean bill of health."

Arykah and Monique looked at each other, then back at Dr. Biesterfield before Arykah spoke. "You're sending me home? What about the biopsy?"

"A biopsy isn't needed."

Monique looked confused. "I don't understand, Doctor Biesterfield."

He scratched his head. "Neither do I. Either my x-ray machine malfunctioned on Monday or I need to go back to medical school."

"What are you saying?" Arykah asked him.

"I'm saying the lump is gone. It totally disappeared."

"Oh my God," both Arykah and Monique squealed at the same time.

Dr. Biesterfield chuckled. "That's pretty much what I said when I saw the x-rays we took this morning. This is unexplainable. I've never seen anything like this in all my twenty years of practicing medicine."

Arykah was on the highest level of spirituality she'd ever been as she and Monique left the hospital. "Monique, can you believe what God did?"

"What did I tell you Tuesday, Arykah? Didn't I say the lump would be gone by Friday? I told you I had the hook up."

They got into Monique's car and pulled out of the hospital's parking lot. "God is awesome," Arykah said.

"No argument there. Since we have the rest of the day off, what do you wanna do?"

"Take me by the church. I gotta get on the altar."

After an hour of kneeling and giving God thanks for her healing and deliverance, Arykah took Monique to Oakbrook Terrace Shopping Center for her annual shoe shopping spree. "Okay, Monique, I'm a single woman with a mortgage, so take it easy on me."

"What's my limit?" Monique asked.

"I'm not gonna give you one. Just act like you got some sense."

Thirty minutes after they entered Nordstrom's, Monique was already carrying around four pairs of shoes, and of course, Arykah bought duplicates for herself. After spending big money in Nordstrom's, they were walking and talking when Arykah's cellular phone rang.

"Arykah, speaking," she answered. She tried to be discreet with her conversation. "Uh-huh. Yes, that's right. No. Absolutely. Yes. No. No. Yes. Something like that. Sure. Okay, thanks for calling."

Arykah knew Monique was looking at her curiously and wanted to question her about the mysterious phone call. She placed her telephone in her purse and nonchalantly walked into Lord & Taylor.

"What was that about?" Monique asked as she followed closely on Arykah's heels.

"What?"

"Don't what me. Who was on the phone, and why were you giving one word answers?"

Arykah picked up a cream colored Baby Phat satin pump and pretended to examine it. "I don't know what you're talking about."

"Oh, so now you've got amnesia?"

Arykah held the pump out to Monique. "Isn't this cute? I wonder if they have this in fuchsia."

Monique snatched the shoe from Arykah's hand. "Don't play with me. I asked you a question."

"I'm sorry, I didn't hear it. What was the question?"

Monique asked the question again and did sign language as if Arykah was deaf. "Who . . . was . . . on . . . the . . . phone?"

"Nobody, wrong number." Arykah walked away and looked at another shoe, but she wasn't getting off that easy. Monique was still close on her heels.

"You got a man you're trying to hide from me?" she asked Arykah.

"A man? What's that?"

"You ain't funny. Who was on the phone?"

Arykah exhaled and looked at her best friend. "Monique, do I be all up in your business every time your phone rings?"

"You're keeping secrets, and that's not right. I know one thing though, you better not be getting your freak on."

"What if I am?" Arykah asked.

A man approached them before Monique could respond. "Hey, Arykah. Hey, Monique."

They turned to see someone who'd been chasing Arykah for three years. Monique was the first to speak. "Hey, Evan, long time no see. How have you been?"

"It's all good. How are you, Monique?"

"I'm fine, thanks."

Evan turned his attention to the woman who had filed a restraining order on him a year ago. He'd been seen lurking outside Arykah's home in bushes, sitting across the street from her job, and standing in the back of the church on Sunday mornings, trying to get a glimpse of her. "How are you doing, Arykah?"

She gave him a dry 'hello,' then excused herself and walked away.

Monique knew he was a thorn in Arykah's side. "So Evan, what's been going on with you?"

"Same old, same old. Still working at the candy factory, living from paycheck to paycheck, trying to make ends meet. I got suspended a month ago for sexual harassment, but I'm back at work now. Still living at home with Big Momma. My dog died on my birthday. I think my neighbors may have poisoned him. I just got over the chicken pox two weeks ago."

If Monique were double jointed, she'd extend her leg backward and kick her own butt for opening up this can of worms with him. Misery loved company, and it truly loved Evan too. She hadn't realized that Arykah had left her alone in Lord & Taylor with Evan.

"Wow, Evan, there's never a dull moment with you, I see," Monique said.

"Nah, it's cool though. My probation is gonna be over soon."

Monique's eyebrows rose. "Probation?"

"I got caught up in a little petty theft thang with Pee Wee, Crusher, Bullet, and Hammer. I'm doing community service cleaning up elephant poop at Brookfield Zoo on the weekends."

Monique knew she needed to end this conversation quick, fast, and in a hurry before Evan confessed to killing folks and preserving their brains in jars of formaldehyde that could be found in a refrigerator in his mother's garage. She looked around the shoe store and didn't see Arykah anywhere in sight. "That's nice, Evan, excuse me a moment." She reached in her purse for her cellular phone and called Arykah. "Where in the heck are you?" Monique yelled.

"I'm sitting outside in the car eating gourmet cheese and caramel popcorn."

Monique was furious. "You better be lying."

Arykah put a mouthful of popcorn in her mouth and crunched loudly in Monique's ear.

A few minutes later, after exiting the mall herself, Monique threw her bags in the backseat, sat behind the wheel and slammed the door. "I can't believe you left me alone with Jeffrey Dahmer's half brother."

"You know I can't be within one hundred feet of that fool," Arykah said.

"You created that monster, Arykah."

Arykah turned her entire upper torso toward Monique. "How did I do that?"

"Don't act innocent. You knew Evan was sweet on you. And you knew he sat in his car across the street from your house looking through binoculars, pleasuring himself while watching every move you made. You chose to sashay around your living room window naked."

Arykah had a guilty smile on her face. "Monique, please, I did no such thing. And even if that was the case, what I do in the privacy of my own home is my business."

"It ain't all that private if your blinds are wide open. And did you have to call the police on him?"

"That nut stole my neighbor's ladder from their garage

and climbed on top of my roof, trying to get in my house."

"You should've had some clothes on," Monique said.

"What I should've done was call Bubblegum, the dope dealer that hangs around the church. For a six-pack and a carton of cigarettes, he would've taken Evan out."

Monique laughed as she drove toward Arykah's house. "Speaking of Bubblegum, Gravy said he was on the side of the church last Sunday selling raw chicken wings and hamburger meat that he'd stolen from a grocery store."

"I can believe that. Two Sundays ago he was selling Krispy Kreme donuts. Now you know the nearest Krispy Kreme to the church is in Bridgeview, which is about thirty miles away, and Bubblegum doesn't have a car. So there's no telling where those donuts came from or how long he had them. But the crazy thing is, folks were buying them."

"Arykah, that is nasty. Everybody knows Bubblegum sleeps next to and eats out of a dumpster."

"Girl, please, folks don't care. Krispy Kremes will do that to you."

Monique shook her head from side to side. "That's a shame. The saints probably gave Bubblegum enough money to overdose. He's a dealer and a user."

She drove into Arykah's driveway and turned off the engine. She and Arykah collected their bags and went inside. They sat the bags on the living room sofa, and Monique opened the boxes and looked at the shoes Arykah had bought her. "I love my shoes; thank you."

"You're welcome, sis. Happy birthday. What are you gonna do tomorrow?"

Monique sat down and leaned back on the sofa and exhaled. "I'm gonna do what I always do on my birthday. Absolutely nothing. I plan to lay in my bed all day. I'll be twenty-nine. This is my last round before I become an old woman."

"I beg your pardon. I'm thirty and as fine as I was when I turned twenty-five."

"That's a matter of opinion, sweetie. I ain't mad at you though, you keep on convincing yourself of that lie."

Arykah threw the shoe she was holding across the room, and it barely missed Monique's leg. "You would say that to the woman who just spent over a thousand dollars on shoes for you?"

"Arykah, please. You know you're a fox."

"You better recognize. Can you get me a glass of water? My throat is dry."

Monique got up and went toward the kitchen, but stopped dead in her tracks as she got to the archway leading into the kitchen. Sitting on the kitchen table was an Atomic Bomb cake lit with a single candle. A dozen helium 'Happy Birthday' balloons were dangling from the ceiling.

Suddenly, a hand firmly gripped Monique's waist from behind. Adonis stood next to her and pulled her closer to his side, then looked down into her eyes and sang "Happy Birthday."

When Adonis finished his solo, Monique wrapped her arms around his neck. "Oh my goodness. Thank you so much. How did y'all plan this?"

Arykah got a large knife from the utensil drawer. "That was the call I got at the mall. Adonis was telling me everything was set for us to come to my house."

Monique hugged her best friend. "You are too much."

Adonis pulled Monique to the table. "The candle is getting low, you better make a wish and blow it out."

Monique leaned over the cake, closed her eyes, paused, then blew out the candle. The three of them sat around Arykah's kitchen table, and the ladies introduced Adonis to Atomic Bomb. Arykah gave her testimony and told him what God did for her that day.

"I told you I was gonna stop what I was doing at ten o'clock and pray," Adonis said.

"Well, it worked. To God be the glory for what He's done," Arykah said.

"Amen to that," Monique agreed.

Adonis excused himself and left the kitchen. He returned a short time later with a small turquoise bag with the Tiffany's logo on it. He sat it on the table in front of Monique. "Happy birthday, beautiful."

Monique couldn't speak.

Being speechless was something Arykah was not known for. "All right, Adonis, the *big* spender."

Monique nervously pulled a long rectangular shaped box from the bag. Inside the box was a five-carat platinum diamond tennis bracelet.

Arykah nearly cursed aloud at the sight of it. She barely caught her tongue before the explicit was released.

Monique couldn't say a word. No one had ever given her anything like that before. She sat at Arykah's kitchen table holding the bracelet, looking at it in total awe.

Adonis gently took it from her hands and hooked the clasp around her right wrist. "It's a friendship bracelet, Monique. Do you like it?"

She rotated the bracelet around her wrist. The diamonds sparkled at every move she made. "My God, Adonis. It's breathtaking."

"But do you like it?" he asked again.

"Heck yeah, she likes it. But if she doesn't, remember that I'm your friend too," Arykah joked.

Monique stood and looked into Adonis's eyes. "I love it, thank you."

While she was standing so close to him, Adonis knew the time was now or never. He leaned forward and kissed her lips softly. Monique gave in to her own temptation and allowed the passion she felt for Adonis to take over her emotions. She stood on her toes and connected with him. Arykah dug into her slice of cake and watched the show.

Monique was the first to pull away. Adonis grabbed her chin and kissed her lips again. He couldn't get enough of her. "Whew, I better leave." He held Monique's wrist up. "If you allow me to love you, there can be more where this came from."

He kissed the back of her hand seductively, then walked to Arykah and kissed her cheek. "I'm glad you're all right. It's good to see you smiling again."

When they heard the front door shut behind Adonis, the two friends squealed with excitement as they made a fuss of Monique's $6,800 gift. Adonis had mistakenly left the price tag in the box.

Arykah reminded Monique of the conversation they had a few nights before about Monique being torn between Boris and Adonis. "Choose wisely, don't be a fool," Arykah said.

"I've been living in the hotel for a month now and Boris has yet to call to see how I'm doing. Not even a phone call to try and get me back home."

"So what are you gonna do?" Arykah held her breath. If

her best friend didn't do the right thing, she would kill her.

Monique glanced at her gift sparkling on her wrist. "I'm calling the wedding off."

"Oh, bah shah," Arykah shouted in the unknown tongue then jumped up and started dancing.

Chapter 9

The loud ringing of her cell phone startled Monique from a deep sleep at seven-thirty, Saturday morning.

"Happy birthday, Baby Girl."

"Thank you, Gravy."

"What are you gonna do today?"

"Stay in the bed," Monique responded lazily as she yawned.

"Stay in bed on your birthday?"

"I may go down to the pool later on, but other than that, I don't have any plans. I just wanna chill today."

"Baby Girl, when you turn sixty-five, that's when you stay in bed on your birthday. At your age you should be painting the town red. I don't understand y'all young folks. I'm gonna cook you a birthday dinner tomorrow after church," Myrtle said.

"Gravy, you're the best."

"Don't you ever forget that."

"I won't. I promise."

"What do you want to be on the menu?"

"You know I love everything you cook, Gravy. Surprise me. Just be sure to make your specialty."

"What's that?" Myrtle asked the question as if she didn't already know the answer.

"Finger lickin' good gravy," Monique said.

After talking with Myrtle, Monique sat up on the bed and thanked God for her twenty-nine years of life. She had great strength and perfect health. As Senior Executive Producer at WGOD, Monique grossed nearly eighty-five thousand dollars a year and for that, she was thankful. She was proud of most of the choices she had made in life. She was an only child, but Arykah filled the void and became the sister she never had.

She sat in the middle of the king-sized bed and thought about Boris, one of the choices she wasn't so proud about. During the two years they'd been together, there were definitely more downs than ups. And then there was Adonis. Monique glanced at her gift. She still couldn't believe she was wearing five carats on her wrist. Adonis said it was a friendship bracelet. Monique wondered how many carats his wife would get.

Her cell phone rang again as she imagined what her life would be like if she were engaged to the other Mr. Cortland.

"Good morning, beautiful. Happy birthday."

Monique's heart melted at the sound of Adonis's voice. "Good morning to you too, and thank you, it is a *very* happy birthday."

"Sounds like someone slept well last night."

She smiled and rotated her bracelet around her wrist. "I did. I slept with my bracelet on. I didn't wanna take it off. I don't know what I would do if I lost it or if somebody stole it."

"Calm your nerves, it's insured. How are you gonna spend your special day?"

"Lying in my bed, watching back to back movies on the *Lifetime Movie Network*."

"That doesn't sound like much fun."

"It would be if you were lying next to me," Monique mumbled.

"What did you say?" Adonis asked.

"Nothing."

"Do me a favor, Monique."

"Anything."

"Walk onto your balcony and look down."

Monique obeyed his request. With her cell phone in her hand, she stepped onto her balcony and looked down eighteen stories and saw a miniature Adonis standing beside a miniature white stretch Mercedes Benz limousine, waving up at her. She squealed in delight and waved to him. "What are you doing, Adonis?"

"You have a nine o'clock appointment. Get dressed and be down here in twenty minutes."

Monique didn't have to be told twice. She ran back inside and tossed her cell phone on the bed. She quickly stripped from her pajamas and skipped into the bathroom.

The doorman escorted Monique out of the hotel. Adonis saw her the moment she came through the revolving doors. She stole an extra fifteen minutes getting ready, but Adonis didn't mind. Looking at her dark flawless skin with her make-up done to perfection and not a hair out of place, he decided she was well worth the wait. He wore a white casual linen shirt and pants set. Monique decided to match him with a white fitted sundress that crisscrossed in the back and draped to her ankles.

"You are unspeakably beautiful today, Monique. I know you must be getting tired of hearing that word. Actually, you're more than beautiful, but I can't think of a more profound word to describe you."

"Adonis, I never get tired of hearing the word 'beautiful', so you can stick with it."

He laughed and guided her into the limousine, then instructed the driver to make a U-turn and head north on Lake Shore Drive.

"Where are we going?" Monique asked.

"I've had this day planned for a week. When you said that spending the day in bed would be relaxing, it confirmed that I'd made the right plans."

"That doesn't tell me where you're taking me."

He looked at her and smiled. "We're going to a place where there's plenty of rest and relaxation."

"Is Arykah in on this?"

"Nope, this is all my doing."

Monique didn't believe him. "Can I call her?"

"Arykah doesn't know anything, but you can call her if you want."

Monique dialed Arykah's home number. "Hey, Arykah."

"Hey. Happy birthday," Arykah greeted.

"Thanks. I'm in a limo headed north on Lake Shore Drive, and I want you to tell me where I'm going."

Arykah lay in her bed not fully awake. "What?"

"What's my destination?"

"Are you tipsy, Monique?"

"No, I ain't tipsy. Do you know where I'm going or not?"

"First of all, I haven't had any coffee yet, so I don't have all of my marbles. But how am I supposed to know where you're going if you don't know yourself? And what are you doing in a limousine anyway? You said you were spending your birthday in bed like you do every year."

"Adonis picked me up this morning, but he won't tell me where he's taking me."

"Sorry, I can't help you, girlfriend. As a matter of fact, I asked Adonis on Wednesday night if he were planning anything for you and he told me he wasn't. So I want you to put that lying devil on the phone."

Monique gave Adonis her cellular telephone. "Arykah wants to have heated fellowship with you."

Adonis brought the telephone to his ear. "Sister Miles, God bless you."

"I'm only holy on Sundays. Why did you lie to me?"

"Because I know you can't hold water," he said.

Arykah was offended. Yes, she was known for her loose lips, but so what? "Oh no you didn't. Now I gotta cut you."

"Let me ask you a question, Arykah. Who told Monique that Sister Cox is pregnant by Deacon Walton?"

"Adonis, pregnancy is something that can't be hidden. Eventually the whole church will know."

"Okay, I'll give you that, but who told Aunt Myrtle that the Bishop's sister-in-law is messing around with Sister Taylor's husband?"

Arykah's tongue was hot when it came to gossip, but she didn't like being called on it. "Look, Adonis, we're not in a courtroom playing *cross examine the witness*."

"I just want you to know why I couldn't trust you with privileged information; you tell everything."

"That's not true. If someone says, 'Arykah, don't say anything,' then I won't. But you have to say those words to me. Now tell me where you're taking Monique."

"It's a secret." He quickly disconnected the line.

*   *   *

Monique saw they were entering the Eden's Expressway. "Can you at least give me a hint, Adonis?"

"Then it wouldn't be a surprise."

"I don't like surprises."

"Your bracelet was a surprise. If you don't like it, I
could take it back."

That was not an option. Monique proclaimed she
would never take it off. In fact, she'd let her loved ones
know that she was to be buried wearing it.

The driver exited at Peterson Road in Skokie, Illinois, a
small suburb just north of Chicago, and headed west.
Monique twitched in her seat as though her underwear
was on fire. "Adonis, the suspense is killing me. *Pleeeease*
tell me where you're taking me."

Adonis refused to answer her, but chuckled at her anx-
iousness. He instructed the driver to turn right at the
next stoplight. Five minutes later, the limousine drove to
the door of Lady Brenda's Day Spa & Salon. Monique
looked at Adonis and smiled broadly.

The driver opened the rear door and Monique stepped
out followed by Adonis. A light skinned African-American
woman, with her hair pulled back tightly in a bun, came
outside to greet them. "Good morning, Monique. Happy
birthday."

Monique was stunned that the woman knew her
name.

"Mr. Cortland, it's a pleasure to meet you. Were you
able to follow the directions okay?"

"Yes, they were very detailed, thank you," Adonis answered.

She looked at Monique. "I'm Brenda Finley, and this is
my establishment. On behalf of my entire staff, we welcome you, and it will be our pleasure to relax your mind,
body, and soul. Mr. Cortland has instructed us to meet

your every need. So tell me how we may service you today?"

Monique did her best to get words to come out of her mouth. "I, uh, I'm, oh my God, um . . . " she stammered.

Adonis stood next to Monique and gently took her by the waist. He loved the effect he had on her. "Lady Brenda, if I may. Monique is already beautiful and flawlessly made. But how about styling her hair any way she likes? I'm sure she'll enjoy a facial and the Swedish body massage you recommended. Be sure to touch up her fingernails and toenails. Those are the services that I personally want for her, and of course, anything else her heart desires. The sky is the limit. I want her pampered from the crown of her head to the tips of her toes. Today is her birthday, so please make sure she's completely satisfied."

Lady Brenda was impressed. "Absolutely, Mr. Cortland. She's in good hands, and I promise she won't be disappointed."

He lightly kissed Monique's lips, placed his hands on the sides of her face, and looked into her eyes. "I want you to clear your mind and allow them to treat you like the goddess you are. Feel free to add whatever you want to the tab. On your special day, I want you to have whatever you want." Adonis's salary as an electrician and what the church paid him afforded him the opportunity to spoil Monique. And his parents' life insurance policies were made available to him when he turned twenty-one years old. He had plenty of money to live a fulfilled life and take care of the woman of his dreams.

"Will you be waiting for her, Mr. Cortland?" Lady Brenda asked.

"How long will she be?"

"Approximately four and a half hours."

"I'll come back for her. That gives me enough time to plan her next surprise."

A woman dressed in a white smock and white pants met Monique at the door to the salon and exchanged her stilettos with a pair of pink plush complimentary slippers. Then Monique was led to a private room where she was instructed to change into a pink plush terrycloth robe. Five minutes later, Lady Brenda escorted her to another private room where a buffet table displayed all of her breakfast favorites.

"Mr. Cortland was very specific in his selections," she told her. "I hope this spread is to your liking."

On the table were fresh strawberries and whipped cream, crushed pineapple, lightly toasted cinnamon bagels, blueberry and banana nut muffins, sausage links, waffles, scrambled eggs, freshly squeezed orange juice, cherry lemonade, hazelnut flavored coffee, lemon iced tea, 2% low-fat milk, and ice water. Twenty-nine roses, one for each year of Monique's life, were scattered along the table.

Monique placed her hand over her heart. Adonis thought of everything and left no stone unturned. She was stunned at the lengths he'd gone to just for her.

Lady Brenda saw the expression on Monique's face. "This is the first time a man has requested first class service such as this. I've been in business for thirteen years and have never been asked to set up a buffet table."

"How much is all of this costing him?" Monique asked.

"Mr. Cortland requested that you not be made aware of the cost." She noticed Monique's bracelet. "That's a gorgeous bracelet."

Monique extended her wrist forward. "He gave this to me last night."

"You have one heck of a fiancé, Monique."

She saw that Lady Brenda was referring to the ring on

her finger. Even though Monique had told Arykah she would call off her wedding to Boris, she hadn't made any effort to do so. "Oh no, Adonis and I are only friends."

"Just friends? Over the years, I've had husbands and fiancées shower their women with unlimited pampering. But today is the first that a man has soared to this magnitude for a *friend*."

Lady Brenda advised Monique to eat all she could within the next half hour. At that time, her pampering would begin.

Almost five hours later, Monique was so relaxed she could barely lift her calves and walk. Every muscle in her entire body was on vacation. She got to the reception area and saw Adonis sitting patiently waiting, reading a magazine.

He looked up and saw Monique, then came and stood next to her at the receptionist's desk. "How do you feel?"

She leaned against him for support. "That was absolutely the most amazing experience I've ever had."

"Did you enjoy your breakfast?"

"Oh my God. Yes, you fed me well; thank you. But it's gone from my belly now."

He looked confused. "What do you mean?"

"I've had my colon cleansed."

Adonis knew what that procedure entailed, and he chose not to expound on the details. "You're a better person than me. I could never get that done."

"It's no big deal. You should try it."

Adonis shivered. "Call it a man thing, but ain't nobody putting a tube in my behind."

The receptionist appeared. "Miss Morrison, how was your experience at Lady Brenda's Day Spa and Salon?"

Monique could only think of one word. "Fabulous."

* * *

In the limousine heading south on Lake Shore Drive, Adonis noticed Monique's new hair color. "I like what they did to your hair. Is it dyed?"

"Not all of it. What I have is called honey blond streaks. They took strands throughout my hair and bleached them."

"It highlights your skin," Adonis complimented.

"The streaks are called *highlights*, so I guess the salon did a good job."

"What else did you get done?"

Monique leaned her head back against the headrest and exhaled. "Everything. They poked, they prodded, they rubbed, and they kneaded every inch of my body. While I was lying on the massage table, they put earphones on my ears, and I listened to water falling from somewhere. The sound hypnotized me. Then they turned me over so that I was laying on my stomach as they detailed my back. Someone took what looked like an oversized wooden rolling pin, kinda like the one that Gravy has in her kitchen, and ran it up and down my spine. I didn't know I was drooling until someone wiped my mouth with a towel. I'm telling you, Adonis, I was so out of it, I didn't even know my own name."

Adonis was impressed, pleased that his money was well spent. "Wow, you make *me* wanna get on the massage table."

"It's a mind blowing experience."

"I'm glad you're satisfied, Monique."

Monique extended her upper and lower limbs and stretched. "I'm satisfied, satiated, and sated."

It was just about two P.M. when the driver brought them to the Buckingham Fountain. From the trunk of the limousine, Adonis retrieved a picnic basket and a large red and black quilted blanket. He led Monique to a grassy spot underneath a huge tree twenty feet away from the fountain. Adonis spread the blanket, set the picnic basket on top of it, then gently pulled Monique down to sit next to him.

"I hope you're hungry," he said to her.

Monique watched in awe as Adonis removed a bottle of sparkling white grape juice, cubed cut cheddar cheese, rolled ham and salami slices, potato chips, red seedless grapes, and an entire Eli's cheesecake from the picnic basket. "How is it that you know what my favorite foods are?"

"Arykah is always helpful. And I told you once before that it's a man's job to know what his date likes and dislikes."

Last week at Houston's, Monique threw a ball into Adonis's court when he made that same statement, but he threw the ball back at her. She wondered what he'd do with the ball if she asks him the million-dollar question again. "Is this a date, Adonis?"

"Monique, this could be a date, just two friends getting together, or a chance meeting. I really don't care what we call it, because it really doesn't matter. By the way, have I told you how exceptionally radiant you are this afternoon?"

"You told me I was beautiful, but you didn't say I was radiant."

"Where are my manners?" Adonis inserted a toothpick into a cheddar cheese cube and fed it to her. "You are radiant, beautiful, sexy, voluptuous, seductive, and flawlessly gorgeous."

Monique smiled shyly and gave him a short wave. "Aw, Adonis, go on."

He obeyed Monique thinking she wanted him to stop the flattery.

"I mean it, Adonis. Go on."

They both laughed, and he poured sparkling grape juice into two flutes. He gave one to Monique and held his own flute out to her. "Here's to you on your birthday. I pray that God will bless you abundantly. I'm talking about bountiful blessings, stupid fat blessings, the 'eyes haven't seen nor ears heard what's in store' type of blessing. The 'just because I'm God, and I can do that' kind of blessing. The type of blessing that makes people ask 'why her and not me? The kind of blessing that just doesn't make any darn sense."

Monique was almost in tears sitting next to him. Adonis was gifted to render her speechless at the drop of a hat. "Who are you?"

He looked at her like she was nuts. "Excuse me?"

"Who are you and where did you come from?"

Adonis pressed the back of his hand against Monique's forehead, searching for signs of a fever. "Are you feeling okay?"

"I'm serious, Adonis. No one has ever covered me in prayer like that before. I've never gotten roses delivered to me. No one has ever upgraded my car. I can't remember anyone ever complimenting me the way you do. Today was my first trip to a spa, compliments of someone else, and this is my first private picnic. I never even got one carat, let alone five of them. This is unreal to me, and it's too good to be true. I feel like I'm living in a dream that I'll eventually wake up from."

Adonis took Monique's free hand and placed it on the center of his chest. "Do you feel my heartbeat? I'm a real person." He moved her hand over to his shoulder and down his left arm. "This is real skin. It isn't a dream. I'm really here, and I ain't going nowhere."

They sat staring into each other's eyes for the longest moment before they were interrupted. A man dressed in a clown suit stood in front of them holding a Polaroid camera. "Would you lovebirds like to have your picture taken for seven dollars?"

"Yeah, we would," Adonis answered.

The man positioned the camera. "Okay, lean into each other, and smile like you just can't live without one another."

Striking the requested pose came so effortlessly. Monique and Adonis sat cheek to cheek, held their champagne glasses up, and smiled.

"That's perfect. Hold that pose."

The man gave them the 3x5 colored photo in a paper frame, collected his money, and moved on.

Adonis admired the photograph. "We look good together, don't you think?"

"You look good and I look good, so we're destined to look good together." The word 'destined' means 'meant to be,' and Monique wondered if she should've let it slip from her lips. "I meant to say two people who look good can't help but look good together."

"You said it right the first time."

Monique thought it would be good to change the subject. "I'm hungry. Are you hungry? I think we should eat."

For the next hour, Monique and Adonis sat, laughed, and ate. Adonis fed Monique ham and cheese as she fed him salami and potato chips. He stretched his legs forward and instructed Monique to lay her head on his lap. He held up a whole grape vine over her mouth and told her to bite off a grape.

She honored his request and looked up at him. "You know, Adonis? You have a way of making me feel like I'm the only female in the world."

He ran his fingers throughout her hair. "If you were my woman, I'd make sure you always felt that way. When I was in music school, I met this guy named Jesse. He reminded me a lot of myself because he saw a woman whom he just had to have."

Monique bit off another grape from the vine. "Did he get her?"

"Let me tell you Jesse's story. Every morning before he went to class, Jesse would see this beautiful woman walk past his dorm room. After two weeks of watching her, he gathered enough nerve to go outside and talk to her. She said her name was Cynthia, and Jesse told her he thought she was pretty and asked if she would consider having dinner with him that evening. Cynthia was reluctant at first, but somehow Jesse talked her into it. She didn't give Jesse her address, but she agreed to meet him out.

"They made plans to meet at Carson's Ribs in Elmwood Park on Harlem Avenue. When Jesse got to the restaurant, Cynthia was already seated in a booth. He said she was so pretty, her face had a glow as though a ray of light was shining down on her. During their conversation, Cynthia didn't want to tell Jesse anything personal about herself like where she lived or worked. He said she even refused to talk about her family. Her excuse was that she didn't feel comfortable sharing personal information on a first date."

"I can understand that," Monique said, biting off another grape.

"How about understanding her ordering two full slabs of ribs for herself and eating three quarters of them? Jesse said Cynthia just about ate both slabs. He only ordered a half slab for himself, and he could hardly finish it."

"That's impossible, Adonis. I think your friend was exaggerating when he told you this story. Two whole slabs? I don't think so."

"That's what I thought too, but let me finish the story. After spending almost ninety bucks on dinner for a chick that chose to keep the conversation to a minimum, Jesse decided that night would be the first and last time he asked Cynthia to go anywhere. When they exited the restaurant, Jesse asked Cynthia where she had parked her car. He would walk her to her car to make sure she got in safely. She told Jesse that she didn't drive to the restaurant. She assured him that she would get safely home on her own. It was late in the evening, and Jesse told Cynthia that he'd feel better about her safety if she allowed him to give her a ride home.

"In the car, she told Jesse to take Harlem Avenue to Roosevelt Road, then turn right. When he got to the corner of Roosevelt and Wolf Roads, Cynthia told Jesse to let her out of the car. She said she would walk home from there. Jesse looked around and saw two cemeteries on the southwest and northwest corners. On the opposite side of the street was a gas station and a church. He asked Cynthia if she were sure she wanted to get out on that particular corner, and she said yes. Jesse persuaded her to give him her telephone number so that he could call and make sure she got home safely.

"She wrote a number on a piece of paper and gave it to him. She kissed Jesse's cheek, thanked him for dinner, got out of the car, and walked across the street toward one of the cemeteries. He just knew there was no way this girl was going inside a cemetery, so he sat there and watched until someone pulled behind him and blew their horn to get him to move. He turned left onto Wolf Road and saw in his rearview mirror that Cynthia was definitely going into a cemetery."

Monique stopped chewing the grapes and held onto every word Adonis was saying.

"Jesse made a U-turn and drove back to the corner of Roosevelt and Wolf Roads and pulled over to the curb. When he didn't see Cynthia anywhere, he pulled out his cell phone and dialed the number she had given him. An elderly woman answered, and Jesse asked to speak to Cynthia. The woman asked Jesse who he was and she wondered why he was calling for her daughter. He told the woman his name and stated that he and Cynthia just had dinner that evening, and he wanted to make sure she got home safely. The woman became very upset and told Jesse that she didn't appreciate him calling her house. She informed Jesse that it was impossible for him to have had dinner Cynthia, because she'd been dead for twenty years."

Monique sat up so fast she made herself dizzy. Her eyes were the size of ping pong balls. "Oh my God."

Adonis saw her eyes buck out of her head. As hard as he tried, he couldn't suppress his laughter.

Monique didn't see anything funny about this story. In fact, it was very sad. "What did Jesse do after speaking with Cynthia's mother?" she asked anxiously. Monique's eyes grew wider.

Adonis grabbed her hands to try and calm her. "Monique, it was a joke. There was no Jesse and there was no Cynthia. I made the whole thing up."

She grabbed a handful of grapes and threw them at Adonis. "That was cruel." Though she wasn't really angry with Adonis, Monique couldn't let him know that. She sat with her back to him and folded her arms across her chest and pouted.

Thinking that he had overstepped his bounds with her, Adonis wrapped his arms around her and pulled her backward into his chest. "I'm sorry, Monique. I didn't mean to spoil your birthday."

She saw the cheesecake next to the basket. She smiled mischievously and grabbed a handful and smashed it in Adonis's face. Because he was caught off guard, Adonis released her. He was willing to take his punishment in stride until he heard Monique laughing at him. He grabbed a handful of cheesecake, and Monique tried to crawl away, but wasn't fast enough. Adonis got a hold of her right leg and pulled her backward.

He turned Monique over and rubbed the cheesecake over her entire face as she squirmed and squealed. They looked at each other and laughed.

"Look what you did to my face, Adonis. The spa had my make-up just right."

"You started it," he said.

"Serves you right for telling that bogus story. Now how do you suppose we get this mess off our faces?"

"I have an idea." Adonis moved closer to Monique and began kissing her face, concentrating on her lip area.

Monique's first instinct was to stop him, but decided against it. Why let an entire cheesecake go to waste? What difference did it make if they ate it out of the tin pan or off of each other's faces? Besides, that was the first time anyone had ever spread anything on her and kissed it off, and Monique enjoyed the attention she was getting.

When Adonis finished cleaning her face, Monique returned the favor. She too concentrated on the lip area.

Adonis walked Monique to her hotel suite. He inserted

her key card into its slot and opened the door. She entered the room and noticed he wasn't following her. "Are you coming in?"

"You don't want me to."

"Why would you say that?"

Adonis scanned Monique from her newly highlighted hair down to her freshly painted toes. "Trust me, you don't want me to."

Monique walked over to the king-sized bed and sat down. "How do you know what I want, Adonis?"

He looked deeply in her eyes. "You're trying to seduce me on the down low, Monique."

She forced a phony shocked expression to appear on her face. "Seduce you? Why would I seduce you?"

"Oh, so I'm reading you wrong, is that it?"

Monique took strands of her hair and seductively placed them behind her ear while staring into Adonis's eyes. He was in the doorway with one foot in the hotel room and one foot out of it. He had a decision to make. Should he enter the room or walk away from it? Monique was trying to act innocent, but she knew exactly what she was doing to him; he was sure of it.

The left side of Adonis's brain was battling with the right side. *"What am I waiting on?"* the left side asked. *"She wants me to get under those sheets. I better go ahead and show her what I'm working with."* Then the right side of his brain said, *"If there's any chance of Monique and I spending the rest of our lives together, I gotta do it right. God won't bless any mess."*

Monique snapped Adonis out of his thoughts. "Are you coming in?"

He looked at her. "You better be glad I'm saved." He sat her key card on the dresser and gently closed the door behind him.

Monique was grateful that Adonis was the strong one. She, herself, had had a weak moment.

Adonis got on the elevator, paced the small space, and gave himself a pep talk. "You did the right thing, man. You did the right thing."

When he reached the limousine, the driver asked Adonis for the next destination.

"Take me home quick. I need to take a shower," he replied.

After watching Monique and Adonis snuggling up in the backseat, the driver knew what kind of shower Adonis needed to take.

A soft knock on the door aroused Monique from her nap at six fifteen P.M. She got up, slipped on her bathrobe, and looked through the peephole. "Who is it?"

"It's Joanie from the front desk. I have a delivery for you, Miss Morrison."

Monique opened the door and Joanie gave her two white boxes.

"Who sent these?"

"I'm not sure, ma'am. I just happened to see them on the counter with your name and room number written on them."

Monique gave Joanie a $10 tip and thanked her. She sat the boxes on the bed and opened the larger box first. On top of the wrapping tissue paper was a small envelope.

Monique read what was written on the inside of the card.

'Your birthday isn't over yet and neither is the celebration. Slip into this number and join me in the lobby in twenty minutes.'
                                    Adonis

Beneath the tissue paper was a red Donatella Versace strapless sequin and satin gown. "Oh, my God" was all Monique could say. She took the dress and stood in front of a full-length mirror and pressed it against her body. There was no denying the dress had cost a pretty penny. She opened the smaller box and saw red Jimmy Choo satin sling back, three-inch heels and a small red satin clutch. Once again, Monique was rendered speechless. She took a shower and got dressed.

She emerged from the elevator with a look that was to die for. Adonis was standing at the front desk dressed in a black custom made Bill Blass tuxedo, white shirt, a black satin cumberbund, and tie. In his hand, he held a red rose wrist corsage for Monique. She came and stood in front of him and Adonis thought she was even more beautiful than when he'd last seen her earlier that day. As usual, her make-up was done to perfection.

Adonis loved the ruby red lipstick she wore. The strapless gown fit her every curve. Monique looked as though she was born in it. Adonis recalled earlier in the afternoon when Monique tempted him. After his cold shower, he got on his knees and prayed for strength. He desired Monique but knew that God wouldn't be pleased if he took her.

He leaned forward and kissed her on both cheeks. "There isn't a word in Webster's Dictionary that describes how lovely you are this evening."

She smiled. "You're quite dapper yourself."

Adonis couldn't help but notice her bright smile. Against the red lipstick, Monique's teeth stood out like stars against a pitch-black sky. "Girl, you make a brotha wanna propose right here and now."

Again, she flashed the stars. He slipped the corsage

onto her right wrist, then held his elbow out for her to slip her arm through. "Shall we?"

"We shall," she answered excitedly.

Outside, in the waiting limousine, Adonis placed a blindfold over Monique's eyes. Again, she had to wait to find out her destination.

At Navy Pier, Adonis guided Monique out of the limousine. Because she couldn't see, she took each step like she was walking on eggshells. Adonis wrapped his arm around her waist for support. "Monique, just relax and walk normal. I got you. I promise not to let you fall." After a few more steps, he brought Monique to a stop. "Okay, we're here. Are you ready?"

"Yes," she said excitedly.

Adonis slowly lifted the blindfold. Monique saw the word **ODYSSEY** in big bold letters displayed on the side of an oversized yacht. She was stunned as she looked from the yacht to Adonis. "I don't understand. What did I do to deserve this?"

"You were born," was his answer.

At the top of the gangplank, an elderly Caucasian man wearing a white military jacket, white pants, white patent leather shoes, and a white hat with a black rim greeted them in style. "Good evening, Mr. Cortland. I'm Captain Gaynes."

Adonis shook the Captain's hand, then presented the woman on his arm. "Good evening, Captain. May I present, Lady Monique Morrison."

Monique extended her hand to the Captain who kissed her knuckles softly. "Miss Morrison, you are truly a jewel. Happy birthday, and welcome aboard the Odyssey. Mr. Cortland's description of you is justified; you're breathtaking."

"Thank you, Captain." She blushed.

Adonis and Monique were led to the formal dining room. It was designed to hold up to two hundred people. Monique noticed only one table set for two people in the center on the room. "Where are all of the people?" she asked the captain.

"You and Mr. Cortland have the entire dining room to yourselves this evening."

She looked at Adonis. She just couldn't believe how much effort he'd put into making her birthday a very special one. It was a birthday she'd never forget. "Who *are* you?"

He chuckled and guided her to their table and pulled out her chair. Captain Gaynes informed them that in ten minutes, the boat would sail out onto Lake Michigan and return to Navy Pier at approximately midnight. When the Captain walked away, the waiter approached their table with a bottle of Cristal. "Good evening, Mr. Cortland. My name is Bryson, and it's my pleasure to serve you."

"Thank you, Bryson." Adonis extended his hand toward Monique. "The lady's name is Monique."

Bryson bowed to Monique and smiled. "Happy birthday, Miss Monique."

He held the bottle out to Adonis. "Would you care for a glass of champagne before dinner, sir?"

Adonis looked across the table at Monique for permission. They were away from the public eye. They didn't have to worry about church folks seeing them sip alcohol and spread their business throughout the church. But if there was ever a time to celebrate, it was then. Monique felt like Cinderella. But she wasn't living a fairytale. The limousine she rode in wouldn't turn into a pumpkin come midnight.

She smiled. "Just one glass."

Bryson filled Adonis's flute, then stood and waited. Adonis took a swallow and nodded his head. Bryson then filled Monique's flute, set the bottle of champagne in a bucket of ice on the table, and walked away.

The sound of Kenny G and his saxophone flowed throughout the dining room.

Monique looked all around her. Lavender silk drapes cascaded down the walls. The lavender Berber carpet looked as though Monique's and Adonis's feet were the first to have treaded on it. Antique chandeliers adorned with Swarovski crystals dangled above every table. Monique would be willing to bet her paycheck that the dinnerware on the table before them was from the 19th century. Pure elegance was all around.

"How much did this cost you?" she asked Adonis.

"Why? Are you gonna reimburse me?"

"This is too rich for my blood. It's Saturday night, no doubt the busiest night for this yacht, which means you had to compensate for at least one hundred people in order to have it privately. I can't believe you did this."

Adonis leaned back in his chair and looked at her. "You know what your problem is, Monique? You don't value yourself, and you don't know your true worth. You're so used to settling for whatever life throws at you instead of going after what you really deserve. You gotta get out of that mindset, because there's so much more in life God wants you to have."

She chose not to comment, but he definitely gave her something to think about. They each took a sip of champagne, then Adonis stood and extended his hand to her. "Dance with me."

Monique placed her hand in his and followed Adonis out onto the deck. He pulled her close to him and placed his open palm against her lower back. Monique pressed her voluptuous bosom against his chest and laid her head on his shoulder.

"You smell so good," Adonis said.

Wrapped in each other's arms, they swayed back and forth under the full moon for an entire hour.

Bryson walked out onto the deck and lightly tapped Adonis's shoulder. "Dinner is served, Mr. Cortland."

Filet mignon, lobster tails, scalloped buttered potatoes, steamed asparagus with almonds, and dinner rolls were what Adonis chose for the menu. Monique was in heaven.

Chapter 10

On his way to the shower Sunday morning, Adonis walked past Boris's bedroom and saw him standing at a mirror tying his tie. "What's up, cuz?"

Boris glanced at his wristwatch. "You're just wakin' up? It's almost nine thirty."

"I overslept."

"You were missing in action yesterday, man. I called your cell at least five times. Is it working?"

"Yeah, as far as I know," Adonis answered.

"So what chick had you so occupied that you were unavailable?"

Your chick. "What makes you think I was with a chick?"

Boris tightened his tie around his neck and looked at his cousin. "Because the only other time you disappeared for a whole day was when you and that girl, Francis, was creepin', and you didn't want her old man to know."

"Boris, that was six years ago. I ain't seen or heard from Francis since."

"Well, don't keep me in suspense, who is she?"

"There is no *she*. I was paged to a job site yesterday morning. A few houses in Markham lost power, and it took all day to get it back on." Adonis despised the fact that he had to lie about spending time with Monique. It's something that he wanted to share with the world.

"I wonder why I didn't get that page. I'ma have to check that out. Working on a Saturday pays double time," Boris said.

Adonis tried not to panic. Boris had connections at the electric company, and he'd gotten Adonis hired right after he graduated from music school. Boris had seniority over Adonis, which meant he would've been called for overtime before Adonis. If Boris investigated and found out there was no power outage, Adonis would have a lot of explaining to do.

Boris picked up his pager from the nightstand and looked at it. "Aw man, you know what, cuz? My battery is low. That's probably why I didn't get the page."

Adonis exhaled a sigh of relief so loud, Boris looked at him. "You all right, cuz?"

"Yeah, I'm cool. I'ma hop in the shower and get ready."

Boris put on his suit jacket and walked past Adonis. "See you at church."

Boris tried to get Kita's attention throughout morning service, but to no avail. She too was missing in action yesterday with a non-working cellular phone. When Boris called her apartment that morning, Cherry informed him that Kita had left for church already.

Even as she marched past the organ into the choir stand, it seemed to Boris that she purposely ignored him. Immediately after the benediction, Boris gave the musicians his weekly preparation speech for the upcoming rehearsal. He noticed Kita was quickly exiting the sanctuary. She was halfway down the street when he caught up with her.

"Kita, slow down," Boris called out.

She stopped and turned around hastily. "What is it, Boris? I'm in a hurry."

"To go where?"

"That ain't none of your business."

Boris had no clue why she was behaving in such a hostile manner. "What's your problem and where were you yesterday?"

Kita held up her left hand for Boris to examine. "You ain't put a ring on this finger, Boris. I'm three times seven plus four. Do the math, and you'll realize that I'm fully grown and whatever I do is none of your concern."

She turned to walk away, and Boris firmly gripped her by the elbow. "Hold the heck up. You don't walk away from me when I'm talkin' to you. You have your monthly friend or something?"

"Humph, nah that ain't it. As a matter of fact, the color red won't be flowing for a while." Kita snatched her arm from his grip, got in her car and drove away.

Boris stood with his mouth agape and the bottom of his brand new Stacy Adams shoes glued to the concrete.

"Yo, cuz," Adonis called out to him.

Slowly, Boris moved in Adonis's direction as though he were in a trance.

"Why did you rush out of the church?" Adonis asked. "Is everything okay?"

The neighborhood was spinning all around Boris. "You ain't gonna believe this. I screwed up big time, man."

The expression on Boris's face told Adonis that his world was falling apart. "Let's go somewhere and talk," Adonis said.

* * *

In the buffet line at Betty's Soul Shack on south Cottage Grove Avenue, Adonis topped his plate with pork spare ribs, roasted garlic potatoes and gravy, corn on the cob, candied yams, sweet peas, and white rice. Boris chose to go with a simple lettuce, tomato and cucumber salad. Once they were seated in a booth, Adonis gave thanks to the Lord for their food then looked at Boris's plate. "That's all you're eating?"

Boris was still in a state of shock from the bomb Kita had dropped on him. "I ain't hungry."

Adonis dug into his potatoes and gravy. "What's going on with you, cuz? Is this about you and Monique?"

"Nah, it's Kita."

Adonis rolled his eyes in the air. He'd rather discuss a boring tennis match than engage in conversation about the church ho. "What about her?"

"She's pregnant."

Adonis almost dropped his fork. *"What?"*

"Yeah man, she just told me."

"How can she be pregnant? You ain't use nothing?"

Boris didn't answer. Adonis laid his fork on his plate and looked directly into Boris's eyes. "Cuz, I know you weren't dumb enough to touch that girl without putting a glove on. Come on, man, please tell me you ain't that stupid."

Boris sat his elbows on the table and placed his face in the palm of his hands. "I made a mistake; what else can I say?"

"You mean a *grave* mistake because a baby ain't the only issue you gotta worry about."

"What do you mean?"

"We're talking about Kita, Boris. She's nasty."

Boris frowned. "Nasty how?"

"Come on, cuz, stop playing. Kita is well known around Chi-town, and it ain't because she can sing. You need to see your doctor and get yourself checked out real fast."

Monique walked into Myrtle's living room using the spare key Myrtle had given her. "Ooh, Gravy, I smell it. I smell it."

Myrtle yelled from the kitchen, "Come on in the kitchen, Baby Girl."

Monique saw Arykah sitting at the table already indulged in homemade buttermilk biscuits and gravy. "What are you doing here? This is *my* birthday dinner."

Arykah licked her fingers clean. "Be that as it may, in church this morning, Mama Cortland extended me a cordial invitation to feast at her dinner table, and I graciously accepted. The devil will have on a pair of drawers made out of popsicles before I turn down a home cooked meal."

"You could've at least waited 'til I got here before you ate." Monique rolled her eyes at Arykah and walked to Myrtle standing at the sink washing dishes. She kissed her cheek. "How was church this morning, Gravy?"

"Church was real good. Bishop preached like a fool. He came out of the pulpit and walked across the deacons' laps, whooping and hollering."

Monique sat down at the table while Myrtle prepared her plate. "The bishop clowned this morning, huh?"

"Like a fool," Myrtle said.

"Like a *baldheaded* fool. He almost made *me* cut a step," Arykah added.

"Well, Apostle Donald Lawrence Alford wasn't a punk this morning either. He told us that if we can see our dreams, we can seize our dreams. Then he asked us how badly we wanted our dreams. Before he finished taking his text, half the church was on the floor. The folks over at Progressive Life-Giving Word Cathedral are straight up ghetto when it comes to praising God. They don't care who's watching. I looked around and saw people falling like dominos. One brotha leapt so high, I swear his shoes were at least three feet off the floor. It was like everybody was having seizures. And that's when it happened."

Arykah and Myrtle asked at the same time. "What?"

"Well, I was just standing and watching everybody get their praise on, and the Holy Spirit asked me what my problem was. I answered that I was just getting a feel for things. Then the Holy Spirit said, 'Oh, I got something for you to feel.' Next thing I knew, I started having a seizure like everybody else."

Arykah and Myrtle laughed at Monique's description of morning service at Progressive Ministries.

"Y'all go ahead and laugh, but I'm telling the truth. We were running around the church and jumping over pews. It's like doing something you wouldn't want anyone outside of the church to see you do because they wouldn't understand it. An unsaved psychiatrist would highly recommend the entire congregation, from Apostle Alford on down, be committed to a psych ward. Crazy praise is the only way to describe it."

The three of them laughed so loud they didn't hear Adonis come in the front door.

"What's so funny?" he asked.

Monique averted her eyes to the plate of food Myrtle sat in front of her.

"Ain't nothin' funny," Myrtle said with an attitude. "Where is your cousin?"

Adonis kissed her cheek. "He went home after church. He said he had a headache."

"Hey, Adonis," Arykah spoke.

"Hi, Arykah, it's good to see you. How are you doing, Monique?"

She looked into his eyes. "I'm fine, Adonis; how are *you*?"

"I'm cool," he answered, but didn't return her gaze for fear that the love he felt for her would show.

"You want something to eat?" Myrtle asked him.

Adonis knew that if he told Myrtle that he'd eaten food other than what was on her stove, she'd curse him out, and then ask God for forgiveness later. "Nah, Auntie, I ain't hungry. I just came to see you."

"Well, say happy birthday to Baby Girl. Yesterday was her big day."

Arykah decided to be messy. "Yeah, her birthday was yesterday, Adonis. You didn't know?"

"Uh, nah, uh, happy birthday, Monique."

"Thanks," she said without looking up from her plate."

Myrtle sat down at the table with Monique and Arykah. "So, were you able to stay in bed and relax like you planned, Baby Girl?"

Adonis stood behind Myrtle and leaned against the sink with a silly grin on his face.

Arykah went to the stove and pretended to refill her plate while portraying the same silly grin as Adonis.

"Yeah, I had a nice, relaxing day, Gravy," Monique said.

Arykah brought her plate back to the table. "Monique, are you sure you spent the entire day in your suite? I called your room several times yesterday and never got an answer."

She glared across the table at Arykah. "That's because I unplugged the phone so I could get some rest."

Myrtle turned around and spoke to Adonis. "Speaking of telephones, I called your cell phone a few times yesterday and didn't get an answer. Where were *you* all day?"

"I was at work," he quickly answered.

"On a Saturday?" Myrtle asked.

Arykah relished looking at the sweat beads that formed on both Adonis and Monique's faces.

"Yeah, Auntie, a few houses lost power in Harvey. It took all day to get it back on again. I left my cell phone in the work van."

"That wasn't on the news last night. Why did the city lose its power?" Arykah asked, knowing full well that Adonis was fabricating a story for his and Monique's sake.

If Myrtle wasn't sitting between them, Monique would've destroyed Arykah's shin under the table with her stiletto.

As he answered Arykah, Adonis slightly gritted his teeth to let her know she was working on his last nerve. "We never figured it out. Almost half of a block in Markham was without power for about fifteen hours."

Myrtle looked at him confusingly. "Harvey or Markham?"

Arykah could no longer hold in the silent laugh. She pretended to cough to let it out. Monique closed her eyes and prayed that Adonis would be able to pull this off.

"I meant to say Markham; I mean, Harvey." Adonis nervously grabbed a plate from the dish rack and began to fill it with potatoes and gravy.

"I thought you said you weren't hungry," Myrtle said to him.

"Gravy, as usual, you put your foot in this gravy," Monique said, trying to get Adonis off the hot seat. But as Monique lifted her fork with her right hand, Arykah shrieked.

"Where did you get that beautiful bracelet? Is it a birth-day gift?"

Monique felt her bladder begin to betray her. Before Myrtle could address the bracelet, there was a loud shatter behind her. She turned around and saw Adonis's broken plate on the kitchen floor. Mashed potatoes and gravy were splattered all over the place.

"Boy, what the heck is wrong with you?" Myrtle fussed. "I just mopped this floor."

Adonis nervously knelt to clean up the mess. "I'm sorry, Auntie, it slipped."

Myrtle got the broom and dustpan from the pantry. "Get out of the way, I'll clean it up. Sit your clumsy behind down somewhere."

"I'll buy you another set of dishes, Auntie."

"You sho will," Myrtle said as she swept.

Adonis sat at the table. He and Monique stared fiercely at Arykah. She knew they were glaring in her direction, but refused to give them the satisfaction of looking up. Only one spoonful of mashed potatoes remained on her plate, however, Arykah savored it and made it last until Myrtle joined them all at the table. Then and only then would it be safe to look up.

On Monday morning, Adonis sat at his desk to enjoy a cup of strong black coffee before heading out to a job site. He thought about Boris and what he was going through. He couldn't understand why Boris would willingly surrender a heavenly treat for a hellish trick. The more Adonis thought about it, Boris's situation could actually work in his favor. Monique had yet to admit to him that she was totally done with Boris. Now that there was an illegitimate baby about to surface, it could be the pep in her step to run straight into Adonis's arms.

He tossed and turned all night contemplating whether or not to inform Monique that the man, whose engagement ring she was wearing, was on the verge of becoming a not so proud papa. However, Boris was his cousin, and they shared the same bloodline, so Adonis opted to say nothing. And as Arykah would say, 'Pregnancy is something that can't be hidden. Eventually, the whole church will know.'

Adonis decided to sit back, relax and watch the karma and fateful chips fall where they may.

"Good morning, Adonis."

He looked up to see Dan Thurman, Boris's supervisor. "Good morning, Mr. Thurman."

He gave Adonis a sealed white envelope. "Can you make sure Boris gets his paycheck?"

"Why are you giving his check to *me*?"

"He called in sick this morning. He said he came down with the flu over the weekend and asked if I could give his paycheck to you."

Boris was gone when Adonis left the house that morning. He assumed Boris got an early start for work. This is the first that Adonis had heard about him having the flu. "Sure, I'll make sure he gets it."

When Mr. Thurman left his desk, Adonis called home. It was possible that Boris got halfway to work, then turned around. That way he and Adonis could've easily missed each other in passing. After three rings, Monique's voice filled the telephone line. "*You've reached the Cortland-Morrison residence. This call is very important to us. Please leave your name, number, and a brief message after the beep, and your call will be returned as soon as possible.*"

Adonis could've disconnected the call when the voicemail picked up, but he looked forward to hearing Monique's voice whenever he could. Adonis thought it good that her voice may soon come from a different voicemail in the near future; maybe from a house that he and Monique would share together as husband and wife.

He dialed Boris's cellular phone and got his voicemail. "Hey, cuz, it's Adonis. What's this about you having the flu? Next time you ditch work, let me know. I was almost a lousy cover for you. Anyway, I got your check."

It took Boris forty-five minutes to come down from his second high. He sat in an alley with his back propped up against a dumpster and his belt tied tightly just above his elbow. He gave Bubblegum another crisp $20 bill, then extended the belted arm forward a third time.

Bubblegum tapped the heroin filled syringe, then inserted the needle into the crease of Boris's arm. "Somebody sho' ticked you off, huh? Fifteen bucks is the most you've ever spent on this stuff. Not that I'm complaining, but what's the deal? I mean, it's been years since you've paid me a visit."

With his vein reloaded, Boris leaned his head back against the dumpster. The blood throughout his entire upper torso became warm. The last time he dealt with drugs was when Monique threatened to leave him for good a year and a half ago ago. His mood swings and carelessness were tearing them apart. Boris swore to her that he'd never touch the stuff again.

"I'm about to be a daddy, man," Boris said sluggishly.

"That ain't necessarily a bad thing. You're gettin' married anyway, right?"

"Man, Monique left me about a month ago."

Bubblegum sat next to Boris. "So who's pregnant?"

"A girl named Kita."

"Kita Mitchell? The girl who goes to your church?" Bubblegum asked.

With barely opened eyes, Boris looked at Bubblegum. "You know Kita?"

Bubblegum chuckled. "Do I *know* her? I'll tell you how well I know Kita. Her birthmark, shaped like a heart, is on her left breast. She has a small mole at the top of her right butt cheek, and if you look on the inside of her upper left thigh, you'll see a purple hickey. I put it there last night. That's how well I know Kita."

The weight of Boris's own head became too heavy for his shoulders. He freely let it fall to his chest.

Theresa walked into Monique's office and saw her frantically rumbling through file cabinet drawers. "Good morning, Boss Lady. What are you looking for?"

"My date planner. I have to finalize a couple of out of town trips. Have you seen it?"

"The last time I saw it, you were taking it home so that you and Boris could select a date to view wedding invitations."

Monique paused. *Oh, my God.* It was the second week of July, and she had forgotten to cancel the order for her and Boris's wedding invitations. They were due to arrive that week. She did, however, call the church to alert the secretary that the wedding was off. Another church event could be planned for September sixteenth.

"Then it's gotta be at the house." Monique looked at her wristwatch. It was 9:30 A.M., a time when Boris should be at work. "Theresa, I'm gonna run to the house and get my date planner. I should be back in an hour."

"I wanna know what you did on your birthday."

Monique held up her right wrist. "For starters, I got this."

Theresa gasped at the sparkling diamonds. "Adonis?"

"The one and only. You're looking at five carats, girl-friend."

"For five carats, I know you dropped your g-string and gave him some nooky."

Monique looked at her secretary shamefully. "Do you eat with that mouth, Theresa? Is your mind always in the gutter?"

Theresa rotated the tennis bracelet around Monique's wrist. "You did something to get five carats."

Monique put her purse on her shoulder. "Goodbye, Theresa. I'll be back in an hour."

"And I'll be waiting to pick up where we left off."

Monique waved goodbye to her secretary as the elevator doors closed.

At the electric company, Adonis peeped into his supervisor's office. "You wanna see me, Jack?"

"Adonis, there was an F-four twister in Detroit last night. It's been reported that power lines, over a five-mile stretch, are all over the place. The city is soliciting volunteers from northern Illinois, eastern Iowa, and southern Wisconsin. I don't know the extent of the damage, but what I saw on the news wasn't pretty. Everything is in total chaos. You're trained highly for this, and you're one of the best I've got. Joe Cummings is already on board, but he needs a partner. Are you interested?"

There was no hesitation. "I gotta get home and pack a duffle bag. "

As Joe Cummings drove the company van out of the parking lot, Adonis called Monique's cellular phone. In her hurry to escape Theresa's interrogation, it sat forgotten on top of her desk. After the third ring, Adonis left a message. "Hey, black beauty. I guess you're busy. I called to let you know that I'm on my way to Detroit to try and do damage control. I have no clue when I'll be back. Depending how things are in Motown, I'll try and call you later. I miss you already."

Monique pulled into the driveway and pressed the 'up' button on the garage door opener that was clipped on her visor. Satisfied that neither Boris nor Adonis were home, she closed the garage and parked her car in the driveway. On her way to the front door, Monique couldn't help but notice the neatly mowed lawn. Surely, Adonis was responsible for its dark green texture.

It had been weeks since Monique had seen the inside of her home. She looked around the living room and saw that absolutely nothing had changed. The aroma of Issey Miyake cologne was fresh in the air. Monique had no idea how close she had come to running into Adonis at the house. He had rushed home, packed a duffel bag and was back out the door only five minutes before Monique had arrived.

She glanced at the photos of her and Boris sitting on the mantel above the fireplace. In one photograph, Boris stood behind Monique with his arms wrapped around her waist. Staring at their smiles in happier days, Monique had to admit that in that particular photo, she and Boris looked like a match made in heaven.

She searched the bookshelf next to the entertainment center for her date planner but didn't see it. She moved to the dining room, but the date planner was nowhere in sight. In the kitchen, Monique saw it was spic and span. Not one dirty dish could be found. Neatly stacked glasses, plates, and utensils were in the dish rack. Monique noticed the old Crisco Oil can that she used to store left over bacon, chicken, and fish grease was no longer on top of the stove. She could smell the freshly waxed floor beneath her feet.

Monique opened the refrigerator and saw a twenty-four pack of Miller's Genuine Draft, a gallon of drinking water, a pitcher of grape Kool-Aid, and a bucket of chicken on the top shelf. She looked in the bucket and saw a crispy thigh and a wing. On the second and third shelves were carry out containers from at least seven different restaurants. Monique figured the reason the kitchen was so clean was because nobody was cooking anything.

She walked into the second bedroom that was used as a home office and a mini gym. On top of the desk, Monique searched through books, papers, and junk mail, but still couldn't find her date planner. The only other place it could have been was in the master bedroom. Monique passed the bathroom and saw that it too was spotless. The smell of disinfectant penetrated her nostrils. The toilet seat was up, a sure sign that bachelors resided on the premises.

Unknown to Monique, just before she walked into the master bedroom she had shared with Boris for the past two years, the entry light on the security alarm panel next to the front door lit up.

On the dresser, Monique saw three bottles of perfume she'd left behind. The levels of perfume were lower than she remembered. The bottle of Ralph Lauren was almost empty. She put all three bottles of perfume in her purse. She opened the closet door and saw it was full of Boris's clothing. Boris had managed to take over Monique's side of the closet. The space where her blouses, dresses, and slacks once hang had been replaced with gym shoes, jeans, and athletic wear. Had Monique seen any female clothing not belonging to her, she would have introduced them to a pair of scissors.

The dresser drawers she used were empty. Next to the bed that was decorated with a comforter set Monique had never seen before, was a nightstand with her date planner lying on top of it. She fumbled through it before turning around and facing Boris standing in the doorway.

"What's up?" he asked her.

In the two words he spoke, Monique knew he was as high as a kite. Boris's eyes were bloodshot red and glassy. His pupils were dilated. Monique hadn't seen those eyes in over a year. She remembered the dangerous and uncontrollable side of Boris when his veins were loaded. She thought that if she didn't confront him on his latest drug use, things would remain calm and she could leave the house without a problem arising.

"Nothing. I just came by to get my date planner. Why aren't you at work?"

"I didn't feel like going today," he said. Boris could hardly hold his head up. His speech was slurred, and Monique gave him credit for having enough sense to stay away from live wires.

"Well, I gotta get back to the station," she stated.

"Who put those rims on your car?"

"What?" She asked the question allotting herself time to answer him.

"Who bought those rims for your car?"

"I did," she lied.

"What brand are they, Monique?"

She couldn't answer Boris because she really didn't know the answer. "I don't know. I liked them so I bought them."

"Those are Lowenharts, and you can't afford them.

Who detailed your paint and who bought you new floor mats?"

"Why were you roaming through my car, Boris?"

"You got a dude spending money like that on you? You spreading your legs for him?"

"You gave up your right to know my business when you started messing with Kita."

"Kita? I don't care about her."

Monique shrugged her shoulders. "Oh, well, that's on you. I gotta get back to the office," she said, but made no attempt to move past him. She wanted him to willingly step aside.

"We can't talk?"

"There's nothing to talk about, Boris." When Monique adjusted her purse strap on her shoulder, Boris caught a glimpse of her sparkling tennis bracelet.

"What the heck is that on your arm?"

Monique didn't answer. She clutched the date planner against her breast and proceeded to squeeze past Boris standing in the doorway to the bedroom. He grabbed her wrist to examine the diamonds. "Who gave this to you?"

Not only was Boris high, but also drunk as a skunk. Monique smelled stale alcohol on his hot breath. There's no telling what he'd do to her when he was in that state of mind. She knew she'd better get out of the house. She snatched her arm from his grip. "Let go of my arm. Don't you ever put your hands on me."

Boris glared at Monique the way a predator does when it is waiting for just the right time to pounce on its prey and devour it. "Who in the heck are you talking to?"

She allowed him to take her there. "I'm talking to your crazy behind."

In a split second, Monique was pinned up against the

hallway wall by her throat. In no time, though, Boris had gone from being angry to loving Monique. He kissed all over her face.

"I miss you, baby. I miss you so much. Please come back home."

With all of her might, Monique tried to peel Boris's fingers, one by one, away from her throat, but she wasn't strong enough. The more she fought, the tighter his grip became. "Boris, let me go," she strained to say.

With his free hand, Boris attempted to unbutton Monique's blouse. "You smell so good."

"Let me go, Boris."

He kissed Monique's neck. "You don't want me no more? You will always be mine."

Fear crept into Monique. She knew she had to do something drastic to get Boris off of her. She sent her right knee full force into his groin. He released her and yelled out in pain. He covered his groin with both hands and Monique slapped his face. "Boris, are you crazy?"

He fell to his knees in pain. "I'm sorry. I'm sorry."

Monique clutched her date planner and ran past Boris, out to her car. She buckled her seatbelt and reached for her cell phone and became horrified that she didn't have it with her. She realized that she must've left it on her desk. She'd just have to call Arykah when she got back to the radio station. She backed out of the driveway and proceeded to head back to the radio station. She turned on the radio and heard Heather Headley singing the second half of her latest release.

"Why you wanna hurt me so bad? I wish I could go back to the day before we met."

Monique could've written that song herself. Was it possible that another woman was going through the same

crap with her man? Monique turned the volume up as
Heather sang the words that came straight from Monique's
own soul.

Fifteen minutes later, a distraught Monique walked up
to Theresa's desk. "Any messages?"

She saw that Monique was agitated. "Are you all right?"

"I ran into Boris at the house."

"At this hour?"

"He decided not to go to work today. He chose to get
drunk and high instead."

Theresa saw that Monique was anxious as she spoke.
"What did he do, Monique? Did he hurt you?"

"No."

"But he tried to, didn't he?"

"Theresa, I'm fine. Are there any messages?"

"No messages, but you left your cellular phone on
your desk. It rang five minutes after you left."

Monique went into her office and shut the door behind her. She sat at her desk and listened to Adonis's
message that he'd left on her cell phone, then she dialed
his number and got his voicemail.

"Hi, I'm sorry I missed your call. I saw the news this
morning. It's just like you to run to the rescue. Please be
careful. I'll talk to you soon."

If there was ever a time she needed to be wrapped in
Adonis's arms, it was right then.

Theresa brought Monique a cup of hot lemon tea and
sat it on her desk.

"Thank you, Theresa. Can you get me the number of
calls that came in from last night's show? And call the studio and ask Jasper to play "When Sunday Comes" by Darryl Coley. I need to hear that right now."

Five minutes later, WGOD aired Monique's request.

* * *

Later that afternoon, Theresa pressed the intercom button. "Arykah is on line two."

Monique picked up the extension. "Hey there."

"Hey yourself. What time are you getting off today?"

Monique glanced at the clock on the wall. "I won't be here too much longer. Theresa and I had a lot of paperwork to sort through. How was your day?"

Arykah squealed into the telephone. "I sold two houses today."

"Congratulations. I might be in the wrong business. Maybe I should go to house-selling school."

Arykah chuckled. "There is no such thing as house-selling school. You enroll in realty classes. Anyway, I feel like celebrating. What are you doing tonight?"

Monique exhaled. "Spending another celibate evening alone."

"Monique, you're celibate by choice."

"You better be celibate too, Arykah."

"Girl, please."

"Don't *girl please* me. We always do things together."

"Some things, not all things. Shopping, dieting, getting our hair and nails done are things we do together. But saying no to a gorgeous man? No way, sis. I can't roll with you on that one."

Monique laughed. "I can't believe you said that."

"I need deliverance, pray for me. What do you wanna eat tonight?"

"How about pizza?"

"Pizza, Monique? I told you I sold not one, but *two* houses, and you want pizza?"

"Well, since you got it like *that*, let's go to Gibson's Steak House on Rush Street."

"Let's do the darn thing."

* * *

"So big spender, how much did the houses sell for?" Monique asked Arykah after the waiter had seated them in a booth.

"One estate in Olympia Fields sold for six hundred thousand, and the other in Orland Hills sold for four hundred-eighty thousand."

"How much of that goes into your pocket?"

"Ten percent of each sale."

Monique did the math. "So you're one hundred eighty grand richer than you were on yesterday?"

"Give or take a few thousand, yes," Arykah said proudly.

Monique snapped her fingers in the shape of the letter Z. "All right. Independent women are doing it for themselves. So when are you gonna settle down and share your wealth with a husband?"

"When one can match my income. I'm not taking care of a man; it's *his* job to take care of me. What I want is a rich man who's blind and deaf."

"Arykah, that's crazy," Monique said.

"No, it's not. I would love to have a husband who can't hear me when I tell him I'm going to the mall or can't see the Visa statement when it comes in the mail, but can afford to pay for my shopping spree."

They were laughing when the waiter brought their drinks to the table. "Are you ladies ready to order?"

Arykah opted for a steak and lobster tail platter. On the menu, Monique saw that it cost $250. She was going to settle for the $45 chicken Caesar salad. She looked across the table at Arykah. "Uh, just so we're clear, this *is* your treat, right?"

"Yes, it is."

"I'll have what she's having," Monique told the waiter.

When he walked away, Arykah buttered a hot roll and bit into it. "So how is Adonis?"

"Adonis is wonderful. He's working in Detroit today."

"Why Detroit?"

"A tornado ripped through the city yesterday and did a lot of damage. I saw it on the news this morning. Power lines are down all over the place."

"Wow, he could be there for a while. Can you survive that?" Arykah asked.

"How many times do I have to tell you that Adonis ain't—"

"My man." Arykah finished Monique's statement.

"That's right, he's not," Monique confirmed.

"But does *Adonis* know he's not your man? He may feel the amount of money he's shelling out and all the time you spend with him constitutes as being your man."

Monique rotated the diamond bracelet around her wrist. "Adonis and I have talked, and we have an understanding."

The waiter brought their salads to them.

"So do you know if Boris went to Detroit too?" Arykah asked.

"Heck no, that fool didn't go. He didn't go to work today either."

"How do you know?"

"Because I went to the house to get my date planner, and he was there. He was drunk and loaded."

Arykah was in the midst of pouring blue cheese dressing onto her salad but paused. "What? He's back on drugs?" Arykah had once been a witness to one of Boris's mood swings when he was under the influence. "He clowned today, didn't he?"

"Yep, he asked who put the rims on my car, then he grabbed my wrist and grilled me about this bracelet. I knew he was getting ready to snap, so I tried to get out of the bedroom, but he pinned me against the wall in the hallway. Then he started kissing me and saying how much he missed me, and he wanted me back home. He tried to unbutton my blouse, and that's when I kneed him where it hurts."

Arykah's mouth was wide open listening to Monique. "Oh my God. What happened next?"

"I slapped his face. He apologized, then I left."

"Thank God you were able to get away from him, but you know Boris is getting ready to flip the script, don't you?"

"What do you mean?"

"The new rims and bracelet put something on his mind. Before today, Boris didn't know another man existed in your life. He doesn't have any solid proof, but trust me; he knows someone is sniffing you. That's why he behaved the way he did today. I bet if you started paying attention and glance in your rearview mirror from time to time, you'll see Boris's Navigator at least two cars behind you. Get ready for the 'I'm sorry' phone calls."

"You think so, Arykah?"

"Girl, I *know* so. Boris is a man, and they never vary from the 'I'll do anything to get you back' script. Men can't take the fact that even though they are the ones who messed up, the women they wronged are being treated right by another man."

"That is so true. My Nana in Louisiana had a saying: 'You don't miss your water 'til your well runs dry.'"

"Trust me, sis. Boris's throat is feeling parched right about now. You and Adonis need to play it cool from now on, because Boris is gonna be on you like yellow on pee."

Monique laughed out loud. "Arykah, your mouth is something else."

Arykah paid no attention to what Monique had just

said to her. She kept on talking. "And the fact that he tried to get some nooky from you tells you that everything between him and Kita ain't peachy. You need to tell Adonis what Boris did to you today."

"Uh-uh. I can't tell Adonis that Boris put his hands on me."

"Why not?" Arykah asked.

"Because Adonis will put a serious hurting him."

Arykah put a forkful of salad into her mouth and shrugged her shoulders. "So what's the problem?"

Kita answered a knock at the door. She taught summer school, but was home sick today. "Who is it?"

"Boris."

She exhaled loudly and opened the door. "What do you want?"

"I called the school earlier and found out you were home. What's wrong with you?"

"I'm dizzy, and I'm puking my guts out, but other than that, I'm just peachy," she answered sarcastically.

Boris stepped into the living room and closed the door behind him. "Where's Cherry?"

"She's going to church straight from work. What do you want, Boris?"

"I just came by to see how you're doing."

Kita looked into his eyes. "Are you high? Why would you come to my house when you're high?"

The effects of Boris's visit to Bubblegum earlier that day had yet to wear off completely. "Ain't nobody high."

"I can tell by your eyes and you can hardly pronounce your words. Did you drive here like that?"

"I told you I'm not high."

"You *are* high, and I'm not gonna deal with you when you're like this. Get out," Kita demanded.

"What?"

She stood in his face. "I didn't stutter. I said, get out."

Boris stood still. "Nah, I ain't going nowhere."

Kita placed her hands on her hips. "You ain't going nowhere? Oh, we're gonna see about this." She walked to the telephone on the cocktail table and dialed 911, then looked at Boris. "You're getting your drunk behind out of here."

"Nine-one-one, what's your emergency?" the operator asked her.

"Can you send the police to—"

Boris snatched the telephone cord from the socket and proceeded to hold Kita hostage. He sat on the floor with his back against her living room door. He refused to let her leave the apartment or use the telephone. Kita got up from the sofa and went to the bathroom.

Boris followed and pushed the door open when she tried to close it.

"I gotta pee, Boris."

"So pee."

"We're on the third floor. You think I'm gonna jump out of the window?"

Boris didn't respond. He leaned against the doorway and folded his arms across his chest. Kita was forced to relieve her bladder in his presence.

"You're acting real stupid, Boris. You can't hold me hostage forever. What are you gonna do when Cherry gets home?"

He watched as she flushed the toilet and washed her hands. "Tell me what I wanna know, and I'll leave. Whose baby are you carrying and how long have you been messing with Bubblegum?"

"Who I'm pregnant by ain't your business. Don't concern yourself with an issue that has nothing to do with you."

"How do you know it's not *my* baby?"

Kita laughed in his face. "Because I'm three months along. And you can't make me happy, let alone pregnant. You don't satisfy me, Boris. As soon as you leave my bed, somebody else comes right over to finish what you couldn't."

"If you ain't satisfied, why are you with me?"

"*With you*? I ain't *with* you."

Boris was getting hotter by the moment.

"I don't want your drunken, crack head behind, Boris. You think I'm gonna get with you so you can do the same crap to me that you did to Monique? The only thing you can do for me is what you've been doing, paying my bills."

That comment infuriated Boris, and it sent him into a rage. For the second time in one day, he wrapped his hands around a woman's throat and pinned her against the wall. But unlike Monique, Kita was from the streets. As soon as Boris slammed her back against the wall, she swung her left fist at his eye. Immediately, he released her, but she kept swinging. The second punch was open-handed. Three of her acrylic coated fingernails left long scratches on Boris's face. He yelled out in pain and felt the welts on his jaw.

He saw blood on his hand. "You crazy broad."

"Oh, I'm a broad today, huh? Well, I'ma show you just how crazy this broad is." Kita ran into the kitchen and pulled a large butcher knife from the cutlery. By the time Boris caught up with her, she was standing flatfooted with the knife in her hand ready for him to make a move.

Boris looked at the knife and chuckled. "What are you gonna do, Kita, stab me?"

"I will dice up your crack head behind like bell pepper and onion. You wanna fight? Come on with it."

After the early dinner with Monique, Arykah attended a finance meeting at the church. As she was leaving, she looked into the sanctuary and saw the praise dancers rehearsing. Cherry was conducting the routine, but her sidekick was nowhere to be seen. When Arykah turned to leave, she bumped into a woman who was coming out of the ladies room. "Excuse me . . . Tracy, right?"

"Yes, I'm Tracy, and you're Erica?"

"Actually, it's Arykah. It's pronounced like Eureka, the vacuum, but it's with an A. I was looking for Kita Mitchell. Is she rehearsing tonight?"

"Kita won't be dancing or singing for a while."

Arykah's eyebrows rose. "Oh, really? Why is that?"

"She's been sat down because uhh . . . " Tracy paused, then made a gesture with her hands forming a bump on her belly.

"Tracy, it's time for your dance solo," Cherry announced sternly from the sanctuary door.

"It was nice talking to you, Arykah." Tracy walked into the sanctuary.

Cherry stood with her arms folded across her chest, glaring at Arykah. Arykah turned the corners of her mouth upward in a slight sneer, indicating to Cherry that she didn't get to Tracy fast enough. The beans had been spilled. Cherry watched as Arykah turned on her heels and sashayed out of the church.

Arykah couldn't get all the way in her car before she dialed Monique's hotel room. "Girl, are you sitting down?"

Monique lay across her huge bed watching television while enjoying a pint of Chunky Monkey ice cream. "Why do you ask?"

"I just had an interesting conversation with Tracy."

"Who's Tracy?"

"She's the newest praise dancer. When I left the finance meeting I peeked in the sanctuary and noticed Kita wasn't practicing with the other dancers, then I bumped into Tracy on my way out of the church. I asked if she knew where Kita was. She said Kita won't be dancing or singing for a while."

"Why?" Monique asked.

"She's pregnant."

"Did Cherry say anything to you?"

"That tramp knows better."

"Humph, so Kita is pregnant, huh?" Monique was glad that she'd made the right decision to call off her wedding to Boris.

"Yep. That broad is pregnant," Arykah said.

"I wonder if Boris knows."

"Probably so. That could be the reason he was jacked up and acting crazy this morning."

"You know what, Arykah? You could be right."

"I'm willing to bet my commission check on it."

Chapter 11

On Tuesday morning, Monique lay in her bed watching the six o'clock news. The anchorwoman on *NBC* Channel 5 announced that more than half of the city of Detroit was without electricity or telephone service. "If you look over my right shoulder, you will see a path of destruction the F4 twister left behind. Thousands are homeless; seventy-four people are confirmed dead, and that number is expected to rise due to the number of people who are still unaccounted for. President Obama has declared a state of emergency. Policemen, firefighters, as well as electricians from the entire state of Michigan and nearby states have volunteered their services. Rescue workers have labored all through the night and are still working tirelessly, cleaning up debris. These men and women of honor are going above and beyond the call of duty to make sure that every name among the missing persons list is accounted for. You are looking at approximately three million dollars worth of damage, and that number is expected to rise as well. It could be weeks before the city, affectionately known as Motown, is up and running again. Reporting live from Detroit, I'm Latricia Collins."

Monique felt a queasiness rumbling through her abdomen. She silently prayed that God would bring healing to the city of Detroit. She couldn't imagine having had her family and everything she'd built snatched away in the blink of an eye. Monique dialed Adonis's cellular telephone, but was unsuccessful in reaching him. She thought about the conversation she had with Arykah on yesterday.

"Wow, he could be there for a while. Can you survive that?"

A few days without Adonis would be a piece of cake, but weeks without him was a different matter. Again, Monique dialed his cellular number and heard the familiar message. *"Your call cannot be connected at this time. Please try your call again later."*

Monique sat up on the bed and exhaled. She didn't know why she allowed herself to get so worked up over Adonis's absence. They were only friends. She ran her fingers through her hair and spoke to herself. "Get a grip, Monique. He's not your man."

She got out of the bed and dragged her feet, which felt like twenty-pound weights, into the bathroom and started the water in the shower. While she was humming beneath the cascading water, she didn't hear her telephone ring.

After a quick ten minute shower, Monique stepped from the tub and heard a familiar voice. Without even thinking of grabbing a towel, she ran and stood in front of the television soaking wet. Her heart pounded against the walls of her chest when she saw his face. She pressed the volume button on the remote control to hear him clearly.

"It grieves my heart deeply to see so many lives taken," Adonis said.

The reporter spoke to him. "Tell me, Mr. Cortland, how has being here in the midst of destruction affected you personally?"

"It has definitely humbled me. From day to day we take the gifts of life for granted. Being here watching these people search for their loved ones and reacting to their loss has shined a new light on how precious life is."

"I'm sure Detroit appreciates your thoughtfulness and unselfishness in the part you're playing to help make this place whole again."

"I'm honored to have been asked to help."

The reporter looked into the camera. "There you have it, folks. Adonis Cortland is an electrician who came all the way from Chicago, and he's just one of many who volunteered his time. I'm Latricia Collins for Channel 5 News."

Monique lowered the volume on the television and heard a beep come from her cellular telephone. She saw that someone had left a message. She prayed it was from Adonis as she dialed her voicemail.

"Good morning. I was wondering if you'd consider having dinner with me tonight. I'm on my way to work. Call me when you get this message. I love you, and I miss you."

Disappointed that the caller wasn't Adonis, Monique erased the message and threw the cellular phone on the bed. She went into the bathroom to dry off. "You must be out of your doggone mind, Boris."

* * *

Arykah had a few choice words when Monique filled her in on Boris's message. "Heck no, you won't consider having dinner with him. Boris is a baby late and a diamond tennis bracelet short. You won't even sit and fart with him, let alone eat with him. I'll tell you what you *need* to consider, Monique. Consider the fact that Boris is quick to dismiss your feelings and only focuses on his own when he decides to 'do tha fool'. Consider how he openly disrespects and embarrasses you in public. And consider how he conveniently gets his act together when he runs out of options. After you've considered all of that, call that fool and tell him that you will *not* have dinner with him."

Just after lunchtime, Theresa set a bouquet of roses on Monique's desk.

"Who are those from?" Monique asked.

"I didn't steam the envelope open, but my guess is Adonis."

Monique excitedly stood and sniffed a single rose as she tore open the envelope and pulled out the small card. Even during a crisis in Detroit, Adonis still found time to send her roses.

Please call me, Boris.

She placed the card back into the envelope and sat down. Theresa looked at her. "Let me guess. He's missing you something terrible, and he can't wait to see you."

"Guess again, Theresa. They're not from Adonis."

"Whaaat? You are just sowing your wild oats all over the place, huh?"

When Monique didn't answer, Theresa snatched the envelope from her hand and read the card. "Oh, heck to the no. Boris is trying to worm his way back in. I know you're not going to call him, Monique. You want me to throw this bouquet away?"

"No. Call the florist to have these roses picked up."

Theresa wrote 'Return To Sender' on the front of the envelope and followed Monique's instructions.

An hour later, Monique's cellular phone rang. She recognized Boris's work number and allowed his call to go to her voicemail. The intercom on her desk buzzed.

"Yes, Theresa?"

"Boris is on line two."

"How ever many times he calls, I'll be in a meeting."

At ten minutes to six, as Monique was leaving for the day, her cellular telephone rang again. Myrtle Cortland's name appeared on the caller ID. "Hey, Gravy. How are you? " Monique answered.

"This is Boris."

Monique felt her stomach drop. Her first instinct was to disconnect the call, but she knew she couldn't avoid him forever.

"Hello? Monique, are you there?"

"What is it, Boris?"

"How are you?" he asked.

"Fine."

Boris paused. Apparently he was waiting for Monique to inquire about his well-being but she said nothing. "I'm doing good too."

"Is there a particular reason you called?"

"If you're busy, I could call you back."

"That won't be necessary. Just tell me what you want."

"I wanna know why you sent the flowers back."

"I didn't want them."

"You love roses, Monique."

"How would *you* know? You've never sent me any before."

He exhaled into the telephone. "I can see you're not gonna make this easy for me."

"Make what easy?" she asked.

"My apology."

"Oh, is that what the roses represented? An apology?"

"Well, I was kinda hoping they would be an ice breaker."

Monique chuckled sarcastically. "Well, you kinda hoped wrong. After all that you put me through, those flowers didn't impress me, Boris. And from what I hear, you're getting ready to be a daddy. I know doggone well you don't think we're getting back together so I can raise an illegitimate baby."

"Kita told me that the baby wasn't mine."

"You know what, Boris? I don't even care. As far as I'm concerned, both you *and* Kita deserve each other." She disconnected the call and shut the power off.

She saw the huge baby blue box sitting on her desk first thing Wednesday morning. '**Blessed Events Consulting**' stared back at her in big bold black letters. Monique knew the wedding invitations were due to arrive any day. They were supposed to be addressed and mailed in two more weeks, just six weeks prior to the wedding.

Monique knew she should just tell Theresa to shred the contents in the box, but since the invitations were sitting on her desk, she couldn't help but open the box to read one.

Monique remembered sparing no expense when it came to selecting the ivory invitations with the glossy front. She was very choosy with the Lucida Calligraphy type font in gold letters.

Monique and Boris
On this day we dedicate our love to one another
Monique Lynnette Morrison
And
Boris Dexter Cortland
Invite you to share in the ceremony in which their hearts
and souls will be joined in holy matrimony
Saturday, September 16th, 2010
at 3 o'clock in the afternoon
Morning Glory Church of God In Christ
17 Rockway Lane
Chicago, Il
Wishing Well Reception Immediately Following Ceremony

It was halftime at the Dodger Stadium and the Los Angeles Lakers were ahead of the Boston Celtics by eight points. The cheerleaders were on the court shaking what their mothers had given them. It was the playoffs and game number seven. If the Lakers continued to play hard, they would win their 15th NBA Finals Championship. The team's starting line-up would open up the fourth quarter. Boris and Monique had flown from Chicago to the west coast for this special event. They sat courtside directly beneath the south side net.

The cheerleaders finished their routine with a Chinese split and pompoms in the air. The lights dimmed and the display board lit up showing the exact words the announcer said. Monique looked up and saw her name.

MONIQUE MORRISON, YOU'RE ALL I EVER WANTED AND SO MUCH MORE THAN I DESERVE. I LOVE YOU

WITH ALL OF MY HEART. WILL YOU MARRY ME? FROM BORIS

The spotlight was on Monique's face. The roaring rumbling through the stadium sounded as though the Lakers had just scored the winning point with less than a second to go. Boris was down on bended knee with a diamond ring in his hand. Monique smiled at him and nodded her head. The crowd cheered louder as Boris stood with Monique and embraced her. Fifty minutes later, the Lakers jumped and danced around the court because they had earned their rings. Monique was just as excited and danced on the sideline; she got her ring too.

Theresa snapped her fingers twice in Monique's face. "Hello, is anyone home?"

Monique blinked her eyes, sat up in her chair, and placed the invitation back in the box. "Good morning, Theresa."

"According to the smile on your face, I'll say it's a very good morning or maybe it was a very good night."

Monique shook her head at Theresa. "Is getting freaky all you ever think about?"

"Basically, yeah. What's in the box?"

"My wedding invitations."

"Wedding invitations? Are you still marrying Boris?"

"I forgot to cancel the order."

"That didn't answer my question, Monique. I thought the wedding was off."

Monique became agitated at Theresa's interrogation. She cocked her head to the side and looked at her secretary. "Did I tell you that?"

"No, but I just assumed."

"You should never assume anything, Theresa."

"So, what are you saying?"

Monique leaned back and crossed her left leg over her right knee. "I'm saying that I need you to get me the number of calls from last night's show."

Theresa knew that was Monique's way of dismissing her without bluntly telling her to mind her own business.

On her way back into her office, after an hour-long meeting, Monique stopped at Theresa's desk. "Any messages?"

Theresa didn't look up from the spreadsheet she was working on. "No."

Monique proceeded to her office. "If Boris calls, put him through."

"What?"

Monique stopped dead in her tracks and turned around to look at Theresa. It wasn't the question that stunned Monique, but the high-pitched tone that accompanied it. She was sure Theresa meant the *what* to be a *why*. "Did you not hear what I said?"

"Oh, I heard you, Monique, but I don't understand it."

Monique came and stood directly in front of Theresa's desk. "Let's get something straight here. *You* work for *me*. *I* give the orders, and *I* ask the questions. It's not the other way around. When I give you a direct order to do something, I expect it to be done without an interrogation. If you can't handle that, let me know and I'll find a secretary that won't involve herself in my personal life. You're not privileged to know my business. I'll tell you what I want you to know. Never again are you to second guess or inquire about anything that I do or what I tell *you* to do. *I'm* the boss. Is that understood?"

A pregnant pause presented itself before Theresa spoke. "Yes . . . *Miss* Morrison."

"Oh, so I'm Miss Morrison now, huh?"

Theresa didn't respond. She brought her attention back to the spreadsheet. Without another word, Monique went into her office and slammed the door.

Monique exited her office at ten minutes to six and found Theresa gone. Her usual 'Goodnight, Boss Lady' didn't flow from her lips that evening.

As Monique drove toward the Loop, she thought what an excellent secretary Theresa was. What happened that day was partly Monique's fault. If she hadn't shared her personal issues with Theresa, the disagreement wouldn't have occurred. How could she expect Theresa not to have an opinion on what she'd been told? She knew Theresa was only looking out for her best interest. Just like everyone else who loved Monique, Theresa was tired of the way Boris treated her. It really wasn't the fact that Theresa was in her business that had set Monique off. Monique was frustrated because of the situation she was in. She didn't want to be a victim of a broken engagement, and she didn't want to be in love with her ex-fiancé's cousin. Monique knew that God loved her. But if Adonis was the better man for her, why hadn't God allowed her to meet him before meeting Boris?

Before Monique got to the hotel, she stopped at a party store and bought three 'I'm Sorry' helium balloons for Theresa. Tomorrow morning at work, Monique would call a truce. After securing the balloons in her car, Monique proceeded to her hotel. Had she taken Arykah's advice to glance in her rearview mirror every now and then, Monique would have noticed Boris's Navigator, weaving and bobbing in and out of traffic, exactly two cars behind her.

From across the street, Boris watched the valet drive Monique's car into the garage of the Chicago Hilton. He read the balloons she carried inside. Instantly he became enraged with jealousy, wondering what man she was there to see with make-up balloons. Just the thought of another man touching her the way he was no longer entitled to infuriated Boris. He sat in his SUV for over three hours waiting for Monique to emerge from the hotel. At precisely 9:30 P.M., Boris had given up waiting. He started his engine and burned rubber when he sped away from the curb.

Upstairs in her suite, Monique lay across her bed watching the nightly news. She listened intently as the anchorwoman gave the latest details of the clean-up and rescue mission in Detroit.

"There are still over sixty people who are unaccounted for, and the death toll is rising by the hour. Reporting live from Detroit, I'm Latricia Collins."

Not only had Monique prayed for Adonis's and the other rescue workers' strength, she prayed for the anchorwoman's strength as well. It seemed Latricia Collins was on duty in Detroit twenty four hours a day. Monique pressed the power button on her remote control, turned onto her side and exhaled loudly. If she could just touch Adonis's face or wrap her arms around his forty-eight inch chest and inhale his natural masculine scent, she would be satisfied.

She reached for her cellular telephone on the nightstand. Maybe God would have special mercy on her when she dialed Adonis's number. When she turned her telephone on, the small envelope showed she had a voicemail. She keyed in her security code and brought the telephone to her ear. She was almost positive the message would be from Boris.

"Hello, beautiful."

At the sound of Adonis's voice, Monique quickly sat up on the bed to listen to the rest.

"I've been trying to call you for the past two days. The phone lines are down all over Detroit. My cell phone couldn't reach Chicago, but I guess I got lucky tonight. I'm so tired; I've only had about five hours of sleep since I got here. What you see on the news is nothing compared to the devastation and destruction here. Today, I lifted a pile of two by fours and found an unresponsive year old baby girl. It tore me up real bad. I didn't know what I was getting into when I agreed to come here. I know for a fact that I will never volunteer for anything like this again. I don't know when I'll be able to call you back. I hope all is well with you. Bye."

Monique saved his message and quickly dialed Adonis's number. She heard an operator say, *"Your call cannot be connec . . . "*

Disappointed that she couldn't speak with him, Monique pressed the power button and sat the cellular phone on the nightstand. She then lay down and snuggled her pillow. "Adonis, please come home."

Chapter 12

On Thursday morning, Arykah sat in her car. She glanced at her wristwatch and exhaled. Her client was twenty minutes late, and she was pressed for time. She had another house showing on the other side of town in an hour. It was a good thing for Mr. Powell or Howell or whatever his name was, that Arykah had had her morning cappuccino. Without her early morning cup of joe, she wasn't the easiest person to get along with.

In her rearview mirror, Arykah saw a shiny, black, late model Lincoln Town car drive up behind her. She moved her eyeballs to her driver's side mirror. She got a glimpse of perfect size twelve, burgundy Stacy Adams stepping onto the pavement. Arykah couldn't see the face of the man wearing the tailor made charcoal gray, single-breasted Bill Blass suit with burgundy stripes walking her way. She did, however, see the newly manicured nails on the tips of long dark fingers.

Diamond cufflinks glittered in the sunlight. The wind blew in the direction he was walking, and Arykah got a whiff of Tiffany's Man before he got to her car door. She did a quick make-up check in the rearview mirror.

Suddenly, the man was at her car door. "Miss Miles?"

Oh, God, that voice. If Arykah didn't know any better, she'd swear that Barry White was alive and standing next to her car, speaking to her right then. She looked up at a bald, chocolate colored man with even toned skin. She got caught up in his dimples even though he wasn't smiling. The reason he was late had to be because he'd just left his barber's chair getting his beard and goatee trimmed. He was absolutely gorgeous.

Hershey's must pay him top dollar to sell his skin and put their name on it, Arykah thought. "Can I lick you?" The words flowed from her lips beyond her control.

"I beg your pardon?"

Arykah could've died at that exact moment. That was the most humiliating thing she had ever done. "Oh, my God. I can't believe I said that, Mr. . . . "

"Howell, Lance Howell," he answered, displaying a huge grin.

Arykah opened her car door and stepped out. "I apologize, Mr. Howell. I was thinking out loud."

Lance gently grabbed her hand and kissed her open palm. "No apology is necessary, and the answer is yes."

Arykah's equilibrium was off. He smelled delicious, sounded heavenly, and was more handsome than all of her past boyfriends put together. And did he just kiss her open palm? She looked at him confusingly. "To what?"

"Your question."

Arykah's entire face got heated. She stood in the street not knowing what to do or say.

Lance sensed her embarrassment and chose to change the subject. "So, this is Oakbrook?"

"Yes. Oakbrook Terrace actually." She guided him toward the estate he had called about. "There is an excellent country club on the grounds that I'm sure you and the Mrs. will enjoy."

"There isn't a Mrs.," Lance said.

Arykah almost did a two-step but she kept her professional composure. "Oh? You mean a man of your caliber who owns a construction company and can afford this house isn't married?"

"Nope, not yet."

Arykah turned the key in the lock and opened the door to a two-story foyer. "Just as you requested, this home has five bedrooms and six baths. The master suite is on the first level and takes up the entire left side of the estate."

Lance walked through the great room and stood looking out of the floor to ceiling windows at the backyard. Arykah came and stood next to him. "There's plenty of room for children to run and play."

"Yes there is, but unfortunately, I have no children."

I'm gonna double my tithes and offerings on Sunday for this, Lord. Arykah was becoming more and more impressed with Lance.

Lance followed Arykah into the oversized kitchen that had two islands. "With no wife or children, I doubt this room will get much use. I know how finicky you bachelors are."

"Oh, it will definitely get used. I'm also a chef."

Don't play with me, Jesus. "Are you really? What's your specialty?"

"Whatever is requested. I can master anything."

I bet you can. "Would you like to see the rooms upstairs?"

Going up the winding staircase, Arykah pointed out the Berber carpet and cherry oak railing. Lance couldn't care less about the railing or anything else Arykah was talking about. Walking up behind her, he focused on her plus size smooth calves and metallic ankle strap three-inch stilettos she wore. Arykah opened the door to a room at the top of the stairs. "This room can be used as a gym or home-office."

She allowed Lance to enter the room first. He took off his suit jacket and swung it over his right shoulder. His muscles protruded through his silk, burgundy shirt.

My, my, my. Arykah thought.

After the tour of the house, Lance turned to Arykah. "Miss Miles, I love it. It has everything I want."

"I'm glad to hear that. The asking price is six hundred thousand dollars. Will that work for you?"

"Let's discuss it over dinner this evening. Will that work for *you*?"

"Are you asking me out on a date?" She prayed that he was.

"Only to discuss business."

Okay, Lord. I'll take that. Of course she'd break bread with a man who's contemplating on blessing her bank account with an enormous commission. She smiled.

"Sure, I'd like that. Where should we meet?"

"Here," Lance said.

Her eyebrows rose."Why here?"

"Because I'm going to cook for you."

Her smile grew wider. "Mr. Howell, that—"

"Lance," he interrupted.

"Okay then. *Lance*, that would be wonderful, but I can't allow you to use the kitchen if this house doesn't belong to you."

Lance wasn't going to take 'no' for an answer. "Well, then let's make it happen."

Arykah watched him retrieve a checkbook from his interior suit jacket pocket. He signed his name on the bottom right line and gave the blank check to her. "You can fill in the rest."

This was way too good to be true. Surely she was being punk'd. Arykah expected Ashton Kuchter to come busting out of the closet in any moment. She looked around the room for the hidden camera.

Lance was handsome, owned a construction company, could afford any house of his choice, knew his way around a kitchen, and he was single with no children. She thought that he must sell drugs. Arykah wondered if he were saved. She hoped to God he was saved, because if he wasn't, she wouldn't waste her time. Lance looked wonderful on the outside, but how was his spirit? It wouldn't take long for an unsaved man to start asking questions like, 'Why do you have to go to church every Sunday?' or 'Can't you skip Bible class this time?' She'd been down that road before, trying to convince a man to get saved, and found it to be too much work.

Arykah knew she'd better nip this in the bud. "Lance, what church do you attend?"

"I've been a member of Freedom Temple Church Of God In Christ my entire life."

Arykah held her breath, waiting for his answer and was able to release a sigh of relief. "I've heard many good things about that church. Who's the pastor?"

"*I'm* the pastor."

Arykah's knees buckled.

Theresa saw the balloons on her desk and walked to the door of Monique's office, all smiles. "Thank you for my balloons."

Monique looked away from the computer and toward Theresa. "You're welcome. Come on in and have a seat."

"Okay, let me get my pad and pen."

"You won't need them for this," Monique said.

Theresa shut the door behind her and sat across from Monique. "What's up?"

She turned to save the document on her screen then swiveled her chair around to face Theresa. "First, I owe you an apology. I'm not sorry about what I said yesterday, but I do apologize for the way I spoke to you. I understand that you care for me, and I appreciate that. However, the decisions I make about my personal business are not to be questioned by you or anyone else. I've made many mistakes, and I know that I'm not done making them. But when I confide in you about some things, Theresa, I just want you to listen and not judge me. I hope we can put what happened yesterday behind us and continue to be friends."

Theresa smiled. "I'd like that, Monique. And I'm sorry for overstepping my bounds."

Monique stood and came around the desk to hug her secretary. "Thank you."

On her way out of the office, Theresa turned to Monique. "I'm going down the street to the café. You want anything?"

Monique smiled at her, glad that she and Theresa had resolved their issue. "A large white chocolate mocha latte with cinnamon would be nice."

Ten minutes after Theresa had left, Monique was sitting at her desk looking over the instructions Mr. Wiley had given her on rotating the deejays hours. The telephone rang, and it wasn't until the fourth ring that Monique remembered her secretary was away from her desk. She hastily picked up the extension. "WGOD, Monique Morrison speaking."

"Good morning, Monique."

She rolled her eyes in the air. *Not him again.* "Boris, how are you?" she asked dryly.

"I'm good. How are you?"

"I'm fine. What's up?"

"Do you have some time to talk?" he asked.

She looked at the clock on the wall. "I have a meeting with a couple of my deejays in fifteen minutes."

"Okay, then I won't hold you up. I just called to see how you're doing."

"All is well with me, Boris."

"Yolunda Rena Cooper from Blessed Events Consulting called the house and left a message yesterday. She wanted to know if we received the wedding invitations and if they were to our satisfaction."

"The invitations arrived here at my office."

"So how are they?"

"They're perfect, Boris. Yolunda does great work. She was highly recommended to us. They're exactly what we wanted."

"You probably shredded them, right?"

Monique exhaled. Where was this conversation going? "No, Boris, I didn't. But I will if you want me to. It was *your* check that paid for them."

Boris heard the hostility in Monique's voice. The conversation wasn't going the way he had hoped it would. "Of course I don't want you to shred them. What I want is for us to address and mail them."

A sarcastic chuckle escaped her lips. *This fool is crazy.* "You must've paid a visit to Bubblegum this morning. Why waste folk's time in getting dressed and coming to the church for a wedding that's not going to happen?"

"Our wedding is still on the church's calendar."

"No, it's not."

"Monique, please don't do this."

Was he serious? Her voice rose. "Please don't do what, Boris?"

"Don't break us up."

Monique's voice raised an octave higher. "You're telling *me* not to break us up? I'ma tell you what broke us up. When you decided to chase after the church ho, *that* broke us up. And when you decided to do whatever the heck you wanted to do without giving me a second thought, *that* broke us up. So don't call my job trying to put this crap on my shoulders, Boris. *You* screwed up, not me."

It was extremely rare that Monique lost her temper. Boris knew that whenever she let heated words flow like that, there was almost nothing he could do to calm her down.

"Baby, I'm sorry for all of that. I know I was wrong, but I can't change the past. I know I messed up, and I'm living with that."

"I didn't say you messed up, I said you screwed up. There's a big difference. Don't get it twisted. You're ticking me off because you want to down play this situation."

"I know you're upset, and you have every right to be."

"You're doing it again. I didn't say I was upset, I said I'm ticked off."

Boris couldn't win for losing. "I'm sorry."

"You're always sorry. Every time you screw up, you expect me to forgive your crap just because you apologize. When am I gonna stop hearing those worthless words come out of your mouth? See, evidently you don't know what it feels like to devote your heart, mind, body and soul to someone who doesn't appreciate it. Well, guess what, I got somebody loving on me now. There's somebody who actually cares how my day goes. It feels good to be appreciated, loved, respected, and needed. I can't tell you the last time I had to put gas in my own car.

"You didn't even call me on my birthday, Boris. But I'll tell you how much icing was put on my cake anyway. First of all, this bracelet I'm sporting was a gift and it came from Tiffany's. And on the morning of my birthday, I was chauffeured by limousine to a spa where I, Monique, was pampered and treated like royalty. Absolutely no expense was spared for my satisfaction. Then I was treated to a picnic. And it didn't stop there. I was taken aboard a yacht for a private dinner over Lake Michigan, and I was dressed for the occasion. So I had my cake, and I ate it too. All of it. This is how I'm living now, so you can keep the drama. I no longer have to tolerate it."

Monique didn't care that she may have told too much of her business to Boris. He needed to know that she wasn't miserable without him. That she wasn't sitting around feeling sorry for herself. But more importantly, she wanted him to know that she was better off without him.

"Baby, I can do all of that for you. I can change," Boris pleaded.

"Uh-uh. We've tried that change thing, remember? This is not the first, second or third time we've gone through this. I've learned that people can't change who they are on the inside. You're just ignorant, Boris."

"Baby, I need you." He sounded pitiful.

"You don't need me, you need a woman you can manipulate and abuse her self-respect. Well, I'm not that girl. So see ya." Monique slammed down the telephone and walked out of her office on her way to her meeting.

Theresa had returned from the café, so she stopped at Theresa's desk for her mocha latte.

When the elevator doors closed, Monique's extension rang again.

"WGOD, Miss Morrison's office," Theresa answered.

"Hi, Theresa. Can I speak to Monique?"

"Hi, Boris. I'm sorry, Monique is in a meeting."

"I was just talking to her a minute ago."

"I understand that, but she's in a meeting right now."

Theresa heard a click in her ear.

Later that evening, Arykah paid a visit to Monique's hotel room.

"This is a surprise. What are you doing here looking like you just stepped out of *Ebony* magazine?" Monique asked.

"I'm passing through on my way to Oakbrook Terrace."

"You're showing a house *this* late?"

Arykah sashayed into the room and sat on the bed. "Nope, I have a dinner date."

Monique closed the door and leaned against it. "Whaaat? You mean the great and wonderful Arykah Miles will grace a man with her company?"

"Not just a man, but *the man*."

"Who is *the man*?" Monique asked.

"Well, first of all, I had the easiest sale of my career this morning."

Monique lay across the bed. "Oh, really? Tell me about it."

"Yesterday, I got a call from a man named Lance Howell. He wanted to see the six hundred thousand dollar estate for sale in Oakbrook Terrace on Caridine Lane. I set up an appointment for us to meet at the estate this morning. He was almost a half hour late, but when he finally showed up, baby, baby, baby. This man stepped out of a brand new, black Lincoln Town car wearing Bill Blass on his buffed up torso and Stacy Adams on his feet. Monique, he wore Tiffany's Man cologne, and you know how good that stuff smells."

"But was he fine?"

"No, he wasn't fine. He was *foine*. And his voice sounds just like Barry White's."

"Did you pinch him to make sure he was real?"

"Oh, he's real all right. He's dark with flawless skin and his mustache and goatee were trimmed perfectly. I accidentally asked if I could lick him."

Monique's eyes grew wide, and she sat up on the bed. "Please tell me you didn't. I told you that your mouth was gonna get you into trouble one day."

Arykah raised her right hand in the air. "I promise you, I did. And he said yes."

"Oh my God. You didn't do it, did you?" Monique was really worried. At times her best friend could be hot to trot.

"No, but I was tempted to."

"He bought the house?"

"With a blank check."

"What do you mean a blank check?"

"This is where the dinner date comes in to play. He said he loved the house, so I made him an offer. He asked if we could discuss it over dinner. When I accepted his invitation, he told me to meet him at the estate tonight and he would cook for me."

Monique's eyes grew wider. "He cooks too?"

"Yeah, girl. Lance owns a construction company, *and* he's a chef."

Monique stood from the bed and stared at Arykah. "Oh my, this story just keeps getting better and better."

"I'm not finished yet. I told Lance that I couldn't allow him to use the house if he didn't own it, and that's when he signed his name on a personal check and told me to fill in the rest."

Monique couldn't take anymore. "Girl, if you don't shut up, I'll faint."

"Hold on, I might have something for you to faint about in a minute. You know I try to stay away from men who aren't saved, right? If Lance wasn't in church, I wasn't gonna waste my time having dinner with him. I asked what church he attended, and I was happy when he told me that he'd been a member of Freedom Temple Church Of God In Christ his entire life."

"Arykah, that is such a plus. So, he's a C.O.G.I.C. man, huh? Who pastors that church?"

Arykah displayed all of her thirty-two teeth. "*He* does."

Monique gently lay down on the floor, crossed her arms over her chest and closed her eyes. "Lord, you sent her a pastor? I done seen it all. You can take me now."

Five minutes after Arykah left, Monique's telephone rang.

"I'm gonna spank those hips when I see you," the voice on the other end of the telephone said.

"You're always spanking me for something, Gravy. What did I do this time?"

"You ain't rang this phone in awhile."

"When was the last time *you* called *me*, Gravy?" Apparently, Monique didn't know who she was talking to. Her flip lip was about to get her into major trouble.

"First of all, who's the doggone momma, me or you? Second of all, have you lost what sense you had, talking to *me* like that? You're cute and everything, but I will still snatch a knot in your behind."

Monique knew she'd better check herself before Myrtle did it for her. "I'm sorry, Gravy, it's been a rough day."

"I don't give a rat's behind what kind of day it's been. I had nothing to do with that. Don't you ever use that tone with me again, Baby Girl. Do you hear me?"

"I said I was sorry, Gravy."

"I heard what you said. Tell me what happened today that almost got your teeth knocked out."

Now that Myrtle was calm, Monique teased with her. "You think you can take me, Gravy? You can't punch hard enough to knock my teeth out."

"I'll have you looking like a snaggled toothed pumpkin on Halloween. Adonis can vouch for that. When he and Boris were little, I wouldn't let them go outside and play until I got home from work. They knew my normal time getting home was about six thirty. My neighbor, Shirley, told me that Adonis would be outside playing with his friends until six o'clock, then he'd come in the house so I wouldn't catch him. The next evening, I left work early, and sure enough, as soon as my car turned onto the street, I saw his lil' tail take off running toward the house. He ran so fast, all I saw was the dust he left behind."

Monique was laughing hard. "What did you do, Gravy?"

"When I walked in the front door, he and Boris were in the living room watching T.V. Adonis's chest was heaving up and down like he was having an asthma attack because he was tired from running. He had tears in his eyes because he knew I was gonna get that butt. I walked over to him and asked why he was outside. When he parted his lips to speak, I punched him dead in the mouth and knocked out one of his teeth. I didn't even give him time to explain because if this house wasn't on fire, he had no business outside."

"You were tough on them, huh, Gravy?"

"Chile, I had to be. The boys were taller than me when they were just twelve years old. It was nothing for me to reach up and knock the heck out of them. I still have Adonis's tooth upstairs on the top shelf in my closet. I keep it in one of those purple Crown Royal bags with the yellow drawstring."

"Crown Royal bag? What are you doing with that, Gravy?"

"If you are without sin, Baby Girl, cast the first stone. In other words, mind your own business."

"I may not be able to cast the first stone, but I can surely cast the second or third one."

"I don't think so. I know too much of your business. You're engaged to my son, while at the same time, courting my nephew. Humph, you can't even cast the hundredth stone."

When Myrtle mentioned Monique's engagement to Boris, she thought it was a good a time as any to tell her about the decision she'd made.

"Um, Gravy, I canceled the wedding." After she spoke, Monique held her breath.

"Well, it's about time." Myrtle was pleased.

Chapter 13

Adonis turned his key into the lock and opened the door. Boris was sitting in front of the television with a half empty forty-ounce bottle of beer on a dinner tray next to his La-Z-Boy. Adonis set his duffle bag by the front door and walked into the living room. "Whaddup, cuz?"

"Just chilling. How was Detroit?"

Adonis wanted to leave the problems of Detroit where they were. "It was a mess, but I don't wanna talk about that. What's going on with you? How was choir rehearsal last night?"

"I canceled it," Boris said as if he didn't have a care in the world.

"Why?"

"Because I didn't feel like going."

By the look on Boris's face, Adonis knew his troubles had gotten worse while he was away. "You all right, man?"

In Boris's hand was a white envelope. He held it up for Adonis to take. Inside, Adonis saw the card he had bought for Monique the day her car was detailed.

"How could you do this to me, cuz?" Boris asked.

Adonis felt his knees weaken. How in the world had Boris found out, and how did he get his hands on that card? Surely Monique wasn't careless enough to have given it to him.

Boris stood and looked at Adonis. "Huh, cuz? Why didn't you tell me Monique had a dude on the side? You talk to her."

Adonis exhaled a sigh of relief, happy that his and Monique's cover hadn't been blown. He didn't know how he would have handled the situation. "I don't talk to her all that much and she's never mentioned another dude. I doubt if Monique would trust me with something like that anyway, since you and I are cousins."

"Yeah, I guess you're right." Boris sat in his La-Z-Boy again.

Adonis looked inside the card and silently thanked God that he didn't sign it. "Where did you get this card?"

"From her glove compartment the other day. She came by here to get something and I searched her car and found it. Did she tell you some dude got her car detailed and put Lowenharts on it?"

"Nah, she didn't tell me that."

"And she's wearing a bracelet he bought from Tiffany's."

Adonis eyebrows raised. "She told you that?"

"Yeah, man. I called Monique today to see if she would have dinner with me. She went off and cussed me out."

"Cussed you out? Monique?" Adonis found that difficult to believe.

"She may as well have cussed. I'm telling you, she snapped. I told her that I was sorry for what happened with Kita and how much I loved and missed her. That's when she confessed to having somebody on the side. She told me some guy took her to a spa for her birthday and took her on a picnic, then on a dinner cruise."

Adonis was stunned that Monique would volunteer this information. Boris walked to the mantel and looked at a photograph of him and Monique. "I did something stupid the day she was here."

"Like what?"Adonis asked.

"When I saw the rims on her car and the bracelet she was wearing, I lost it. I was drunk and high, and I did something I shouldn't have."

Adonis felt his blood get warm. "What did you do?"

"Monique tried to leave, but I wouldn't let her. I grabbed her arm and tried to kiss her, but she kneed me hard and got away from me. I wish I could relive that day and take it all back."

Adonis was furious but he couldn't let it show. How dare anyone touch the woman he loves? "Did you hurt her?"

"Nah, cuz." Boris didn't say a word for the longest moment. "I just wanted to make things the way they used to be before . . ."

"Before Kita?"

"Yeah, man, before that skeezah. It turns out the baby ain't mine."

"Whose is it?"

"Heck, I don't even think *she* knows. I found out she's been screwing Bubblegum."

Adonis voice rose. "The dope dealer?"

"Yep, and it ain't no telling who else she's been dealing with."

"How can you be sure the baby isn't yours?"

"Because I started messing around with Kita about two months ago. She's almost three months pregnant."

Adonis studied the scratches on the left side of Boris's face. "What happened to your jaw?"

"I went to Kita's house to confront her about Bubblegum, and we got into a fight."

Adonis shook his head from side to side. "I'm gone three days, and all heck breaks loose?"

Boris looked at the photograph again. "I gotta fix this, cuz. I gotta get my woman back, but she won't give me the time of day."

And she never will if I have anything to do with it, Adonis thought.

At precisely 7:30 P.M., Arykah arrived at 9130 Caridine Lane. Before she turned her engine off, Lance was at her driver's door.

"How did you know I was here?"

Lance reached for Arykah's hand to help her out of the car. "A queen is always looked out for. I'm glad you could make it."

Arykah chuckled. "Are you kidding? You bought a house on first sight. Of course I would make it." They walked hand in hand into the two-story foyer. Arykah looked all around the empty space. "I have to admit, Lance, this is a beautiful estate."

"I'm pleased with it. I wanna thank you for loaning me the keys while the paperwork gets processed."

"I gotta tell you that this is highly unusual for me. But your credit checked out as well as the check you gave me, so I didn't see the harm. But this is only for one night. The good thing is that we can probably short close on this estate sometime next week."

In the kitchen, Arykah saw a table and four chairs that weren't there when she sold Lance the house earlier that day. Lance sat her at the table and draped a white linen napkin across her lap. "I hope you're hungry."

The aroma coming from the stove intoxicated Arykah. "Yes, I am. Whatever you're cooking smells delicious."

"It's veggie lasagna salad; one of my many specialties."

"Sounds intriguing," Arykah smiled. "What's in it?"

Lance took a pan covered with aluminum foil from the oven. "Well, let's see. There are broccoli florets, a little bit of garlic, tomato paste, ricotta cheese, balsamic vinegar, olive oil, shredded carrots, zucchini, spinach, Asiago cheese, salt, and black pepper."

As Lance went down the list of ingredients, Arykah prayed he couldn't hear her empty stomach growling. "My God, that sounds good. Is it *your* personal creation?"

"Unfortunately, I can't take the credit for this dish. I saw the recipe in the *Chicago Sun-Times* many years ago."

Arykah watched Lance take two plates from a brand new box of dishes. He washed and dried them before setting them on the table. He had traded the tailor-made suit for a dark blue T-shirt and very fitting Levi jeans.

"What persuaded you to become a chef?" she asked.

He withdrew two glasses from a different box and placed them in the dishwater. "I'm the eldest of three kids. When I was eight years old, my father went to the grocery store for milk, but couldn't find his way back home, so I was left to look after my six-year-old sister and five-year-old brother while my mother worked two jobs. I had to cook breakfast and dinner. So I guess it just grew on me."

"Is your mother alive?"

"She's alive and well. I would love for you to meet her."

Myrtle once told Monique and Arykah that when a man

is willing to introduce a woman to his mother, he was interested in a serious relationship. Although Arykah was smiling on the inside, she didn't let it show. "What about your sister and brother? Are the three of you close?"

Lance filled their glasses with ice cubes and iced tea. "My sister, Adrienne, and I are like two peas in a pod. We do everything together. She leads the praise and worship team at church. She's married with a three-year-old daughter, Bianca, who has her uncle Lance wrapped around her pinkie. My brother, Derek, well, what can I say? He has his own agenda on how to live his life. He'd rather sell drugs than work a nine to five to earn a living. I've stopped counting how many promises he's broken about coming to church."

Arykah could hear the disappointment and hurt in Lance's voice as he talked about his brother. "Well, prayer changes things, but you know that already, right, Pastor?"

"You know what, Arykah. It's my assignment to encourage people to pray without ceasing, but sometimes I have to wonder if God hears my own prayers."

Arykah didn't comment, but she could definitely relate to Lance. There had been many a day when she was forced to ask, "God, did you hear me?"

He brought the pan of lasagna to the table and sat opposite of Arykah. "Since you're a guest in my soon to be home, why don't you bless the food?"

"I'd love to," Arykah happily responded. They bowed their heads, and she petitioned the throne of grace. "Father God, first and foremost we thank You for this day, a beautiful day we haven't seen before. We honor You, Lord, as our Comforter and Keeper. We acknowledge that no one else can do for us what You can, and for this we're grateful. I am especially thankful for my new friend, Lance Howell, and I thank You for this fellowship. We're thankful for this meal, and please bless it along with the hands that prepared it. We pray, Lord, that thy will be done and that the mailbox outside would soon display the name 'Howell.' We exalt Your name, and we will be so ever careful to continue to glorify You in everything we do. In your darling Son, Jesus' name, we thank You. Amen."

Lance opened his eyes and looked across the table at Arykah. "Wow, that was excellent. Are you a prayer warrior or intercessor?"

"I don't know about all of that, but believe me, I stay in God's face."

Arykah put a forkful of lasagna in her mouth, and one would've thought she'd taken a bite out of heaven. "This is so good."

"Thank you. I put a lot of heart into it."

Arykah paused for a minute. "Lance, there's something you should know about me."

"I'm listening," he said.

"I'm ghetto," Arykah confessed.

He chuckled. "Explain *ghetto*."

"Ghetto means asking you to wrap me a plate of this lasagna to take home so I won't have to buy lunch tomorrow."

Lance laughed out loud. "I love your sense of humor, Arykah. Tell me about yourself."

"Be careful what you ask for. I've got a lot of history. Pick a subject."

"Your parents."

"I don't have any. From what I've been told, my mother hemorrhaged to death while giving birth to me. The doctors could only save one of us. On my birth certificate, the space designated for my father's name is blank. I was bounced around from foster home to foster home until I was eighteen. I held jobs at every fast food restaurant in the city of Chicago while paying for my realty classes. Six years of hard work paid off. I'm the only African American female in my region that sells at least two estate homes a month."

"That's very impressive."

"I love what I do," Arykah said.

The more she talked, the more Lance wanted her to talk. "Can I get personal?"

"You can ask my age, but not my weight."

He chuckled again. "I know better than to even go there, but now you've piqued my curiosity. How old are you, and how much do you weigh?"

Arykah drank iced tea before she answered. "I'm thirty, but only a husband is entitled to know a woman's weight."

"Thirty?" Lance shrieked. "I would have guessed you to be twenty-four."

That comment brought a smile to Arykah's face. "You better watch yourself. Flattery will get you everything."

"Will it get me an answer to my next question?"

"Depends on the question."

"Are you seeing anyone?" he asked.

"What do you mean by *seeing*?"

"Dating someone exclusively."

"No."

"Can I ask why?"

Arykah cocked her head to the side and looked at Lance. "I'm sorry, I was under the impression that you were a pastor of a church. Maybe I should change your occupation status to Private Investigator."

"You intrigue me, Arykah." The look on Lance's face melted Arykah. His eyes pierced her soul. "I wanna know everything about you."

Arykah laid her fork on her empty plate. "Okay, now you're getting into my baggage. Are you sure you wanna do that?"

That statement made Lance even more interested. "I definitely wanna do that, but let's take our dessert into the great room."

"Dessert? Lance, I'm stuffed. Plus I'm trying to watch my weight."

"Why don't you let me do that for you. I've been watching it ever since you got here, and it looks great."

Arykah knew she was cute that evening; thankful that Beyoncé made it easy for big girls to strut their stuff in House of Dereon jeans. Lance couldn't take his eyes off of Arykah's voluptuous backside. The way she strutted in the denim bottoms paired with four-inch gold stilettos and a navy wrap around blouse from Ashley Stewart, qualified Arykah to compete on *America's Next Top Model*. She was big, she was black, she was beautiful, she was bold, and as Tyra Banks would say, she was *fieerrce*. "Remember what I said about flattery," she smiled.

"I figured you to be a woman who loves strawberries."

"Yes, I do. What did you make for dessert?"

"Strawberry pavlova. It's sort of a baked strawberry soufflé."

Arykah couldn't resist. "I'll have a very small slice, but I'm gonna visit the little girl's room first."

When Arykah joined Lance in the great room, she saw him sitting on the floor with his back against the wall. He held a saucer with a large slice of strawberry Pavlov on it. He patted the space on the floor next to him. "Come sit with me."

She stepped out of her stilettos and walked across the huge, vacant room and sat next to him. When she became comfortable on the hardwood floor, Lance inserted a forkful of the dessert into her mouth. Arykah's eyes rolled into the air. "Oh my God. Are you sure you're a pastor? Because it's probably a sin to make something this delicious. It can be addictive."

"Before I was called into the ministry, I was a full-time chef at the Drake Hotel. Baking sweets was one of my favorite things to do. Why are you single, Arykah?" He wasn't letting her off the hook.

"I was hoping you forgot you asked that."

"If you don't feel comfortable talking about it, that's fine. But I really wanna know."

"Let's talk about you first. Why are *you* single?"

Lance fed her another bite. "How are you just gonna flip the script like that? We were talking about *you*."

"But now we're talking about *you*."

Lance looked into her eyes and smiled. "You are slick, but okay, we'll do this your way. Five years ago, I was engaged to Gwendolyn, the love of my life. She was beautiful and possessed everything I desired in a woman. If I started a sentence, she'd finish it. One Wednesday in January, I closed the deal on my construction company. I called Gwen with the good news, and we made plans to celebrate that evening.

"About three feet of snow had fallen that day. She loved cheesecake, so I decided to take her to the Cheesecake Factory in the Loop for dinner. My realtor's office was Downtown, so Gwen was gonna meet me when she got off from work. She taught pre-school on Fifty-Third Street. It was so much snow, it looked crazy outside, and I knew I should've told Gwen to just go home, but I got caught all up in the excitement of owning my business. I just prayed she would make it safely.

"We were supposed to meet at the restaurant at five o'clock. At five-thirty, I called her cell phone, but didn't get an answer. I didn't think too much of it because Gwen always blasted gospel music when she drove, and sometimes couldn't hear her phone ringing.

"At six o'clock, she still hadn't arrived at the restaurant, but I chalked it up to bad weather and traffic. I went and sat at the bar to wait for her. The bartender had the television on, and I remember looking at *The Cosby Show* when it was interrupted by breaking news. There was a fatal car accident on the Dan Ryan Expressway headed inbound to downtown."

Lance paused, and Arykah grabbed his hand and squeezed it. "Lance, you don't have to—"

He held up his hand to silence her. "No, it's okay. I knew it was her. I could feel it. When Gwen's car flashed across the screen, I fell off of the barstool. An eighteen-wheeler lost traction and slammed into her. The paramedics said she died instantly and didn't suffer. I haven't seen or met another Gwendolyn yet."

Arykah ran the palm of her hand across Lance's left cheek. "I am so sorry."

"With nine months of therapy and trying to get over the guilt of not telling Gwen to just go home, I'm okay."

"There's no way you could've predicted what would have happened, Lance."

"I was told that hundreds of times, but it still didn't take away the pain."

Arykah didn't respond. She let her eyes fall to the floor.

"Your turn," Lance said to her.

She sat with her back against the wall, took the saucer from Lance's hand, and fed him dessert. "I was in love too. Madly in love with a guy who meant more to me than life itself. His name was Eric, and we lived together for two years. According to me, he could do no wrong.

His poop smelled like roses, and the sun rose and set at his command. Having spent my whole life moving from home to home, I yearned to hear the words 'I love you,' and when Eric said them to me, nothing or no one else in the entire world seemed to matter."

She inserted another forkful of Pavlov into Lance's mouth. "In the early part of our relationship, Eric and I got along perfectly. I loved him, and I really believed he loved me too until I started noticing changes in his behavior."

"What kinds of changes?" Lance asked.

Arykah fed him again. "He started getting home later than usual from work and receiving phone calls on his cell phone in the middle of the night. And little petty stuff that normally wouldn't faze him, started to tick him off. Things like strands of my hair in the bathroom sink, stuff like that. Eventually his complaints got personal. He told me the gap in my teeth was too wide, and my hair wasn't long enough."

Lance was stunned. "Excuse me? I don't mean to cut you off, but your gap is too wide?"

"That's what Eric said."

"Smile for me," Lance requested.

"No."

"Come on and smile with your fine self."

Arykah displayed a wide grin. "Flattery, flattery."

Lance focused on her teeth. "You have a lovely smile, and I don't see a gap."

Arykah brought his attention back to her story. "One day Eric got mad at me about something I did. I've forgotten what it was. I probably scrambled his eggs too hard or didn't put enough fabric softener in his boxers. Anyway, he just came right out and admitted to sleeping with another woman, but he said he didn't love her. He admitted to being attracted to how thin she was, and said if I lost weight, he'd leave her alone."

Again, Lance was stunned. *"He said what?"*

"Yep, that's what he said. So willingly giving up my self-respect and self-esteem, I tried my best to lose weight to hold on to Eric. No matter how hard I exercised or how little I ate, the weight would not come off. His complaints turned to insults, which tore my heart out. Suddenly, I was too fat to lie next to at night. Some nights Eric slept on the sofa to keep me from trying to seduce him. He said he wasn't attracted to me anymore."

Lance hadn't met Eric, but he was angry with him. "Okay, can I say something here? I want you to know that it wasn't your weight that put Eric on the sofa; it was the fact that he'd already been with the other woman not too long before bedtime. Men need time to recharge. I don't care what size a woman is, if she's lying naked next to a man, he's gonna try and get her. The *only* reason a man won't touch her is that he's already satisfied."

"You think so, Lance?"Arykah asked.

"I *know* so. Finish your story."

"Well, Eric's insults grew into verbal abuse. He told me over and over that I was too fat and unattractive to ever become anything in life, and no man would ever want me. One day he came home and asked why I was there. He made me feel like I was trespassing."

Lance couldn't help but interrupt Arykah again.*"He asked you what?* Why did you stay there and take that crap from him?"

"He drilled into my head that no other man would want me, so I stayed. That way I could at least say I had a man. And I know this sounds crazy, but I thought he loved me."

"That wasn't love, Arykah. A real man doesn't try to change his woman's appearance. He loves her for who she is."

"It took me two years to figure that out. I got into church and realized Eric had issues with himself, but took his frustrations out on me. God gave me the courage to pack my bags and leave that fool alone. I heard through the grapevine that he's on his third wife."

"Third? How old is he?"

"Eric is thirty-four."

Lance shook his head. "That's a shame. He's changing wives like he changes drawers. He's searching for completeness in women, but he won't find it. Eric has to be complete and whole within himself before he takes a wife. Until he realizes *he's* the problem and gets himself some help, many more Mrs. Eric's will come to pass."

Arykah stood and stretched. "Well, that's my story."

He looked at her full figured torso standing before him. "I want you to walk away, then come back to me," Lance said.

"Why?"

"Because I'm asking you to."

Arykah took the empty saucer to the kitchen sink. On her way, she glanced over her shoulder to look at Lance, and sure enough, he was watching her. She came back and stood in front of him. Lance got on his knees and placed his hands at Arykah's underarms. She held her breath as he ran his hands down the sides of her body, all the way to her ankles.

He looked up at her. "Eric was a fool. You are beautiful in every way imaginable. Don't ever let a man convince you otherwise."

Arykah exhaled.

*   *   *

There was a knock on Monique's hotel room door at nine o'clock P.M. She thought it was Arykah and wondered what she was doing back at the hotel. She looked through the peephole, then yanked the door open and ran into Adonis's arms. She caused him to lose his balance.

He stumbled backward. "Whoa, can I get a hello?" He smiled.

Monique kissed all over his face. "Hello, when did you get home?"

"A few hours ago."

It dawned on Monique she was standing in the hallway wearing a very short teddy. She brought Adonis inside and closed the door. "I missed you."

"I missed you more." He looked at her nightgown. "Looks like I'm just in time."

"In time for what?"

"To tuck you in."

"Don't start anything you can't finish," she teased.

He grabbed Monique by the waist and pulled her to him. "Oh I can definitely finish, but God is watching. I suggest you cover those big, sexy, chocolate legs."

Monique obediently slipped into her long robe and tied the belt into a knot. "Tell me about Detroit."

Adonis exercised wisdom and stayed away from Monique's bed. He sat in a chair next to the dresser. "Detroit was difficult."

She sat on the end of the bed. "I saw you on the news."

"I wish they would've interviewed somebody else; I wasn't in the mood. Right before that, I found a baby girl under a wall."

"I got your message about that. It must've been difficult to have dealt with something like that."

Adonis ran his hand over his bald head. "*Hard?* Try almost impossible. But the worst part came when her parents saw how limp she was lying in my arms."

"I'm sorry, Adonis. I can't imagine the trauma, but I'm glad you're home."

"I'm glad to be home. So what's been going on around here?"

Monique shrugged her shoulders. "Nothing."

"Nothing, huh? Are you lying to me?"

"Nope."

"I think you are."

"Why?"

"Because I talked to Boris tonight."

"Oh really? What did he tell you?"

"Well, first of all, are you aware that he has the card I gave you?"

Monique frowned. "What are you talking about?"

"When I got home, he gave me the card, and he looked upset. At first I thought he knew that I had given it to you, but then he asked why I didn't tell him you had another man. It's a good thing I didn't sign it."

"He must've taken it from my glove compartment when I went to the house on Monday to get my date planner."

"Boris told me what he did to you."

Monique's eyebrows rose. "He did?"

"Yeah, and it took all that was within me to keep from lighting into him. My blood was boiling while I was sitting there listening to him."

Monique smiled. "Adonis, my protector. I love when you talk like that."

A sparkle on her wrist caught his eye. "I see you're wearing the bracelet."

"And I'm gonna keep on wearing it. Ooh, guess what? Arykah is on a date as we speak."

Adonis leaned back in the chair. "Whaaat? Whose funeral will we be going to next week? Arykah reminds me of black widow spiders that kill after mating."

Monique laughed. "I'm telling."

"And I'll deny it. I'm afraid of Arykah."

"The man is the pastor of a C.O.G.I.C."

Adonis's mouth fell open. "Get out of here. Are you serious? How did they hook up?"

"She sold him a house today; a huge house in Oakbrook Terrace. He asked her out, and she accepted. Tonight he's cooking dinner for her."

Adonis couldn't get over it. "I can't see it working." He shook his head from side to side.

"Why do you say that?"

"We're talking about bossy, bold, neck rotating, loud, finger pointing, can't stay out of nobody's business, ain't never wrong, *and* might I add, cussing Arykah, with a pastor. I just don't see it."

"Well, maybe he's just the right man to tame her."

"Humph, I'll be praying for the brotha. He's gonna need chains, handcuffs, and a whip to tame Arykah."

"Then it should be easy, because Arykah likes chains, handcuffs, and whips."

Adonis laughed as he stood and walked to the door. "I gotta go see Aunt Myrtle. I didn't tell her I was going to Detroit; she left six messages on my voicemail. I would let you listen to them, but you don't need to hear that kind of talk."

"I'm used to Gravy's mouth. Earlier, she called and told me that she was gonna snatch a knot in my behind.

Be prepared for her to drop kick you in the chest when she sees you."

"I did a few pushups earlier. Maybe it won't hurt much."

Lance walked Arykah to her car. "I really enjoyed your company tonight, Miss Miles. I hope we can do this again."

"I've never had a man cook for me before. We can definitely do this again."

He opened the driver's door, and Arykah got in. He gave her a plate wrapped in aluminum foil. "Don't forget tomorrow's lunch."

She smiled at him. "Thank you, Lance, for everything. I needed to hear what you said about Eric."

"I'll be teaching Bible class tomorrow night. Why don't you stop by?"

"I wish I could, but I'm showing a house in Naperville tomorrow evening."

Lance couldn't let Arykah leave without setting up a definite date with her. "How about Sunday morning at eleven o'clock for morning worship?"

"I'll be there."

He shut the door and watched her back out of the driveway. Arykah gave him one last smile and a wave before driving down the street. Lance stood in the driveway until Arykah's car was out of sight.

On her cellular phone, Monique saw Arykah's name and number flashing. "Hey, First Lady."

Arykah chuckled. "I could get use to that."

"After only one date? It must've been a good one."

"It was better than good, Monique."

"The way you say that, I'm afraid to ask how much better."

"Let's just say that Lance is a keeper, and there will definitely be a second date. He invited me to Bible class tomorrow, but I can't make it. I am gonna be at Freedom Temple on Sunday morning though. You wanna go with me?"

"Maybe next time. Your first visit should be solo. And make sure you're drop dead gorgeous; hat and all."

"*Hat?*" Arykah shrieked.

"Yes, honey. All first ladies wear big hats and bad suits."

"I am not a first lady, Monique."

"Watch your mouth, the devil is listening."

"Maybe I can find something at Lord & Taylor," Arykah said.

"Let's do breakfast Saturday morning. That way we'll be at the mall when it opens."

"That works for me. So what did you do this evening?"

"Oh, I didn't tell you, Adonis is home. He stopped by to see me."

"Did y'all do the freaky deaky?"

"Didn't you just leave the presence of a pastor, Arykah? He should've sprinkled holy oil on you."

"Hot oil maybe," Arykah joked.

"Arykah, if you're gonna be spending time with this man, you gotta watch your mouth. And you have to practice celibacy."

"I know you're right, Monique. I'm going down in sackcloth and ashes and rededicating my life and body to God."

"Where in the heck have you been?" Myrtle scolded Adonis as soon as he walked in her front door.

"Thanks for asking how I'm doing, Auntie. How are *you*?"

"Never mind that, you told me you were gonna help me wash the outside of my windows."

"Auntie, I've been out of town working. I had to go help out in Detroit. A tornado went through and trashed everything."

"You couldn't call?"

"The telephone lines were down. I don't know why Boris didn't tell you that I was out of town on business. Why didn't you get him over here to help you?"

"Don't get me started on his no good, trifling behind. He's too busy getting caught almost becoming a daddy."

Adonis sat on the sofa. "You know about that?"

"Yeah, I talked to Baby Girl this evening. She told me what's been going on. Does she know you're back?"

"Yeah, I just left the hotel."

Myrtle glared at him. "Y'all better not be doing it, Adonis."

He couldn't believe what Myrtle just said to him. He placed his hand over his heart. "Auntie, you shock me. Monique is my cousin's fiancé." Adonis wasn't aware that Monique had officially called off the wedding. Myrtle didn't think it was her place to tell him.

"Look, boy, the only people you and Baby Girl are fooling are yourselves and maybe Boris, but I know better."

"I don't know what you're talking about." Adonis wasn't about to confess anything.

"I'm talking about how the two of you try so hard not to say no more than hello or goodbye when you're around each other. Folks do that when they don't wanna be found out."

"Auntie, whatever you think you're seeing ain't there.

And as far as Monique and I doing it, that ain't happening. We're virgins." Of course, Adonis knew Monique may be celibate now, but she was certainly no virgin. He had made the statement to throw his aunt off.

Myrtle laughed so hard at Adonis, tears came to her eyes. "I know for a fact that Baby Girl ain't pure, and you ain't no more a virgin than I am."

Chapter 14

On Friday morning, Arykah walked into her office and smelled the roses before she arrived at her desk. The beautiful bouquet consisted of four red roses, four yellow roses, and four orange roses. The vase sat in the middle of her desk. A small white envelope, with her name written on it was propped up against it. She knew the roses were from Lance, and her smile couldn't have been wider as she tore open the envelope.

Thank you for a lovely evening. I had a wonderful time. I'm looking forward to Sunday morning.
Lance

Arykah placed the card into the envelope and sniffed the roses before sitting down. She reached inside her purse for the church's business card Lance had given her. She dialed the number to the church with a huge smile on her face. Thanks to Lance, Arykah was no longer ashamed of her gap.

"Freedom Temple, may I help you?" the secretary greeted.

"Yes, is Lan . . . uh, Pastor Howell available?"

There was a pause before the secretary spoke. "Who is this?"

Whatever happened to 'May I ask who's calling?' Arykah thought. There was a definite attitude in the woman's voice. Arykah could've sworn she was talking to a jealous wife. "My name is Arykah Miles."

"Is the pastor expecting your call?"

"No, but I—"

"Well, he's in a marital counseling session and can't be disturbed."

"Oh, I don't want to disturb him. May I leave a message for him?"

"What's the message?"

Clearly the woman was hot and bothered by her telephone call. But Arykah was from the old school. Of course she could have easily 'gone there' with the woman and told her to thank *Lance* for the roses he sent and to tell him that she had a wonderful time last night. However, as much as Arykah wanted to be messy, she opted to behave like an adult and do the right thing. "Will you please ask him to call me when he becomes avail—"

"Is this for a counseling session?"

"No, I just—"

"Well, what's the reason for your call?"

Arykah was itching to read this woman, but she remembered what Monique had said to her just last night. *"Arykah, if you're gonna be spending time with this man, you gotta watch your mouth."*

"The reason I'm calling is to speak—"

"Are you a member of this church?"

"No, I'm a friend." Finally, Arykah was able to give a complete answer.

"What kind of friend?" the secretary asked nastily.

Arykah lost the battle. She allowed the enemy to take over her emotions. *I'm sorry, Monique.* "A very close and personal friend. Please tell Lance that I've received my roses, and they're beautiful. On second thought, I'd rather tell him that myself. Have Lance call me on my private line. He has the number, thank you."

"You just *had* to go there, didn't you?" Monique asked when Arykah called to inform her about the call with the church's secretary.

"You should've heard her, Monique. She was all up in my business."

"Well, you better get used to it. Lance is a pastor, and you know how women in the church are. They will speak to the man of God and won't even acknowledge the woman on his arm. You need to learn how to deal with that in a decent, not ghetto, manner. There's a way of putting folks in their places nicely, and when you walk away, they'll be like, 'Did she just check me?' And you know women don't like it when their single pastor brings a woman from outside of the church in to become his wife. So my advice to you is to put on the whole armor of God, and get ready to deal with the women."

"Humph, if anything, those broads better get ready to deal with *me*."

"What did I tell you about your mouth, Arykah?"

"I forgot. Tell me again."

"Look, sis, obviously Lance sees something in you that he likes and you have to respect his status. He represents righteousness, and the moment you step foot in his church as his guest, every area of your life will be under scrutiny. People will remember your face. You've got to be careful in everything you do from the places you hang out at, to the people you associate with and definitely your conversations. First ladies carry heavy burdens. Women in churches confide private and very personal information in their pastor's wife. They're going to be depending on you for counseling and support. It's your job to convince them you're trustworthy."

"I understand all of that, Monique, but I'm not gonna let anyone walk over me or disrespect me."

"Arykah, disrespect comes with the territory you are about to tread on, but it's how you handle the disrespect that makes all the difference. I haven't met Lance, but from what you tell me about him, he sounds like a down to earth guy. Chances are if someone belittles you, especially in his presence, you won't have to open your mouth. Lance will put them in their places."

"You think I should tell him about the call with his secretary?" Arykah asked.

"What are you gonna tell him? That she tried to find out who you were and why you called? Actually, there's nothing to tell. Single pastors must be careful of the women who call them. Do you know how many ministers get into trouble counseling women in a one on one session? Often it's a trap that women set. Next thing you know, it's their word against his that something inappropriate was said or done. It's a secretary's job to cross-examine every call that comes in for the pastor. Maybe a man's call would have been sent through to Lance with no problem. Who's to say? But you can't fault his secretary for doing her job. She did exactly what she was suppose to do."

"What about her nasty attitude, Monique? She wouldn't let me get a word in edgewise."

"Her attitude could be based on a lot of things. Maybe she's having a bad day or maybe she's got a crush on Lance. Whatever her issue was, you shouldn't have made it *your* issue. You were out of line telling her that Lance sent you roses because it was none of her business. He may not have wanted her or anyone else to know, and you can best believe the whole church will know before this day is over. First ladies or women who date ministers shouldn't discuss their relationships with anyone. What you and Lance do is y'all's business, always remember that. Lance needs to be assured that the time you and he spend together is private. He should know that he can let his hair down, kick back and act a fool with you, and his congregation won't find out about it. Do you understand what I'm saying, Arykah?"

Arykah exhaled loudly. "Yeah, I guess."

"Look, sweetie, dating a minister is serious business, and not everyone can deal with it. You have a choice. You can go into this knowing that in the beginning you may only be received by a handful of people and accept that, or you can tell Lance that a relationship with him isn't something you want to pursue right now. If you choose the latter, understand that you may be giving up the man and life God intended for you to have. If you choose to be with Lance, there will be times you may feel like you're walking through a lion's den. But know that you're not walking through it alone. I'll walk with you, and I'm sure Lance will too. And remember one very important thing. Always, always address him as Pastor when you're in the presence of others. Never disagree with him in public, and no one should ever know that the two of you are angry with one another, because people will use that to come between you."

Arykah ran her fingers through her hair frustratingly. "You know, the more I think about this, the more I'm convinced I can't do this."

"Why? Because you don't want to face the challenge? You wanna give up on the relationship before it gets started?"

"I can't deal with the pressure."

"What pressure, Arykah? The hardest thing you're gonna have to deal with is keeping your legs closed and controlling your mouth. If you can master those two things, everything else will fall into place."

Just then Theresa stormed into Monique's office. "Adonis is on line three, and he's upset."

Monique looked at her. "Upset?"

"Yes, and he's yelling."

She spoke into her cellular telephone. "Hold on a minute, Arykah." Monique picked up the third line. "Adonis?"

He was hysterical. "He didn't see it, Monique! He didn't see it!"

She didn't have a clue what Adonis was talking about. "Who didn't see what?"

"His work boots were untied and he tripped. He tried not to fall on it, but he couldn't help it."

Without knowing it, Monique became hysterical too. "*Who?*"

Adonis yelled into the telephone. "Boris. He fell on six hundred volts! The ambulance is taking him to Christ Hospital! I'm on my way to get Aunt Myrtle!"

Monique didn't respond. She quickly slammed down the telephone, then spoke into her cellular phone. "Boris was electrocuted. I'm going to Christ Hospital."

"I'll meet you there," Arykah said.

When Monique rushed into the emergency waiting area, she saw Myrtle on her knees praying. Adonis stood from a chair, and Monique hurried into his arms. She saw that his eyes were puffy and red.

"How is he?" she asked.

"We don't know anything yet. He was unconscious when the ambulance left the job site."

Monique released Adonis and knelt next to the only real mother she'd ever known.

"Boris is strong, Gravy. He's gonna be all right." She stood Myrtle up and sat her in a chair. Adonis sat next to Monique.

"How did it happen?" she asked him.

"He tripped on his boot lace. Thank God he wasn't wearing steel toes. His partner, Paul, said he was walking ahead of Boris when he heard him fall. When Paul turned around, he saw Boris lying on the third rail. He was moving like he was having a seizure. Paul was able to kick Boris off the rail with the rubber sole on his boot. Had Boris been grounded, Paul wouldn't have been able to help him."

"Grounded?" Monique asked.

"You're grounded when you wear earrings, chains or watches. The metal feeds the electricity and it fries you."

"What about Paul? How is he?"

"Paul's cool. His rubber sole insulated him. He's still at work."

Arykah rushed into the waiting room and sat next to Myrtle, then kissed her cheek. "What happened?"

Adonis told the story again for Arykah's benefit.

"What did the doctor say?" Arykah asked.

"We don't know anything yet," Myrtle answered sadly.

The four of them witnessed a doctor approach a man

and his young son who were also in the emergency waiting room. Adonis and Myrtle overheard minutes before Monique arrived that the man's wife was eating breakfast with friends when she choked on a piece of bread and stopped breathing. The doctor shook his head from side to side and patted the husband's shoulder with compassion. The son yelled to the top of his lungs. The father grabbed and held him while trying to fight back his own tears. The doctor and a nurse led them behind two double doors.

Myrtle placed her face in her hands and cried. "Sweet Jesus, please let my baby be all right."

For the next ten minutes, Monique and Arykah held Myrtle's hands. Adonis was silently praying when Boris's doctor came to them. He stood directly in front of Myrtle. "Ms. Cortland?"

Myrtle searched his face. He wasn't smiling or frowning. "Yes?"

"Boris is conscious, and he's very lucky."

Myrtle cried a sigh of relief. "Oh, thank you, Jesus. Thank you, Lord."

Adonis, Monique and Arykah wiped tears from their eyes. The doctor allowed Myrtle and Adonis to see Boris. Twenty minutes later, Adonis came and told Monique that Boris wanted to see her, and Monique hurried to be by Boris's bedside.

She pulled up a chair and sat next to his bed. Three machines were hooked up to Boris's body. Monique saw IV's dripping in both of his wrists. With Myrtle out of the room, Boris opened up to her. "I'm sorry." It was a struggle for Boris to speak.

Monique saw tears running from the corners of his eyes to his ears. "Shhh, save your strength."

"No, I need to say this to you. I know I caused you a lot of pain, and I'm sorry. I was shocked when Momma said you were here."

Monique placed her hand in his. Seeing Boris in that vulnerable state reminded her of the reason she had fallen in love with him two years ago. "Of course I would be here, Boris. I don't hate you, I'm just sick of the way you treat me."

"Monique, if you give me one more chance, I swear to God I won't mess up again."

"Boris, now is not the time to talk about this. Let's get you well first."

"Please, Monique. Come back to me, baby. Please. I'm miserable, and I can't make it without you. I may as well be dead without you in my life."

"Don't talk like that, Boris. That's morbid."

"Whatever I gotta do to get you back, baby, I'll do it. I love you more than I love myself. I need you Monique, I swear I do."

A nurse came in and demanded that Boris rest. Monique stood and kissed his forehead lightly. "Get some sleep. I'll see you later."

In the waiting room, Monique told Myrtle, Adonis, and Arykah that Boris was resting. Arykah stood and placed her purse strap on her shoulder. "I gotta get back to the office. Momma Cortland, call me if you need anything."

"Yeah, I gotta get back to work too. Auntie, you want a ride home?" Adonis asked.

"No, I'm gonna stay awhile. I'll catch a cab home later."

"I'll stay with Boris, Gravy. Let Adonis take you home," Monique said.

The three of them stood in shock looking at Monique.

"Are you sure?" Myrtle asked her.

Monique didn't look into Adonis or Arykah's eyes. She knew what they were thinking. She focused on Myrtle. "Yeah, I'm gonna stay the night with Boris."

Adonis wanted to repeat Myrtle's question, but decided not to do it in the presence of his aunt and Arykah.

"I need you to find a house for me as soon as possible," Adonis said to Arykah in the hospital parking lot, on the way to their cars.

"She's not going back to him," Myrtle said.

"Yes she is, Auntie, I know she is."

Later that evening, Monique sat at Boris's side, feeding him applesauce. With each swallow he took, she wiped the corners of his mouth with a paper napkin. It wasn't until that very moment when Boris truly realized what he had given up. There was absolutely no comparison between Monique and Kita. As a matter of fact, no woman could measure up to Monique.

"Thanks for staying," he said to her.

"Gravy wanted to stay, but I figured you wouldn't want your mother helping you to the bathroom and bathing you. I'm sure Adonis would've stayed if he could have, but he had to get back to work. Oh, Arykah was here too, so make sure to thank her."

"I bet I'm the last person Arykah wants to hear from."

"I wouldn't say the *last* person. She did drop everything to come see about you."

"She probably wanted to see for herself that I was dead."

"I'll have you to know that Arykah's ways are slowly but surely changing. She happens to be dating a pastor."

"Have you met him?" Boris asked.

"Not yet."

"That's because he doesn't exist. Arykah hates men,

and she definitely wouldn't get with a pastor. She's got too many demons inside of her."

"Be that as it may, I can vouch for her and say that one by one, the demons are coming out. She knows she has to give up a lot if she wants to be with the man."

"Yeah, but how do you go from being a witch to being a pastor's wife?"

"Ooh Boris, don't call Arykah a witch."

"She *is* a witch and she casts evil spells on people. If this pastor does exist, and personally I think he doesn't, because a man of the cloth should be able to spot a witch from a mile away, but if he's hooking up with Arykah, he needs to be warned."

When the nurse on the third shift came to check Boris's vitals, Monique went to the payphone in the lounge area to call Arykah. Because of the rules of the hospital, she couldn't use her cellular phone. "Hey, what are you up to?"

"That's what I want to ask *you*," Arykah said.

"What do you mean?"

"You know what I mean, Monique. Why didn't you let Mother Cortland stay with Boris?"

"Because she would've had to bathe him and stuff. I knew he wouldn't be comfortable with that."

"Why not? She's his mother. And besides, there are professional nurses who get paid to do that stuff for patients. How do you think it made Adonis feel to hear you say that you'd spend the night with Boris?"

Monique closed her eyes. "I don't even wanna know, Arykah."

"He thinks you're going back to Boris."

"Why would he think that? That's crazy."

"Is it?" Arykah asked.

"Yes, it is. Boris's accident doesn't change anything."

"Well, you could've fooled me. By the way, how is he?"

"He's good. The doctor said Boris may be released as early as tomorrow."

"Have you talked to Adonis?"

"I'm afraid to call him."

"You're gonna have to face him sooner or later, Monique. You may as well get it over with."

"I don't see what the big deal is, Arykah. Adonis and I are only friends."

"If you and Adonis are only friends, why are you so defensive?"

"Because I shouldn't have to explain what I do. Adonis ain't my man, and he knows that."

"You think he does, but actually he doesn't. Do you remember the conversation we had in my living room the night you found out about the lump in my breast? I told you to end things with Adonis because he was serious, and he would end up getting hurt when you go back to Boris."

Monique became upset. "What are you talking about, Arykah? I haven't gone back to Boris. Is it wrong for me to be by his side after a near death experience?"

"That's for Boris's mother to do. It's one thing to rush to the hospital to see about him, and it's another to bathe him and spend the night with him, Monique. You two don't even live together anymore, or has that changed?"

Monique didn't answer Arykah.

"Oh my God. Monique, please tell me you're not moving back home."

"It's only temporary, Arykah. Someone's gotta be there to take care of him."

"And you're the only person who can do that, right? You think you can take care of Boris better than his mother could? What the heck is wrong with you, Monique?"

"I know it will be awkward with Adonis living there, but we'll just have to work it out."

"That's one thing you ain't gotta worry about, because Adonis won't be there."

"Why?"

"Somehow, he knew you were gonna have a change of heart. He said he saw it in your face. When we left the hospital, he told me to find a house for him. It just so happens that a three bedroom in Chatham was put on the market this morning. Adonis decided to take the rest of the afternoon off. I took him and Mother Cortland to see it."

"And?"

"He bought it."

Saturday afternoon, Monique made Boris comfortable in their bed. She dressed him in his silk, black pajamas and propped his pillows against the headboard before giving him the remote control to the television. In the kitchen, she sat a pot of water on top of the stove in preparation for homemade soup. While she waited for the water to boil, Monique couldn't resist going downstairs to the basement. Everything Adonis owned was gone. She heard the telephone in the kitchen ringing and ran upstairs to answer it.

"Hello?"

"Hey, Baby Girl."

"How are you doing, Gravy?"

"I'm fine, how's Boris?"

"He's okay. He's lying down. You wanna talk to him?"

"No, I'll let him rest. Do you need any help with him?"

"Nah, I don't think so. I'm making chicken noodle soup for him right now. The Bishop called Boris this morning and prayed for him over the telephone."

"That's good. I'm glad the Bishop took time away from his out of town engagement to bless Boris. How long will he be off from work?"

"His doctor has him off for the next two weeks."

"Well, I guess I'll come over every morning and sit with him."

"You don't have to do that, Gravy. I had scheduled two weeks of vacation for the wedding but I'll just take them now. So I'll be here with Boris."

"Baby Girl, are you sure you know what you're doing?"

Monique spoke softly into the telephone. "I love him, Gravy."

"Humph, well that's all I needed to hear."

"You think I'm doing the wrong thing, don't you?"

"You're gonna be my daughter in-law whether you're with Boris or Adonis. It's a win-win situation for me. My concern is *you*. Do you wanna go back to the way things were with Boris?"

"I don't think it will be like that this time, Gravy. Boris almost died, and I think that experience has got him lookin' at life differently. In the hospital, we sat up all night talking. And we prayed together, Gravy. That was a first for us. Boris said some things to me that he'd never said before. He held my hand and apologized at least twenty times, then he repented to God openly. I've never seen him cry that way before. But I'm concerned about Adonis. I haven't spoken with him. Arykah told me he bought a house."

"Yeah, he did. It's a nice house too. And it's best he moved out. His heart is broken, but Adonis will get through this. He's staying with me until he can move in the house. Listen, after church tomorrow, I'm gonna come by there and cook Boris's favorite meal."

"I'm sure he'll love that, Gravy. My water is boiling; I gotta dice the vegetables. I'll give you a call later on."

An hour later, Monique served Boris a bowl of chicken noodle soup on a small tray. "I need to tell you something, Boris. It's about Adonis."

"What about him?"

"He bought a house yesterday, and he moved out of the basement."

"Yeah, I know," Boris said.

Monique was stunned. "You know?"

"I forgot to tell you that he called the hospital yesterday while you were at the nurses' station getting my release papers. He told me he had a feeling you were moving back home, and he wanted to give us our space."

"That's all he said?"

"I told him I was gonna do everything in my power to make things right between us. He asked if I wanted him to take some time off to stay here with me, but I told him that you were taking some vacation time."

"What did he say about that?"

"He reminded me how special you are and wished us well. Adonis is my cousin, but he's closer to me than any real brother could ever be."

Boris was asleep when Arykah called Monique's house. "Hey, you ready to go to the mall?"

"I've completely forgotten about that."

"That's okay, the mall doesn't close until six thirty. I'm on my way to get you."

"Arykah, I can't leave Boris. He just got home from the hospital."

Arykah's voice rose. "So doggone what? Boris ain't handicapped. He can't do without you for a few hours?"

"He's very weak, and I need to be here when he wakes up."

"So, what are you doing, sitting on the edge of the bed listening to him snore? I bet every now and then you put a small mirror beneath his nose just to make sure he's breathing, don't you?"

"That's not funny, Arykah."

"I ain't trying to be funny. I wanna know why Boris can't manage without you for a little while."

"Because he may need my help getting to the bathroom."

"Does he need your help aiming in the toilet too?"

"That's not fair, and you know it."

"Whatever Monique, I'll talk to you later."

Saturday night, Adonis ran hot water in the bathtub for his aunt. Myrtle was asleep in the living room rocker in front of the television, when Adonis tapped her knee. "Auntie, your bath is ready."

Myrtle opened her eyes and looked at him. "Thank you, sugar. I'm gonna do the dishes first, because after my bath, I wanna get right in the bed."

Adonis helped her to stand. "I washed the dishes already, Auntie. And I washed the outside of all the windows while you were asleep. So you can stop bugging me about that."

"Why didn't you wake me up to help you?"

"Because I knew I could get it done faster without you breathing down my neck telling me I missed a spot."

"Did you put Epsom salt in the bathwater?"

"Nah, I didn't know how much to put in."

Myrtle held on to Adonis's arm for support as she walked slowly to the bathroom. "Seems like my arthritis is getting worse. These old knees of mine ain't worth two cents." She got the carton of Epsom salt from beneath the bathroom sink and poured about three tablespoons in the bathwater.

Adonis left Myrtle to her bath and went into his bedroom and lay across the bed. He thought about Monique and wondered what she was doing at that moment. He should've seen the sign long ago that she wasn't serious about leaving Boris. The fact that she didn't take off her engagement ring was a dead give-away. From his wallet he removed the picture they had taken at the Buckingham Fountain.

Adonis looked at Monique's smile. Truly, she spread the sunshine in his life. What would he do now? He placed the photo back in his wallet, then stretched his arms behind his head. "Lord, how did You let this happen? I asked You, no I didn't ask, I begged You not to allow me to fall in love with Monique. Don't You remember me taking all of that money to the altar? I paid You good money not to let this happen, and You didn't keep up Your end of the bargain. So what am I supposed to do now, Lord, huh? What am I supposed to do?"

After her bath, Myrtle poked her head into Adonis's room to say goodnight. She saw him lying on his back with his hands extended behind his head, staring at the ceiling. Myrtle walked in and sat on the bed next to him and saw tears streaming from his eyes to his ears.

"Love hurts, doesn't it, son?" she asked.

Adonis sniffed, but didn't answer Myrtle's question.

"You wanna talk about it?"

"There's nothing to talk about, Auntie. I put myself out there when I knew she was my cousin's fiancé. But I didn't care about that. Monique didn't come to me, I approached her. And I can't get angry with her because she never confessed to me that she ended things with Boris. But that's not even the point, Auntie. It was wrong for me to even go there with Monique. Boris and I are blood. I should've known better."

Myrtle wondered why Monique hadn't told Adonis that she'd called off the wedding.

"Adonis, if I ask you a question, will you tell your Aunt Myrtle the truth?" He looked at her. "Yeah, Auntie, I'll always tell you the truth."

"I know we joked about this the other day, but I need to know. Just how close were you and Baby Girl?"

He knew what Myrtle was really asking him. "We haven't slept together, Auntie. I have too much respect for Monique to let that happen."

"The way you talk about her and the way your eyes light up at the mention of her name is the way a person behaves when there is a soul tie between them and someone they love."

"You know what, Auntie? Monique and I are meant to be together, I know it. We connect in every way. I wake up thinking about her. I go to bed thinking about her. I smell her perfume in the air at work, and I stop what I'm doing and look around for her face. She's got my nose open so wide, I can smell things that are a mile away."

Myrtle ran her hand along Adonis's arm for comfort. "I hate to see you going through this because you're a good man. I just hope and pray that Boris gets himself together and realizes what he's got. Sometimes it takes for us to get the heck literally knocked out of us before we say 'Yes, Lord.' Maybe this experience was a wake up call for him."

"Yeah, maybe," Adonis said.

* * *

Arykah sat in the middle of her bed watching the *Life-time Movie Network* channel and eating a pint of Baskin And Robbins chocolate chip ice cream. After talking with Monique, she was so angry that she decided not to go shopping for something new to wear to Lance's church. In her closet was a brand new fuchsia two-piece linen suit she recently purchased at Neiman Marcus. She'd wear it with her brand new fuchsia satin sling back pumps. The telephone on her nightstand rang, and she answered on the first ring.

"Hello, Arykah. Did I wake you?"

A huge grin appeared on her face. "No, but it wouldn't matter if you did. You're the only one who can do that."

"Oh, really?" Lance asked.

"Yes. How was your day?"

"Busy. It's summer, and everyone wants to get married. So my days are filled with marital counseling."

The mention of marital counseling brought back yesterday's conversation with his secretary to Arykah's mind. "I called you yesterday. Did you get my message?"

"No, I didn't. What time did you call?"

"I called the church when I got to work and saw the roses you sent. I wanted to thank you. They are beautiful, Lance."

"Pretty flowers for a pretty lady."

"You may not think I'm so pretty when I confess to you what I've done."

"I don't understand."

Arykah slowly inhaled and let the air out of her lungs. "When I called the church yesterday, your secretary wasn't pleased."

"Let me guess. She was real short and nasty to you, right?"

"Yes, she was, but how did you know?"

"Sister Gussie Hughes is an old timer. She's a charter member that never let me forget that she changed my diapers when I was a baby. She, along with the other mothers of the church, have a hard time accepting the fact that lil' Lance is now thirty-five years old. Mother Hughes has been the church clerk for as long as I can remember, but I think it's time for her to retire because you're not the only one she hassles that calls. She also makes it known that as soon as her granddaughter, Sharonda, gets out of jail and delivers her third child, she and I will get married. Mother Hughes jumps down the throat of every woman who smiles at me. I apologize that she was out of line with you."

"I wish I'd known all of this before I did what I did yesterday," Arykah said.

"What did you do?"

"Well, I kinda got angry at the way she was talking to me and purposely let it slip that you sent roses to me."

Lance chuckled. "That explains why the cup of coffee almost spilled when she slammed the mug on my desk."

"I'm sorry, Lance. I let her get the best of me, and I shouldn't have. Are you worried about the church finding out about us?"

"Arykah, I'm a grown man. I'm entitled to a private life. Mother Hughes and everyone else will have to accept that. If they choose not to, I will encourage them to worship at one of the many churches they pass on the way to Freedom Temple."

Boris turned onto his side and wrapped his arm around Monique's waist. She removed his hand. "No, Boris."

"Why not? It's been awhile."

"I don't care. I'm not in the mood."

Boris put his arm back around her waist. "I can fix that."

Monique sat up on the bed. "I said no. And if you love me, you'll respect that."

"Okay, Baby, chill out. We don't have to have sex tonight."

"Not tonight or any other night, Boris," she said sternly.

Boris couldn't believe the words coming out of Monique's mouth. "What?"

"No more sex."

"Why are you keeping yourself from me?"

"Because things have changed. I won't have sex again 'til I'm married. And if you have the strength for sex, you have the strength to go to work." Monique got out of bed and retrieved a blanket from the linen closet. She took it, along with her pillow, and slept on the living room sofa. She had vowed to become celibate, and she was going to stay that way. Monique had finally learned her lesson. Sex before marriage was taboo. She was living proof of it.

Chapter 15

Arykah walked through the sanctuary doors of Freedom Temple Church Of God In Christ and sat down on the last pew in the back of the church. The choir was rendering in song when Pastor Lance Howell saw her enter.

A minute later, an usher was at Arykah's side. "Miss Miles?"

She looked at him wondering who he was and how he knew her name. "Yes?"

"Pastor Howell asked that I escort you to the front pew."

Oh, my God. Arykah glanced at Lance in shock. He smiled and waved her forward. She was aware of the *'who is she?'* stares on many faces. Arykah followed the usher to the empty front pew and sat down. She silently prayed Lance wouldn't ask her to stand and say anything.

After the choir's second selection, Lance took his place behind the podium. "Praise the Lord, saints."

"Praise the Lord," the congregation responded.

"Say amen for the Freedom sanctuary choir."

Many amens flowed throughout the church. Pastor Howell asked the congregation to stand and bow their heads as he led them in prayer. "Father, we thank You for this time when we can share. Father, we understand and can sense in our spirits the need for the church to return back to the great commission, and that is the delivering of souls. We ask, Father, that there will be such an understanding and openness to receive on this morning. Let revelation knowledge flow in the name of Jesus. Cause our hearts to be prepared. God, break the ground of our hearts. Take out the thistles, the thorns and the stones, Lord, so that when the seed is sown, it can germinate and begin to grow and produce fruit in the name of Jesus. And we thank You in Jesus' name. We praise You for the deliverances that are going to take place today. For the victory is ours through the blood of Jesus and we give You glory."

The people were already on fire from the pastor's prayer alone. "Hallelujah, praise God, glory to God," they shouted. "Say your prayers, preacher, say your prayers."

"You may be seated." Lance turned pages in his Bible. "Turn with me to the Old Testament to Isaiah, chapter sixty-one. And this morning, we'll began the series of teaching on the ministry of deliverance."

At that moment, Arykah felt the sermon would be just for her. She knew Lance was going to preach to her about getting over her past with Eric.

"We do understand that in the body of Christ we have some division concerning this subject. But I do believe God wants to bring some clarity this morning concerning the ministry of deliverance. Because if you are in the body of Christ, your assignment is to serve Him. We have an assignment to witness and to set the captives free and

I noticed from the Old Testament, Isaiah begins to speak concerning what is to come and what is to take place once Jesus Christ comes to this earth. Something unique and unusual is to take place once Jesus comes. It had to be spoken by the prophet first. And once the prophet spoke it in the book of Luke chapter four, verse eighteen, it was the fulfillment of prophecy. Are you with me?"

The people were hanging on to Lance's every word. "Amen, Pastor. Teach this morning."

"In verse one, Isaiah said: *The Spirit of the Lord is upon me because the Lord hath anointed me to preach good tiding to the meek. He hath sent me to bind up the broken hearted and to proclaim liberty to the captives and the opening of the prison to them that are bound. To proclaim the acceptable year of our Lord in the day of vengeance of our God, to comfort all that mourn. To appoint unto them that mourn in Zion, to give unto them beauty, the oil of joy for mourning, the garment of praise for the spirit of heaviness, that they might be called 'trees of righteousness', the planting of the Lord that He might be glorified.* How many of you know that He's not glorified in anyone being bound?"

"No, sir. That's right, Pastor," the people responded.

"He gets no glory out of one being sick in their body. For He said with His stripes, we are healed. And healing is the children's bread. Beloved, I wish upon all that thouest may prosper and build. His concern is about souls being healthy, healed and whole. Not oppressed, not obsessed and definitely not possessed."

"Come on and teach this thing, Pastor. Say a word, Pastor, say a word this morning," an associate minister encouraged.

Lance made eye contact with Arykah. "You have the power to speak release and deliverance over your own life. You can command release. That means there's power in your mouth to make things change when you proclaim. There are a lot of folks who are captives and are blind and bruised. And God's anointing must come upon His people to free them. Go with me to Isaiah, chapter ten, verse twenty-seven."

Arykah and the people found the scripture as Pastor Howell read it aloud.

"And it shall come to pass on that day." He looked out at the people and further explained. "The day of bondage that the Word is speaking of is the day that Satan tries to invade your life, the very day the kingdom of God that dwells in the heart of the believer is under attack. That day, somebody say *that day."*

"That day," the people said in unison.

Lance removed his microphone from its stand and began pacing the pulpit. "The day that you're about to give in, and you're entertaining demonic activity, and worldly lust. The day your soul gets confused and you get messed up in your mind and emotions, contemplating on whether you're going to serve God or not. That day is the day when the anointing has an assignment. And it shall come to pass on that day, say 'that day'."

Half of the congregation was on their feet. "That day, that day."

"On that day, His burden shall be taken away from off thy shoulder. Take your hand and pretend to brush something from your shoulder and say get off me, you don't belong here."

The people obeyed their pastor and brushed the enemy off from their shoulders. "Amen, Pastor. Preach this thing."

Lance rushed back to the podium and continued to read from the book of Luke. *"And His yoke from off thy neck.* God did not put the yoke you have on you because He said His yoke is easy and His burdens are light. The yoke God puts on you won't hurt you and cut you and cause you to bleed." He glanced at the text again and read a bit further. *"And the yoke shall be destroyed."* Eyeing the congregation, the pastor said, "Not maybe, not probably, not I hope it will happen, but I'm not for sure. No, no, it *shall* be destroyed. I need about three people to shout, 'It shall be.'"

The entire congregation was on their feet along with Arykah. "It shall be, it shall be, oh yes, it shall be. Preach, Pastor, preach."

"Every one of God's *shall's* are loaded," Lance said.

Many people agreed. "Yes, Lord. Yes, they are."

"It shall be destroyed because of what?" Lance asked.

The people shouted, "The anointing."

"And what is the anointing? It is the presence and power of God on your life. It is the sovereign act of God's love. He chooses whomever He desires to free. Not because we were so wonderful or deserved it, but because He loved us, we're free. How many free folk I got in here today?"

Hands were waving in the air. "I'm free, I'm free. Hallelujah, I'm free."

Lance kept on preaching. "Ministry of deliverance is why God sent His Son, Jesus. Saint John chapter three, verse sixteen says, *For God so loved the world, that He gave His only begotten Son.*

"He wouldn't have given us His Son if He didn't love us. The messed up condition of this world caused God to make a decision. It caused mercy to come on the scene, and it changed the heart of God when He wanted to destroy all mankind. But because of His love for humanity, it caused Him to say, 'I missed that fellowship I had with Adam in the Garden of Eden, and the only way I can get reunited in the fellowship of mankind is that somebody has to pay for this.' Jesus had to come on the scene and become sin to take the punishment that was rightfully ours."

An associate minister in the pulpit, a few feet away from Lance, removed his handkerchief from his suit jacket pocket and threw it at Lance. "Preach, Pastor. Break it down."

Lance was sweating. "Jesus had to be the sacrificial lamb to bear all the sins of humanity so that we can be free forever. So the ministry of deliverance started from the heart of God. And when Jesus came, He represented God's grace at its best. God couldn't do any better than that. He gave His only Son because He was the only one able to set men free. The ministry of deliverance could no longer be ignored because lives and souls were in danger. That's why it's so important for the church of the twenty-first century to embrace the call of the ministry to set captives free, not to bring people to church to entertain their emotions. Because it's their emotions that are not causing them to be set free. The music, the dancing, the shouting, and the praise and worship is not necessarily breaking and destroying yokes. Just because you hear the drums don't mean that everybody's being delivered. You can come to church and hide with your spirit messed up because you won't let God come into the inner chambers of your soul to bring transformation. It's easy to look delivered, but God sees what is hiding in your spirit."

Arykah wiped tears from her own eyes. She had held back until that moment. "That's right, Pastor."

Lance paced the pulpit. "To deliver means to set free, to take and hand over. To take you out of darkness and hand you over to the marvelous light. To take you from ignorance to understanding. Come on somebody. Deliverance releases sin from the sinner. You can be in this world and tempted by sin and not do it. That means you can walk in the midst of mess and stay free. God will place you in the fiery furnace and walk in it with you. You walk around free while everybody else is tripping on your attitude when they know you're going through. They'll look at you and say, 'Girl, how can you be happy when your husband left you with five kids? I'd be going crazy if I were you.'

"It's because of the deliverance of your soul. Because when you're sanctified from it, you can look at it and say *my soul looks back and wonder how I got over*. The ministry of deliverance is an act given by the anointing of God through Jesus Christ to remove emotional, physical, and spiritual bondages in the lives of sinners *and* saints.

Sinners are delivered from sin and placed in the family of God. So now you're a saint, and your soul needs to be dealt with, and your body needs to be worked with. Because when you accept Jesus Christ as your personal Savior, your spirit is born again. You are a new creature in Christ Jesus, old things are passed away and behold all things are become new. But your soul is where your emotions are, where your feelings are, and where your will is. Your mind is where your struggles, called *warfare*, take place. The devil is trying to capture your mind. He wants to set up camp in your mind. He wants to reside and live in your soul. He wants to build houses and rent apartments and hotels in the center of your mind. That's called a stronghold. Whatever issues you're dealing with that are trying to take over God's land and trying to cause you to move from your place of victory to a place of captivity, God said the devil will be dealt with. Look at your neighbor and say, 'Your victory is sure; it's in the bag.'"

The saints were high-fiving one another. "Oh yes, it's in the bag, it's in the bag."

As Lance paced, the musicians accompanied him. "Tell yourselves that today is the day the enemy will no longer control you. Say to yourself, 'Victory is mine.'"

Arykah was the first to shout. "Hallelujah, victory is mine. Thank you, Jesus. Victory is mine."

Lance hooped and hollered as he brought his sermon to a close. "God said, 'I thought it, I purposed it in my heart, and that's what's gonna stand.' Deliverance is ours, people, oh yes, deliverance is ours. Devil, you gotta leave my life. God is getting ready to pull me through this. I don't care how it looks or how it feels. Deliverance is mine. Somebody give Him glory, somebody give Him glory."

The entire church was sending up praises to God. Lance came from the pulpit followed by his elders to lay holy hands. Every person he touched with holy oil fell to the floor. He made his way in Arykah's direction and whispered in her ear. "Your set time is come. Your past is forgotten. In the name of Jesus, you are free."

Arykah closed her eyes, raised her hands toward heaven and began to speak in the unknown tongue as tears ran down her face. Lance touched her forehead with holy oil and Arykah fell into the arms of armor bearers standing behind her.

"Baby Girl, where do you keep your flour?" Myrtle asked Monique.

"It's in the far left cabinet with the seasonings."

"Why don't you have the flour and sugar in canisters on top of the sink like normal women?"

"Maybe I'm not normal," Monique answered.

"I won't argue with that."

At the sink, Monique filled a pot of mustard and turnip greens with fresh water. Myrtle stood at the stove and stirred cinnamon, sugar and butter in a pot of cling peaches. On Monique's way to the stove, and on Myrtle's way to the refrigerator, the two women collided.

"You're in my way, Baby Girl," Myrtle fussed.

"You're in *my* way, Gravy. Before we started cooking, we divided this kitchen in half. You ain't staying on your side."

Myrtle placed her hand on her hip. "How in the heck am I suppose to stay on my side of the kitchen when everything I need is on *your* side? You don't need to be in here anyway. I told you yesterday that *I* was doing the cooking for Boris."

"You don't want me in here, Gravy? I'm trying to help you out."

The expression on Myrtle's face showed offensiveness. "Help *me* out? Did you fix your mouth to say help *me* out? Let me tell you something, you microwavin' heifer, when you met Boris, you couldn't even pour milk in a bowl of cereal. I taught you everything you know. What the heck you mean you're helping *me* out? You bake one good ham, and all of a sudden you're Miss Know How To Cook It All. I ain't forgot about the first time when you called yourself cooking mustard and turnip greens. You had so much dirt in the bottom of the pot, I didn't know if you were cooking the greens or growing them. On your best day in the kitchen, you won't be as good as me on my worst day."

Monique laughed at the sweat on Myrtle's forehead.

"Look at you getting all worked up over nothing. Ain't nobody trying to compete with you, Gravy. But for the record, Boris prefers my cornbread over yours."

"Well, he liked mine until you brought your Betty Crocker wannabe tail around and started putting sugar in it. The way you make it, all we gotta do is put some icing on it and we'll have us a cake."

Monique laughed again. "That is not true, Gravy."

"Yes, it is. Who ever heard of sweet cornbread? If you were a real woman, you would know sugar don't belong in cornbread."

Monique added milk to a pan of homemade macaroni and cheese. "What do you know about being a real woman?"

"See, that's your problem. You were born too late. Real women were born before the sixties. We didn't have that fancy stuff y'all got today. Back then it was unheard of for a girl to be driving a car at the age of sixteen. We walked everywhere we had to go. And we didn't have the pleasure of going to a hospital to have babies. Down south, we had midwives who came to our homes to deliver our babies. There was no such thing as getting a shot in the back to take away the pain of childbirth; we had to suffer to bring our babies in this world. Y'all modern day women whine too much. You whine because it takes nine months for the baby to get here, you whine because the labor pains hurt too much, you whine because the baby's head is too big. And after all that whining, you whine some more because the baby come out looking just like the daddy you ain't seen in the entire nine months."

Monique placed the pan of macaroni and cheese in the oven then sat at the table to knead dough for the cobbler. "Why are you telling me this, Gravy? I ain't had a child."

Myrtle put seven ears of corn into a pot of boiling

water. "And that's another thang. When I was growing up, the girls my age weren't quick to lay with a man. We were scared of getting caught. The birth control we had was our parents' belts. Nowadays all you gotta do is swallow a pill, put a patch on your arm, or get a shot in the butt, and you can lay up 'til the cows come home."

Monique hollered and laughed out loud.

Myrtle peeked in the living room at one of the mothers from the church, sleeping on the sofa. Myrtle, along with a few of the other missionaries from the church, rotated Sundays to make sure that the oldest member of the church got a good home-cooked meal before she returned to her senior citizen's home.

"Girl, hush up before you wake Mother Dobson," Myrtle said.

"What are you doing with Mother Dobson anyway, Gravy? It's not your Sunday to take care of her."

"I know, but Sister Marjorie said she couldn't take her today. I don't mind; Mother Dobson never gives me any trouble. Speaking of real women, Mother Dobson had her first child on top of a kitchen table in Jackson, Mississippi. She said her son weighed thirteen pounds, and she didn't need any stitches. Now, that's a real woman for you."

"Thirteen pounds, Gravy? That's impossible."

"No, it ain't. A real woman can do that."

Adonis came into the kitchen carrying a plastic bag. "I got the ice, Auntie."

"Thank you, sugar. Put it in the freezer for me."

"What else do you need?" he asked.

"Put a pillow under Mother Dobson's neck so it won't get stiff on her."

Adonis set the ice in the freezer and looked at Monique. "Hey."

"Hey." She didn't look him in the eye.

He noticed her bare wrist. "Where's your bracelet?"

"Oh, um, I took it off so I wouldn't mess it up."

"Mess it up how?"

"Well, I didn't wanna get anything on it. Gravy's got me elbow deep in flour and stuff."

Myrtle stood at the stove pretending not to hear them. Before she told Adonis that Sunday dinner would be at Boris and Monique's house, Myrtle had gotten permission from Monique to invite him.

"Where's Boris?" Adonis asked Monique.

"He's lying across the bed lookin' at a football game."

Adonis left the kitchen to go place a pillow under Mother Dobson's head, he then went to the bedroom. "What's up, cuz? How are you feeling?"

"Man, I ain't got no complaints. I'm just glad to be alive," Boris said.

Adonis sat on the edge of the bed. "I feel you, man."

"How was church today? Sorry I had to leave you by yourself."

"It's all good. I held it down," Adonis said proudly.

"Tell the choir not to get too happy I'm gone. I'll be back the Sunday after next."

Arykah walked into the bedroom. "Hey y'all."

Boris looked up at her. "I didn't know you were here."

"I just got here. How you feeling?"

"I'm good, but I wanna know how *you're* doing. I hear you're about to walk down the center aisle."

"You heard a lie."

Adonis looked at Arykah. "You got something against getting married?"

"Nope, it just ain't for me right now. Mother Cortland sent me in here to tell y'all that dinner is ready."

In the kitchen, Myrtle sat Mother Dobson at the table

while she, Monique, Boris, Adonis, and Arykah stood holding hands. "Mother Dobson, will you ask God's blessing on the food please?" Myrtle asked.

Everyone bowed their head, and Mother Dobson talked to God.

Arykah whispered in Monique's ear. "It's gonna take from now 'til next week for her to pray."

"Well, you better wait it out," Monique replied.

"When Momma Cortland told me she was bringing Mother Dobson here, I knew she was gonna ask her to pray over dinner. You know she takes forever. That's why I blessed the food while I was driving here. I'm getting ready to eat."

"Be quiet and show some respect," Monique whispered.

Arykah looked at the old woman who was singing the prayer.

"I wanna thank You, Heavenly Master, for not letting the doctors take my leg off back in forty-five. Then Jesus, I wanna thank You because You been so good to me. Lord, that time I had that bad car accident back in fifty-two, You were with me, Lord."

Arykah whispered to Monique again. "Oh, heck no. I'm not standing here for this."

"Arykah, calm down. She's got a lot to be thankful for. You know she's been resuscitated twice."

Mother Dobson kept on singing. "And then, Maaaster, in sixty-one, You didn't let that stroke take meeee awaaay from here. Oh yes, Lord. You've been soooo goooood to meeee. You been better to me than I been to myself. I just can't thank You enough, God. I thank You for not letting the tornado take me wherever it took my house back in sixty-nine, Lord. I know You're always with me, Jesus."

Myrtle silently motioned for everybody to go ahead and eat.

Mother Dobson sat at the kitchen table and prayed with her eyes closed for another half hour. "In the name of Jesus, we thank You, Lord. Amen." Mother Dobson opened her eyes and saw that every plate on the kitchen table was empty except her own. Everyone was leaning back in their chairs with toothpicks dangling from their mouths.

"Amen, Mother Dobson. Amen, amen," came from around the table.

"Burrrp, amen," was Arykah's response.

Myrtle placed Mother Dobson's plate in the microwave to warm it. Boris and Adonis resumed the football game in the bedroom while Monique and Arykah went into the living room.

"You need to start looking for a dress, Arykah," Monique stated.

"A dress for what?"

"My wedding, what else?"

Arykah's face went blank. "You can't be serious, Monique."

Monique exhaled. "Look, Arykah, don't start with me, okay?"

"I am not going to waste my time looking for a dress when there's not gonna be a wedding."

"I addressed and mailed the invitations this morning. There *will* be a wedding."

Arykah's mouth dropped open. "What invitations?"

"The wedding invitations I forgot to cancel. Now I know it was God who told me not to."

"That wasn't God, Monique, that was stupid talking to you. Why are you doing this? Are you in need of attention? Is that what this is about?"

"I'm getting married, Arykah. Boris and I love each other, and this is what I want to do."

"Have you forgotten what that fool put you through? Why are you allowing him to control you like this?"

"Ain't nobody controlling me, Arykah. I'm doing this because I love Boris, and I want to spend the rest of my life with him. I know you're against this, but I can't worry about that right now because I gotta a wedding to finish planning in only four weeks. Are you in or out?"

Arykah stood and grabbed her purse from the sofa and walked toward the front door. "If you are so determined to destroy your life, you're gonna have to do it without me."

She opened the door and walked out into the pouring rain.

Monique placed her face in her hands and cried silently. Surely she must look like a fool to everyone, but in the hospital, Boris had convinced her that he had a pure heart, and he swore to do right by her from now on. And Monique was glad to know that Boris hadn't impregnated Kita.

Lance opened the door and saw a distraught and drenched Arykah standing on his doorstep. The rain fell so hard Lance couldn't see the houses across the street. "What in the world are you doing out in this weather?"

Arykah walked into the foyer. Because his credit and proof of funds had checked out, Arykah had allowed Lance to move in the estate while they waited for the closing date. Arykah was glad that there was no other offer on the house.

"I was just driving around and somehow ended up in your driveway," she said.

"You're soaked. Is something wrong?"

Arykah hung her head and cried openly. Without giving it a second thought, Lance pulled her into his arms. "Shh, it can't be *that* bad." He held her until her shoulders stopped shaking. "You gotta get out of these wet clothes. Come with me."

Lance led Arykah to the master suite. They walked into one of the walk-in closets and Arykah was amazed at what she saw. The entire closet was filled with women's clothing. Dresses, blouses and pants with the price tags still hanging, took up one half of the closet.

"Lance, what have you done?"

"I'm getting ready to receive my wife. I want everything in place when God releases her to me."

Arykah couldn't help but look at the tags. Every item of clothing was a size 20, her exact size. "When did you do all of this?" she asked.

"My sister, Adrienne, is a buyer for the Ashley Stewart clothing line. I told her to fill this closet with size twenty everything. I was amazed she was able to do this so quickly. Look to your left."

To Arykah's left were at least thirty boxes of shoes stacked neatly on top of one another. She opened a box that revealed black patent leather three-inch heels. She yelped like a puppy when her eyes landed on the red Jimmy Choo and yellow Stuart Weitzman boxes. On all of the shoe boxes, Arykah saw the number 8, her exact size. She smiled and looked at Lance. "I am speechless."

He grabbed Arykah's hand. "There's more." He brought her to a six-drawer dresser in the bedroom and opened the top two drawers. Arykah saw pink, yellow and white nightgowns, pajamas and loungewear neatly folded in the top drawer. She ran her hand along the cotton, silk, satin, and linen materials. The second drawer was filled with ladies underwear; bikini cut, brief cut and boxer cut in every color. The last set of drawers held many ankle socks, knee length socks and booties, every pair in white.

"Lance, you're amazing," Arykah said.

He led Arykah into the master bath. On one side of the double marble sink were two new bottles of Ralph Lauren perfume. That was the only scent Arykah wore. He must've smelled it on her. Next to the bottles of perfume was a comb, a brush and a held hand mirror.

"Open the door next to the vanity," Lance instructed.

Arykah obliged and saw a top of the line curling iron, a hand held blow dryer, bottles of oil sheen spray, a set of hair rollers and boxes of hair and bobby pins. On the bottom shelf were bars of Dove, Caress and Oil of Olay body soap. Next to them Arykah saw Secret and Sure deodorants. Johnson & Johnson baby powder and baby oil were also on the bottom shelf next to a pink toothbrush and a carton of cotton swabs. Arykah was stunned beyond belief. "Lance, is all of this for me?"

Lance was sure that Arykah was his Eve. From the moment he met her, God spoke it to him. He trusted and believed that it would come to pass. One thing Lance knew was true; it doesn't take God long to do anything. "It's for my wife, but until she takes her place in this house, and since you seem to fit her clothes, feel free to borrow from her closet. I'll wait for you in the den."

After forty-five minutes had elapsed, Arykah walked into the den with her hair blow-dried and pulled back into a ponytail. She wore a two-piece silk, copper colored pajama pant set.

Lance looked up from the Bible he'd been studying before she had arrived. "You look comfortable."

"I *am* comfortable, Lance. Thank you."

He closed the book and patted the cushion next to

him. "Come sit with me and tell me why you were upset when you got here."

Lance listened for a half hour, without saying a word, to how Arykah's best friend was about to make the biggest mistake of her life. When Arykah became quiet, Lance looked at her. "Are you finished?"

"I just needed to vent."

"You know, Arykah, you can't make Monique's decisions, and you definitely can't live her life for her."

Arykah stood and walked across the den and stood next to the fireplace. "See, I knew you wouldn't understand, Lance."

"I understand perfectly."

"No, you don't. Monique and I have a special bond, and we've always kept each other from doing stupid and crazy things."

"But sometimes love overrides that."

"Lance, please. What's love got to do with it? Monique is not in love with Boris, and it's obvious he doesn't love her. She's in love with Adonis, I know it. She's just acting out."

Lance scratched his head. "I'ma tell you something about Adonis, Arykah. He's an electrician, right?" Arykah nodded. "Then there's no reason he shouldn't have had his own pad. Couples shouldn't allow grown folks to live with them because something like that always happens. Monique and Adonis were spending too much time together. First of all, Boris and Monique shouldn't have been shacking at all."

"I agree with you, but Adonis had nothing to do with the way Boris treated Monique."

"I didn't say he did, but had he not been living there, he wouldn't have overheard them arguing, and he wouldn't have sent roses to her job to cheer her up."

"He was trying to comfort her, Lance."

"Arykah, that wasn't his place. Monique is his cousin's woman."

"That's besides the point."

"No, sweetie, that's *exactly* the point. Monique cooked Adonis's breakfast and dinner along with special pitchers of grape Kool-Aid. Boris didn't get that kind of treatment."

"That's not true. Monique did no more for Adonis than she did for Boris. Boris is a fool who doesn't appreciate what Monique does for him. He chose to go outside of their relationship to get what was being offered at home. Adonis was the one wiping away her tears; he was there for Monique. Boris never gave her a shoulder to cry on."

"That wasn't Adonis's place."

Arykah couldn't believe what Lance was saying. How quickly had she forgotten that she sang that same song to Monique not long ago. "Are you suggesting that Monique and Adonis should've ignored each other while living under the same roof?"

"I'm suggesting that the moment Adonis knew he had feelings for his cousin's fiancé, he should've moved out. He had no business upgrading her car and sending flowers. But this isn't only Adonis's fault; Monique played a huge part in this. Spending private time with Adonis and accepting his gifts allowed him to get closer and closer to her."

"She didn't have a choice, Lance. Boris was off doing whatever the heck he wanted to do. Adonis took care of Monique, and did all the things Boris wouldn't do."

Lance came and stood in front of Arykah. He gently grabbed her by the shoulders. "I know you want what's best for Monique, and I know you're angry with Boris for the way he treated her, but you can't make excuses for either of them. All three of them did the wrong thing. Boris and Monique were wrong for shacking, Adonis was wrong for allowing himself to fall in love with his cousin's woman, and Monique was wrong for leading Adonis on. Accepting an expensive bracelet and letting him devote most of his time to her was wrong because it sounds to me that Monique never intended to leave Boris for good. You said she kept her engagement ring on, and she didn't cancel the wedding invitations."

"She said she forgot to cancel them," Arykah said.

"No, honey, she didn't *want* to cancel them. And now Adonis exposed his heart by putting it on the front line, and it got shot down."

More tears ran down Arykah's face. "I can't believe how this has turned out. It's not supposed to be like this, Lance. I gotta do something to stop this wedding."

"You can't do that. What you need to do is accept the fact that Monique is an adult, and she's going to do what she wants to do. Right now her mind is made up, and if you try to change it, your friendship will suffer."

"So I'm supposed to just sit back and act like everything is peaches and cream, and go along with this joke? Because that's exactly what this wedding will be, a big joke."

"You have no choice, Arykah. Whether you like it or not, your best friend is marrying a man that you strongly dislike. But Monique needs you right now. The only thing you can do is be the best friend that you are when she calls you for comfort."

"Humph, that will be on the wedding night when Boris tells her he's bringing another woman into their marriage bed."

For the next two hours, Lance held Arykah in his arms and listened to her sniffles. At ten o'clock P.M., she announced she was going home.

"It's storming like a fool outside. You're not leaving this house," he said.

"Lance, I have to work in the morning."

"You can go to work from here. The master suite is stocked with everything you need."

"I don't know, Lance. What will your wife say when she finds out that you let another woman roam through her closet?"

Lance looked deeply into Arykah's eyes. "I don't know, what *would* you say?"

That question reached deep into Arykah's soul. Her stomach dropped as if she were on a roller coaster. "Don't play with me, Lance."

He had Arykah right where he wanted her. The mischievous grin on his face showed it. "What are you talking about?" he asked.

"You know doggone well what I'm talking about. Why did you ask the question like that?"

"I asked a simple question."

"There was nothing simple about it. You put special emphasis on the word 'would' when it should've been on the word 'you.' Then it would've seemed like you were asking my opinion rather than, in so many words, saying that the items in the closet are mine."

Lance decided not to expound on this subject any longer. It was too soon. "Arykah, you can sleep in my bed, and I'll sleep upstairs. And just so you know, I have a real problem with the women that I love driving in bad weather. Please don't do it again."

The women that I love. Arykah was halfway to the master suite when Lance's words hit her.

On Monday morning, the smell of bacon aroused Arykah from a deep sleep. She turned to lie on her back and looked around the bedroom. Waking up in a five-bedroom, six-bathroom house to the smell of bacon every morning was something she could get use to. In the kitchen, Lance sat at the table reading the *Chicago Sun-Times* and drinking a cup of coffee when Arykah appeared.

"Good morning, beautiful," he greeted.

Arykah looked down at her wrinkled pajamas and ran her fingers through her tousled hair that somehow lost the ponytail holder throughout the night. "Beautiful? Maybe you need glasses."

"Maybe you need to accept the fact that you're beautiful to *me*."

Arykah smiled and sat at the table. "Do I smell bacon?"

"You smell bacon, scrambled eggs, grits with cheese, and French toast. Are you hungry?"

Arykah was starved, but she didn't want to touch what Lance had prepared. "I think I'll just pick up a bran muffin on my way to the office, Lance. I'm trying to keep my waistline from expanding."

Lance laid the newspaper down and looked across the table at her. "Arykah, I will say this one time and one time only. I need you to listen real good so that I won't have to repeat myself. What's my name?"

"Excuse me?"

"What's my name?" he repeated.

"Your name is Lance."

"That's right, and 'Lance' doesn't sound like 'Eric.' I'm not Eric. When you deny yourself food when you really want to eat, you treat me as though I'm him, and I don't like that. Haven't I told you that you are beautiful as you are? Didn't I tell you that it's not a woman's outer appearance that matters? Didn't you receive my sermon yesterday? When you left here Friday evening, I was up the entire night writing it.

"I don't ever want to see you deprive yourself of food. If you want bacon, eggs, and French toast for breakfast, then eat it. If you want a cheeseburger for lunch today, then have a double cheeseburger. Get it in your mind that Eric is gone forever. *Lance* is here now, and I don't count your calories." He leaned back in his chair and spoke with a lower tone. "Now, what would be your pleasure for dinner this evening?"

Who would've thought that a man would care for her that way? For years Arykah had been walking around with a self-conscious attitude about her weight. But thank God that Lance was a chubby chaser. "What I would really like is pork roast with garlic potatoes. And I love homemade banana pudding."

He smiled. "Then you shall have it."

"You're so good to me, Lance. What did I do to deserve you?"

He stood her up from the table and looked deeply in her eyes. "It's not you who should be asking that question. Now let's eat."

The first thing Arykah did when she sat at her desk was to call Monique's house.

"I didn't think I'd ever hear from you again," Monique said.

"I'm sorry for everything I said yesterday. I love you, and I'll support you in whatever you want to do. If you wanna marry Boris, I'm behind you one hundred percent."

"Wow, I can tell you got up in the right side of the bed this morning."

"I sure did," Arykah said.

"Thanks for calling me. I need you, Arykah. Can we go

shopping for dresses tonight? Because it's so late, we'll have to buy something off the rack."

"I can't do it tonight, I have plans. But I'm free tomorrow night. Is that good for you?"

"Tomorrow night is good for me. You have plans with Lance tonight?"

"Yes, he's cooking again."

"Girl, you better be careful of the calories he's pouring into you."

"I don't have to do that," Arykah said.

"And why is that?"

"Because Lance said I didn't."

Chapter 16

The Tuesday before Monique and Boris's wedding, Adonis took the day off to move into his house. On his way to return the moving van to the rental place, he saw a Lincoln Navigator turn into the parking lot of the Holiday Inn Hotel on East 95th Street. Adonis's eyes grew wide when he saw **IM BORIS** on the rear license plate. He remembered the day when the license plates had arrived in the mail. Boris couldn't wait to put them on his truck. Adonis turned into the lot of the hotel and pulled into a parking spot, not far from where Boris's Navigator parked.

"Oh, heck no." Adonis couldn't believe it when he saw Boris and a woman get out of the SUV, then walk hand in hand into the hotel. Immediately, he called Arykah's cellular telephone. "Arykah, you ain't gonna believe this. On my way to take this moving van back, I happened to see Boris's Navigator turn into the parking lot of the Holiday Inn Hotel on Ninety-Fifth Street."

"What the heck is he doing at the Holiday Inn? It's early Monday morning. I know he's not with Monique, because I just talked to her ten minutes ago. She said she was on her way into a meeting," Arykah said.

"Nah, he ain't with Monique."

"Did you see the woman?"

"Yep, and I couldn't believe it, Arykah."

She became frantic. "Who is Boris with?"

"Jennifer Ayers."

"Jennifer, from the choir?" Arykah shrieked.

"Yes, and guess what? Jennifer is Taj's woman."

"Taj, the drummer?" she shrieked again.

"What are you gonna do about it?" Adonis asked Arykah.

"Not a darn thing, Adonis. I'm done with telling Monique everything Boris does. It won't change a thing."

Adonis thought about what Arykah had just said. "You're right."

On September 16th, as planned, Boris and Monique stood at the altar, face to face, listening to the words of their bishop. "Dearly beloved, we are gathered in this place to share and to witness these two souls come together in holy matrimony."

Monique could see Adonis over Boris's left shoulder, staring into her eyes. If Monique didn't know any better, she'd swear Adonis was slowly shaking his head from side to side, silently begging her not to go through with the wedding.

"I, Boris Dexter Cortland, take you, Monique Lynnette Morrison, to be my lawfully wedded wife. To have and to hold from this day forward."

Looking into Boris's eyes, as he spoke to her, Monique

wondered if she were the only one in the entire church seeing Adonis moving his head. She forced herself to focus on what Boris was saying.

"To love and to cherish, for richer or for poorer, in sickness and in health. Keeping myself solely unto you until death do us part." Boris slipped the ring onto Monique's finger.

The Bishop gave her the go ahead to say her vows. Before she opened her mouth, Monique again looked at Adonis standing behind Boris. She saw through his eyes that he was pleading with her not to marry Boris. You could've heard a pin drop as everyone, including Boris, wondered why Monique was stalling.

The bishop spoke to her. "Monique, it's your turn."

Monique kept her eyes glued on the man standing behind her fiancé. She opened her mouth and spoke slowly, as though she was in a trance. "I, Monique Lynnette Morrison . . ."

She paused there and reflected back to the words Adonis had spoken to her over and over again. *I appreciate everything you do for me.*

"Take you, Adonis . . . "

The entire church gasped at the same time.

Boris was stunned. "What?"

"Oh my God," Arykah uttered as she stood next to Monique.

The Bishop didn't move or say anything, but then again, what could he say? He'd never had a bride call out the best man's name before. Everyone witnessed Adonis step out of the pulpit and walk down the center aisle. Halfway to the sanctuary door, he stopped, turned around and held out his right hand for Monique to come to him.

Her blood was running warm throughout her veins.

Time stood still as friends and loved ones waited to see what Monique would do.

"You want my arm to fall off?" Adonis said to her.

Through teary eyes, Monique looked at this man standing in the middle of the church. Again, she reflected on his words. *"You know what your problem is, Monique? You don't value yourself and you don't know your true worth. You're so use to settling for whatever life throws at you instead of going after what you really deserve. You gotta get out of that mindset because there's so much more in life that God wants you to have."*

Arykah stepped to Monique and spoke in her right ear. "If you don't seize this moment and go for yours, I'll personally kick your . . . "

Before Arykah could complete her threat, Monique dropped her bouquet, lifted her dress, ran down the aisle, and into Adonis's arms. He picked her up and spun her around twice. As he carried her out of the church, they purposely didn't acknowledge the stunned faces.

Arykah looked at Lance seated on the front pew and gave him the biggest grin. He responded with two thumbs up.

Myrtle sat on the front pew with no visible expression on her face. Boris hung his head and followed the bishop out of the sanctuary.

Outside in the waiting limousine that he had hired himself, as a wedding gift to the couple, Adonis instructed the driver to take them to Midway Airport. Monique didn't say a word. She sat calmly next to Adonis as he made a call on his cellular phone. "Operator, can you connect me to Air Jamaica."

Monique's eyes bucked out of her head.

"When is the next flight to Negril scheduled to leave?" Adonis looked at his wristwatch. "I would like to purchase two first class tickets, please."

Monique felt as though she were in a dream. She refused to open her mouth out of fear that she'd wake herself. She listened as Adonis gave their names and his credit card information. The customer service representative told Adonis their electronic tickets would be at Air Jamaica's airline counter when they arrived at the airport. He disconnected the call and spoke to the driver. "Dude, one hundred bucks has your name on it if you get us there in the next twenty minutes."

Monique looked at him. "Adonis, don't we need passports and birth certificates?"

"Everything we need is in our luggage in the trunk. You can thank Arykah when we get back from our honeymoon. She and I had this planned since Tuesday."

"Honeymoon?" she asked.

With gentle hands, Adonis cupped Monique's face. "Will you marry me on the beach while the sun is coming out of the water?"

A single tear dripped from her eye. "I've always dreamed of getting married on the beach at sunrise. I only shared that passion with Boris, and he thought it was a dumb idea."

Adonis kissed her lips. "Well, he shared it with me, and I think it's a great idea."

Just hours later, they were in the air sipping Mimosa and feasting on caviar when Monique looked over at Adonis. "You know we gotta face the fire when we go back home, don't you?"

"We ain't going back," he said.

That's exactly what Monique wanted to hear, even though

it wasn't true. She sank down in her first class leather reclining chair and let it massage her back. She closed her eyes and made a wish. Monique looked out the window, down at the Atlantic Ocean, and rode the waves all the way to Negril.

Just like candy. I toss and turn in my bed in the morning when I think about you!

THE END

Arykah Miles and Pastor Lance Howell return in Nikita Lynnette Nichols'

forthcoming novel:

LADY ELECT

An excerpt

Chapter 1

Arykah Miles-Howell, and her best friend, Monique Lynnette Morrison-Cortland, along with Monique's cousin, Amaryllis Price, and Amaryllis's best friend and roommate, Bridgette Nelson, sang and danced to the music of R&B group, Kool & The Gang.

"Oh, yes, it's ladies night and the feeling's right. Oh, yes, it's ladies night, oh what a night," the ladies sang.

For the past four months, the full-figured beauties had rotated each other's living rooms, on every third Saturday evening, for their monthly 'Fat Girl' party. This particular evening, the living room in a five-bedroom, six and a half bath estate, in *Covington*, a subdivision in Oakbrook Terrace, was filled with joy and laughter.

As hostess, Arykah changed CDs and led her girlfriends in the electric slide, as each of them held flutes filled with virgin Bahama Mamas.

"Come on, sistas. Step it to the left, now rock it to the right, take it on back, now jump two times. Uh huh, uh huh, now jump again. Now swing it all around and take it to the ground," Arykah instructed along with the CD.

Collectively, the ladies would tip a scale at nearly nine hundred pounds. A lavish buffet table consisting of honey barbeque buffalo wings, taco salad, a tray of rolled salami and ham slices, and fresh baked Hawaiian bread, sat front and center in the home's two-story foyer.

"Ain't no party like a fat girl party," Bridgette, a size 14, and the smallest of the group, said as her bulging eyes roamed over the food. Two dozen Krispy Kreme dough-nuts was the first of the feast to catch the ladies' eyes when they had entered Arykah's front door earlier that evening.

Sweating to the music, Monique was the first to sit down on the plush white Berber carpet to catch her breath. She let her head fall backward on the cushion of the custom made, ivory colored, Nicolette suede chair.

"Come on, cousin. I know you ain't tired yet. This is only the second song," Amaryllis teased.

Monique absorbed the sweat beads on the tip of her nose into a Kleenex tissue. She had become a newlywed just four months ago, and her then size 20 figure had grown larger to a size 22W. "I ain't as thin as I used to be. I can't do all of that bending and twisting and jumping. And I told Arykah that I was on a diet. If she was a true friend, she wouldn't have served all that fat food."

Arykah took a sip of her exotic drink while keeping up with the dance movements. "It's a fat girl party, Monique; you know how we do it. Did you expect me to serve a let-tuce, tomato and cucumber salad? What the heck were you thinking?"

Monique inserted the tissue in her blouse to soak up the wetness in her cleavage. "Well, now that you've mentioned it, a salad with fat free dressing would have been a nice change."

Arykah stopped dancing and placed right her hand on her hip. She then shifted all of her weight onto her right leg. "What? Are we rabbits now? I think there's a bag of carrots in the fridge, you want me to get you some? Keep in mind, Monique, you've inhaled four doughnuts and just about ate all of the salami. And don't even go there about bending, twisting and jumping. Because you ain't got a problem with bending, twisting and jumping for that super fine husband of yours."

Monique chuckled. "That's because Adonis understands that ten good minutes is all I'm good for. And when my ten minutes are up, he does all the work with my two hundred forty-seven pounds."

Bridgette, Amaryllis, and Arykah burst into laughter.

"Does he work it, girl?" Bridgette asked.

"Adonis works it so good; I think he had Energizer batteries implanted," Monique added.

Amaryllis snapped her fingers in the shape of the capitol letter Z. Over the past year, she had allowed herself to balloon from a petite figure eight frame to a size 16. "All right, cousin, I ain't mad."

"I know that's right," Bridgette said.

Arykah was out of breath. She collapsed on the floor next to Monique, panting for air. "Do you remember where we were only four months ago?" she asked Monique. I was doing my realty thing and wasn't even thinking about a man," Monique wiped sweat from around her neck. She thought back to the mistake she had almost made with her ex-boyfriend, Boris Cortland, who just happens to be her husband's cousin. "And I was about to destroy my life. Marrying Boris would have been like committing suicide."

Bridgette and Amaryllis joined Monique and Arykah on the floor. "I remember it like it was just yesterday," Amaryllis said.

"Me too," Bridgette added.

Arykah shook her head from side to side in disbelief. "Monique, when you called out Adonis's name at the altar, I almost fainted. Even though he and I had planned and hoped that things would turn out the way they had, I was stunned that it actually did. I was so happy when you called from Jamaica, and told me that Adonis had proposed to you in mid-air. You said you needed a maid of honor, and I begged Lance to come to Jamaica with me."

"Who would've thought that Lance would propose to you only minutes before Monique walked down that sandy aisle?" Bridgette asked Arykah.

"And who would've thought the two of you would have a double wedding?"

Amaryllis added.

Arykah looked at them both with a gleam in her eyes. "God thought it."

Two hours after the sun had risen over Lake Michigan, Pastor Lance Howell lay in the middle of his California king-size bed. He was waiting for his wife to emerge from their massive walk-in closet. Sunday mornings were fashion show time in the Howell household. Arykah appeared in the closet doorway. She was dressed in a navy Dolce & Gabbana silk sarong dress that tied on the left side of her waist, and hugged every curve of her plus size figure.

"Okay, Pastor, tell me what you think of this one," Arykah said.

Lance exhaled loudly and extended his arms behind

his head. "Cheeks, why do you make me go through this torture every Sunday morning? I think it's lovely on you, just like the other nine outfits you tried on prior to that one."

"What about the length of this dress? My knees are showing."

"So, what?"

"You don't think it's inappropriate for the first lady to show her knees in church?"

Lance got up from the bed and walked over to Arykah. He wrapped his arms around her wide waist and snuggled her neck. "Why don't you just go to church naked so I can watch your butt cheeks jiggle when you walk? You know I like that."

Arykah chuckled. "You need to get saved. If your congregation could hear half of the things that roll off of your tongue, they would vote you out of the pulpit."

Lance playfully tapped his wife's behind on his way to the shower. Arykah's backside was his favorite area on her body. And he'd nicknamed her accordingly. "Cheeks, they can do whatever they want. It won't change the fact that I am in love with my wife."

Arykah took off the dress and laid it on the bed, amongst the other outfits she had modeled for Lance that morning. She slipped into her bathrobe, then followed him into the master bath. She sat at her vanity, next to their his and hers marble sinks. She applied moisturizer to her face.

"So, you and I have a deal, right?" Lance asked from the shower.

Arykah rolled her eyes into the air. She knew what he was referring to, but asked the question anyway. "What deal are you talking about?"

"I'm talking about you allowing Mother Pansie Bowak

to sit in on your counseling session with Sister Darlita Evans after morning service."

"Lance, Darlita asked if I would meet with her to discuss how she should handle her husband's third adulterous affair. It's a private issue, and I think it would be wrong to add a third party to the session. Besides, Mother Pansie doesn't like me."

Arykah faced opposition the moment Lance announced to his congregation that he had married a woman who wasn't a member of The Freedom Temple Church Of God. Lance knew the rules of the church; that it was forbidden for the pastor to marry outside of the immediate church family. Though he was raised to believe that myth, Lance chose to follow his heart.

When Lance asked Arykah to stand, and he introduced her as Lady Elect Arykah Miles-Howell, few people clapped or offered a smile of congratulations. Mother Pansie, along with the entire mothers board, stormed into his office immediately after the benediction to express their disapproval. The mothers pleaded with their pastor to see that it wasn't fair to the hundreds of single women sitting under his nose Sunday after Sunday. Surely he could have chosen a more traditional lady, unlike Arykah Miles, who was much too bold, very outspoken, short tempered, and not likely to be controlled.

"Pastor, think about your reputation. She's not first lady material."

Lance embraced each mother. He thanked them for caring about his wellbeing, then ushered them, one by one, from his office. Truth be told, Lance was in love with the too bold, very outspoken, short tempered, and not likely to be controlled, Arykah Miles.

"What makes you think Mother Pansie doesn't like you, Cheeks?" he asked from the shower.

"She told me so."

"Maybe you misunderstood her. What were her exact words?"

"She said, 'I don't like you.' I wanted to tell her to kiss my behind, but I know I must respect my elders, no matter how old and wrinkled they may be. Plus I promised God that I would stop cursing."

Lance didn't respond right away. He rinsed the soapsuds from his body, then lathered the sponge again. He knew Arykah wasn't exaggerating; Mother Pansie had openly expressed her dislike for his wife on many occasions.

"Pastor, her skirts are too short and her lipstick is too red. Pastor, you shouldn't allow her to wear high heels that tie up around her ankles with diamonds on them. It draws too much attention to her legs. Pastor, first ladies should not be seen with blond streaks in their hair. Pastor, why do you allow her to wear her arms out in the sanctuary? Pastor, why did you allow that woman to keep her maiden name? She's openly disrespecting you when she doesn't carry your name and your name alone."

"As church mother, Pansie Bowak has been counseling the women for years. But I would like for you, as my wife, to take over that responsibility. Just think of it as a training session. I only ask that you allow Mother Pansie to sit in on a couple of marital counseling sessions so that you can get a feel on how troubled marriages should be handled."

Arykah applied Johnson & Johnson's baby oil gel to her elbows and the heels of her feet. "Humph, I already know how troubled marriages should be handled. I believe that if a husband or wife cheats, it's up to the injured spouse to decide if they want to stay in the marriage.

There is absolutely no excuse for adultery. But if the marriage is strong enough to survive it, then to God be the glory. But this Negro has stepped out on Darlita three times. And I'm well aware that the morally correct advice that I should give her is to turn the other cheek. But heck, Darlita only has two cheeks, Lance. And she's already turned them both."

Lance stepped from the shower and wrapped a towel around his waist. He stood behind Arykah and placed his hands on her shoulders. "I'm worried about how you'll handle this situation with Darlita. Remember that God hates divorce."

Arykah was about to file a hangnail when she stopped abruptly and looked in the mirror at her husband's reflection. A serious expression was displayed on her face. "And He hates adultery too."

What was Lance to do? He married a woman who was headstrong and sugarcoats nothing. He imagined Arykah advising Darlita to set the house on fire with her husband in it.

Lance stood Arykah up and turned her around to face him. "I know it's a struggle adjusting to the role as the first lady, but when you're giving advice to the women, you must always refer to the scriptures. You can't give advice based on your personal feelings on a matter. I don't want to see every woman who is dealing with infidelity leave your office with a made up mind to divorce her husband. That's why I think it's important to have Mother Pansie sit in on a couple of sessions."

Arykah turned her head away from Lance. He cupped her behind and squeezed.

"Please, Cheeks. Do this for me."

Arykah smiled even though she knew what she was up against. Mother Pansie was old school and from the

South. She believed that women were inferior to men, and a dutiful wife should always do what she's told.

After the benediction two Sundays ago, a young lady confided in Arykah that she was troubled in her marriage. She confessed that she had been a punching bag for her husband's stress relief method for the past eight months. She told Arykah what Mother Pansie had told her; that if her husband didn't beat her, he didn't love her. Hot under the collar, Arykah marched the young lady straight to Lance's office. "Pastor, we have a problem."

Behind closed doors, Lance listened as the young lady revealed that her husband was facing a layoff. Their mortgage was being threatened, and her husband wouldn't seek counseling to deal with his emotions. She had become subjected to rape and beatings on a daily basis.

Lance looked at his wife and discerned her spirit. The expression on Arykah's face was horrifying. He had married a firecracker, and knew without a shadow of a doubt, that Arykah wanted to advise the young lady to drug her husband, wait until he fell asleep then cut off his member and arms. That was a sure way to cease the torture she was going through.

Lance could've counseled the young lady himself, but wanted to afford Arykah the opportunity to step in as his wife, as his right hand, and as the first lady, to become a mentor to the women in the church.

Arykah was from the streets. She hustled for years to get to where she was. But Lance still saw signs of Arykah's roots taunting her. Though she wanted very much to be delivered from her abusive past relationships, Lance knew he had to continue to cover his wife in prayer and work through her struggles and insecurities with her.

But Arykah was now a pastor's wife. Lance silently prayed for God to write on her tongue. He cleared his throat and loosened his necktie in preparation for damage control. Once he gave Arykah the go ahead, there would be no telling what would come flying out of her mouth.

"First Lady, what do you advise this sister to do?" he nervously asked.

Both Arykah and the young lady sat in chairs opposite of Lance. Arykah held her hands in her own. "I want you to know that God loves you, and He didn't create you to be anyone's punching bag. You are fearfully and wonderfully made. It is unacceptable for a man, any man, to put his hands on you in anger. If Mother Pansie told you that your husband loved you while beating and raping you, she was mistaken.

"Your body is the Lord's temple, and no one, not even your husband, should be allowed to abuse and destroy it. If he isn't willing to seek counseling for his abusive behavior, then you should pack your things and leave. Because the next time he lays unholy hands on you, you may not survive it. And you should seek professional help from an abuse therapist for yourself. It isn't normal behavior for you to have accepted your husband's fury for so long. Ask the therapist to help you find out why you willingly tolerated his mood swings.

"And you have to learn who you are in God. My husband taught me that women must realize their worth and own it. Because if we don't own it, we become vulnerable. And vulnerability is a pathway for the devil to destroy us, often through the very ones who claim they love us."

Lance was well pleased with Arykah's Christ-like attitude. Maybe he could go ahead and sit Mother Pansie down after all. He'd have to wait and see. He tightened his tie around his neck and leaned back in his chair while he watched God work through his wife.

Arykah dabbed the young lady's tears with a Kleenex tissue that she had pulled from a box on Lance's desk. "And you have to always protect your gates. Gates are openings that lead to your soul. Through our eye gates we may have seen our parents become victims of spousal abuse. And because we see it, our souls accept it as normal behavior. That's a trick of the enemy. Our ear gates can become flooded with damaging words spoken to us through verbal abuse.

"I once dated a man who constantly told me that I was too fat, that I wasn't pretty, that I was unattractive, and that I would never be loved by a man. And I believed that lie for years before Pastor Howell deposited a word of release into me. I tolerated that man's behavior because it was what I had become used to.

"And we have to protect the gates of our sexual organs also. Mother Pansie may have told you that it was impossible for a husband to rape his wife, but that was absolutely not true. How do you feel when your husband comes to you for sex?"

The young lady sniffed and wiped her eyes. "I feel violated because he's so rough with me. He never kisses me. Never asks how I feel or if I'm in the mood for sex. He just tells me what he wants, and then takes it from me and demands that I do things I don't want to do. And sometimes he bites my breasts until they bleed. And after he's done, he calls me dirty names."

Arykah was flabbergasted, and Lance was appalled. But he sat silent and let Arykah do her thing that she was doing so well.

Arykah knew all too well what it felt like to be in the arms of a man that didn't love her. Listening to the young lady's story brought tears to Arykah's own eyes. She squeezed the woman's hands for comfort. "When I'm with my husband, I feel safe and secure. I feel protected and adored. He cares what my feelings are. There's no dirty name calling. There's no hurt or pain. Only love, comfort, and security. When a man takes his wife's body by force and inflicts sexual pain upon her, he's raping her. And what you must do is start loving yourself and get out of this relationship because it's not holy, which means it's not of God."

Arykah looked across the desk at Lance to see, through his facial expression, if she had crossed any lines. Lance softly smiled at his wife and nodded his head in agreement with everything she said. He was well pleased.

"Bishop Howell and I will always be here for you, and we want you to feel free to come to us for anything. We are your spiritual parents, and we'll do all that we can to encourage you and keep you strong in the Lord," Arykah assured the young lady.

Lance stood and encouraged the young lady to follow Lady Arykah's advice. He assigned certain scriptures pertaining to strength, courage, and peace for her to study. He led the three of them in prayer for the young lady's strength and peace of mind. The young lady hugged and thanked them both then walked out of Lance's office and closed the door behind her.

Arykah looked at Lance. "You need to deal with Mother Pansie."

That meeting was still fresh in Arykah's mind as she and Lance stood in the middle of their master bath. "Lance, you know what happened the last time Mother Pansie counseled a young lady, but if you want her to sit in on the session with Darlita and me, then so be it."

"Thank you."

"You don't have to thank me. We're a team."

Lance kissed Arykah passionately and guided her back to the bed.

"Do we have time for this before church, Pastor? Don't you have to preach in a couple of hours?" she asked, wanting Lance just as much as he wanted her.

Lance removed Arykah's bathrobe. He let his towel slip from his waist. "This will help me preach real good." He enjoyed his wife in between the Egyptian cotton sheets.

Later that morning, on the south side of Chicago, the sanctuary at Freedom Temple Church Of God was filled to capacity. All fifteen hundred seats had been spoken for. The congregation was in high praise when Lance and Arykah appeared in the doorway entrance to the center aisle.

The praise and worship leader signaled to Adonis Cortland, the head musician, to lower the organs pitch while she announced their pastor and first lady. "Please stand and receive Bishop Lance and Lady Elect, Arykah Miles-Howell."

With Arykah standing on his right, Lance passionately placed his open palm on the small of her back. Arykah wrapped her left arm around Lance's waist, and they walked confidently as husband and wife down the center aisle. As he did Sunday after Sunday, with a smile on his face, Lance escorted Arykah to the first pew and greeted Monique, Arykah's personal assistant, with a peck on the cheek.

Four months ago when Lance walked into the sanctuary for the first time as a married man, he moved his ten deacons from the front left pew to the front right pew. He reserved the front left pew for Arykah, her guests, and Monique. Arykah was now in Lance's full view.

Mother Pansie hadn't taken that rearrangement too

kindly. It had been tradition that the mothers sat behind the deacons on the left side of the church. But with the deacons sitting across the aisle, Mother Pansie had to constantly look at Arykah's back side.

Lance sat in the pulpit with his assistant pastor, Minister Karlton Weeks, to his left. The associates sat on the right side of Lance. Minister Darryl Polk, Minister Tyrone Williams, and nineteen year-old Minister Alfonzo (Fonzie) Kyles, whom Lance was leaning toward promoting to youth pastor, each shook Lance's hand and gave him a good, "God bless you, Pastor."

Lance looked at Arykah, then winked his eye and smiled. She returned the gesture.

Monique nudged Arykah with her elbow and whispered, "I saw that, First Lady. You and the Pastor should know better than to partake in foreplay in the sanctuary."

Arykah chuckled and leaned into Monique for privacy. "If you would've been in our bedroom two hours ago, you would've seen some real foreplay."

Monique gasped, and it caused a few heads to turn their way. She met Arykah's lean and kept her whisper, "On a Sunday morning?"

On the pew behind them, Mother Pansie tried desperately to hear Arykah and Monique's conversation. She saw the wink Lance had given his wife. And because Arykah and Monique were leaning into one another whispering and gasping, Mother Pansie concluded that their conversation may not have been appropriate for the sanctuary. She tapped Mother Gussie Hughes, who sat on the right of her, on the knee and nodded her head in Arykah and Monique's direction.

Mother Gussie, affectionately known as 'Momma G,' hadn't liked Arykah since the day she had first called the church asking to speak to Pastor Howell. As the church's secretary, she had interrogated Arykah about why she was calling. Once Arykah revealed that she wasn't a member, but just a friend of Pastor Howell, Mother Gussie felt she was just another single lady all too eager for the pastor to place a ring on her finger.

Mother Gussie had had her own plans for Lance's future. As soon as her granddaughter would have gotten paroled and delivered her third child, Mother Gussie had planned to bring her to the church and introduce her to the pastor. But only weeks after she had answered Arykah's phone call, Pastor Howell introduced her as his wife.

Mother Pansie and Mother Gussie both turned their noses up at the form fitting, crimson red, knee-length crochet dress Arykah had decided to wear to church that morning. They couldn't help but notice the three-carat diamond platinum studs shining in Arykah's ears. Her lobes were completely hidden. Arykah's hair was pulled back into an elegant ponytail that revealed the matching six-carat diamond tear drop necklace around her neck. As Arykah giggled and whispered in Monique's ear, the mothers saw her bright red lip gloss. Her perfectly decorated eyelids were adorned with false eyelashes.

Arykah felt their stares. She purposely placed her right hand on Monique's left shoulder to give the mothers something to really be hot about. When Mother Pansie and Mother Gussie caught a glimpse of the massive diamond ring, coupled with the diamond tennis bracelet on the first lady's wedding finger and wrist, their breaths caught in their throats.

Arykah heard the gasping sounds and turned around with a smile. "Hello, Mothers. It is so good to see you both on this fine Sunday morning."

The looks on the mothers' faces confirmed to Arykah

what she already knew. They didn't like her and preferred she didn't speak to them. But Arykah didn't wait for a response. She knew it wasn't forthcoming anyhow.

When her mission had been accomplished Arykah turned back around and found Lance's eyes staring into her own. He gave her a half smile and slowly shook his head from side to side, indicating to Arykah that she should be ashamed of herself for meddling with the mothers. She winked her eye at Lance. He smiled broadly, then turned his head to focus on the choir rendering in song.

The mothers hadn't seen Arykah's feet yet. She felt Mother Pansie and Mother Gussie would probably have a heart attack if they saw her red stilettos that were adorned with Swarovski crystals.

Many congregants approached the altar for prayer after Pastor Howell had preached a lengthy sermon on prosperity. The associate ministers came from the pulpit to assist their pastor with laying holy hands on the people. Lance called for Arykah to stand by him when he ministered to women. That was new for Arykah. She hadn't understood what Lance wanted her to do at that time. When he ministered to a woman, he'd ask Arykah to give her an encouraging hug. Arykah felt honored to be in ministry with her husband, it was exhilarating.

The last woman Lance instructed Arykah to hug was Darlita, the woman she was to counsel after morning service. She stood before Arykah with a tear stained face. Because Arykah knew Darlita's story, she immediately pulled her into her arms and began praying for Darlita's strength and sanity. Arykah was the first to pull away when she had finished praying, but Darlita didn't let go. She held on to Arykah as if she were in a safety zone. It was as if Darlita felt that if she let go, her world would collapse.

"Come on, sweetie, let's go to my office," Arykah said.

Monique saw Arykah guide Darlita from the sanctuary and knew that was her cue to grab Arykah's things and follow them. Mother Pansie also saw Arykah leaving the sanctuary with Darlita. As soon as Monique stood to leave, so did she.

Upstairs in Arykah's office, that was adjacent to Lance's and just as large, Monique placed Arykah's Bible and purse on top of the desk and stated that she was going back down to the sanctuary to pay her tithes and offerings.

Soon after Monique had left Arykah's office, Mother Pansie had burst into the room. She was out of breath from climbing two flights of stairs. "First Lady, the Pastor asked me to sit in on this meeting you're having."

Arykah wanted to curse, but remembered her surroundings and the promise she had made to God. "That's fine, Mother Pansie, come on in." Arykah placed two chairs on the opposite side of her desk for Darlita and Mother Pansie, but Mother Pansie had positioned herself comfortably in Arykah's chair behind the cherry oak wood desk.

"That's *my* seat, Mother." Arykah made the statement as calmly as she possibly could, but Mother Pansie was already working on her last nerve. When Mother Pansie had taken her rightful seat, Arykah told Darlita that Pastor Howell had requested that Mother Pansie, the president of the mothers board, sit in on the counseling session.

Before Arykah started the meeting, she silently prayed that the Lord would help her control her emotions, but came to the conclusion that if anything popped off between her and Mother Pansie, it would be her husband's fault.

She opened her right desk drawer to briefly glance at a poem she had written for herself shortly after some of the women at Freedom Temple revealed their true feelings about her position as the pastor's wife. The poem was for her own self encouragement whenever the enemy came upon her to eat of her flesh.

Ain't Goin' Nowhere

Me in my high heels and short skirts
Decorated in things that sparkle and shine
That's right, ladies,
Pastor Howell is all mine

He chose me because I am the cream of the crop
Looking at y'all, humph, do you even shop?
Take a long, wide glimpse of your today
Give it up haters, because I'm here to stay

Don't need to explain nothing to you
Only to the one I'm married to
I see you looking, can't help yourselves
Compared to me, you're like book ends on a shelf

Trying to be a nice woman to you in church
Having to bite my tongue is hurting me so much
My girl, Monique, got my back with her raw words
To make all you wannabe's run like a charging herd

So keep on whispering, talking, pointing, and looking
I promise you, I don't care
Whether you accept me or not
I ain't goin' nowhere

Arykah shut the drawer and kicked off her stilettos under her desk. "Mother Pansie, Sister Darlita is here seeking counsel. Her husband has committed adultery a third time. He isn't a member of this church, and according to Darlita, he doesn't want to give marital counseling a chance."

The first thing that came out of Mother Pansie's mouth to Darlita was, "It's *your* own fault that your husband is unfaithful."

"How in the heck is it her fault?" The words flew out of Arykah's mouth at the speed of lightning before she had a chance to catch them, not that she really wanted to.

Mother Pansie looked at Arykah with raised eyebrows. *"Excuse me?"*

Arykah swiveled her high back leather chair in Mother Pansie's direction. "What do you mean it's Darlita's fault that her husband is unfaithful? What is *his* responsibility to the marriage? Surely you're not suggesting that Darlita forced her husband to put his shaboinka inside of another woman."

Mother Pansies' eyes bucked out of her head. She placed her hand over her heart as if she were going to pass out. She wished Pastor Howell could have been there to witness his wife's outspokenness. "With all due respect, First Lady of *only* four months. If a woman keeps her house and takes care of her husband's needs, he wouldn't stray. And it would be wise for *you* to take heed to this advice I'm giving."

It hadn't bothered Arykah when Mother Pansie reminded her of how long she'd been the pastor's wife. Whether she'd been married for four months or forty years, she would not sit there and allow Mother Pansie to make Darlita think that her husband's infidelity was her fault.

The enemy got the best of Arykah. She forgot that she was there to counsel Darlita. She set her gaze on Mother Pansie. "First of all, my marriage is on point. And you will not sit in my office, in my presence, and convince this sister to accept the blame for her cheating husband. The devil *is* a liar."

Mother Pansie was vested; she had put in her time. She had been the church mother for over thirty-five years. More than half of the women in the church, she helped raise from infants. She refused to let some heifer from the street walk into the church and take over her position and teach the women to be disrespectful and rude. She scooted forward in the chair and pointed her finger at Arykah. "Now see, I done told the Pastor that you weren't first lady material. You need to show some respect. You only been married a short while. What do you know about being a wife? Sometimes a woman's gotta go through—"

Arykah stood up from her desk and raised her voice. She wouldn't let Mother Pansie complete her sentence. "I don't give a rats behind how long I've been married! And as far as respect goes, old woman, you've got to give it to get it."

Darlita sat still. She didn't know what to do.

Mother Pansie stood up. She breathed in hot coals and exhaled fire. She raised her pitch to match Arykah's. "Just who in the heck do you think you're talking to, 'lil girl? You ain't nothing but a two-bit tramp that latched on to the pastor. Ever since you been here, you ain't done nothing but walk around here like you're better than everybody else. I don't care how bright your bracelets and earrings shine or what you're driving. You're still trailer trash, and you need to crawl back under the rock you came from."

Arykah instantly felt herself being drawn into a zone. She stepped out of herself to watch herself perform a scene from the Matrix movie. Arykah had never performed a back bend in her entire life, but at that moment, she was as flexible as a rubber band. In a circular slow motion she bent backward and was getting ready to leap forward over the desk.

"That's enough, Mother!" Lance stood in the doorway to Arykah's office with an expression on his face that she had never seen before. Someone was in trouble. Arykah didn't know whether it was her or Mother Pansie or the both of them.

"You see, Pastor? Do you see what happened now that you've brought this floozy into this church?" Mother Pansie asked Lance.

Arykah was fit to be tied. "Floozy? Who are you calling a floozy?"

Mother Pansie stood her ground. "I didn't stutter. I called *you* a floozy with your fishnet stockings and fake hair. You ain't got no business—"

Lance slammed the door behind him, which cut Mother Pansies' words off. "I said that's enough. I can hear the two of you way down the hall."

Mother Pansie looked at Lance. "That's because your wife doesn't know her place."

Arykah was getting ready to comment, but Lance held up his palm to silence her. "Have you finished your session?" he asked Arykah.

"No, I haven't."

Lance spoke to his wife but focused on Mother Pansies' eyes. "Take Sister Darlita to my office and finish your session."

Arykah hastily grabbed her Bible from her desk and escorted Darlita across the hall to Lance's office.

Lance mentally calmed himself before he spoke to Mother Pansie. "Never again are you to speak to my wife in that manner."

"But, Pastor, she—"

"Never again, Mother. Is that understood? Arykah is my wife, and whatever she does, she does it under my authority. I won't stand for you or anyone else to disrespect her. And effective immediately, *she* will be overseeing the women in marital counseling,*alone*."

Lance may as well have slapped Mother Pansie across her face. She snapped her head back in disgust. *"What?"*

"It's time, Mother. You've held the ball long enough. I have a wife now, and I trust that she can do the job."

Without saying another word, Mother Pansie opened the door and stormed out. Lance would soon realize that he had declared war.

About the author

Nikita Lynnette Nichols is employed at the Chicago Transit Authority. She resides in Naperville, Illinois and is currently writing her next novel.

You can reach the author at

www.nikitalynnettenichols.com

kitawrites@comcast.net

Reader's Group Guide Questions

1. Monique and Boris resided together before marriage. Do you think playing house hurts or enhances a relationship?
2. Was it wrong for Adonis to have developed strong feelings for his cousin's girlfriend?
3. Boris and Adonis were cousins, but were raised as brothers. Describe the difference between the two.
4. Monique had moved out of the house that she shared with Boris because she had grown weary of his disrespect toward her. Why do you think she continued to stay engaged to Boris even after she realized the strong feelings she had for Adonis?
5. Myrtle Cortland never sided with her son, Boris, in his wrongdoings. Why?
6. Arykah had a crush on Adonis from the beginning. At what point had she given up hope of the two of them becoming a couple?
7. Why did Myrtle share with Adonis how his parents had met? Was it wrong for Adonis to follow in his father's footsteps?
8. Monique jilted Boris at the altar? Was that the Christian thing to do?
9. Pastor Lance Howell had fallen for Arykah the moment he had met her. Why do you think that was so?
10. Do you believe that Monique and Adonis were each others' true soul mates?

Urban Christian His Glory Book Club!

Established in January 2007, *UC His Glory Book Club* is another way to introduce **Urban Christian** and its authors. We are an online book club supporting Urban Christian authors by purchasing, reading, and providing written reviews of the authors' books. *UC His Glory Book Club* welcomes both men and women of the literary world who have a passion for reading Christian-based fiction.

UC His Glory Book Club is the brainchild of Joylynn Jossel, author and Executive Editor of Urban Christian and Kendra Norman-Bellamy, author and copy editor for Urban Christian. The book club will provide support, positive feedback, encouragement, and a forum whereby members can openly discuss and review the literary works of Urban Christian authors. In the future, we anticipate broadening our spectrum of services to include online author chats, author spotlights, interviews with your favorite Urban Christian author(s), special online groups for *UC His Glory Book Club* members, ability to post reviews on the website and amazon.com, membership ID cards, *UC His Glory* Yahoo! Group and much more.

Even though there will be no membership fees attached to becoming a member of *UC His Glory Book Club,* we do expect our members to be active, committed, and to follow the guidelines of the book club.

UC His Glory Book Club **members pledge to:**

- Follow the guidelines of *UC His Glory Book Club*.
- Provide input, opinions, and reviews that build up, rather than tear down.

- Commit to purchasing, reading, and discussing featured book(s) of the month.
- Respect the Christian beliefs of *UC His Glory Book Club*.
- Believe that Jesus is the Christ, Son of the Living God.

We look forward to the online fellowship.

Many Blessings to You!

Shelia E. Lipsey
President
UC His Glory Book Club

**Visit the official Urban Christian His Glory Book Club website at *www.uchisglorybookclub.net*